Dressed
-for-
DEATH

Books by Julianna Deering

From Bethany House Publishers

THE DREW FARTHERING MYSTERIES

A DREW
FARTHERING
MYSTERY

Dressed
–for–
DEATH

JULIANNA
DEERING

WITHDRAWN

BETHANYHOUSE
a division of Baker Publishing Group
Minneapolis, Minnesota

© 2016 by DeAnna Julie Dodson

Published by Bethany House Publishers
11400 Hampshire Avenue South
Bloomington, Minnesota 55438
www.bethanyhouse.com

Bethany House Publishers is a division of
Baker Publishing Group, Grand Rapids, Michigan

Printed in the United States of America

ISBN 978-0-7642-1411-0

Library of Congress Control Number: 2015956722

Scripture quotations are from the King James Version of the Bible.

This is a work of historical reconstruction; the appearances of certain historical figures are therefore inevitable. All other characters, however, are products of the author's imagination, and any resemblance to actual persons, living or dead, is coincidental.

Cover design by Faceout Studio
Cover illustration by John Mattos

Author is represented by Books & Such Literary Agency

16 17 18 19 20 21 22   7 6 5 4 3 2 1

To the One who is forever faithful

— One —

"Tell me again why I let you talk me into this?" Drew Far-thering tugged at the starched cravat tied high under his chin and made a face at the little boy sniggering at him from the back seat of the Morris Eight passing on the other side of the road. He felt all kinds of fool driving through Hampshire dressed like a Regency buck, beaver hat, walking stick and all, but those were the rules. At least it wasn't a long drive.

Madeline swatted him with one white-gloved hand. "Leave that alone. Plumfield did a beautiful job tying it, and I don't want it ruined before we even get there."

He sighed, and she leaned over to kiss his cheek.

"You let me talk you into this, darling," Madeline said, "because you adore me and it was the only thing I wanted for our anniversary."

"Ah, yes, the ever-glorious tenth of December, 1932. Still, six months isn't a proper anniversary, you know." He huffed, hiding his smile from her. "You're just trying to set Nick up with your friend Carrie again."

She did look perfectly fetching in her white muslin dress and short Spencer jacket. A broad-brimmed straw hat, trimmed with silk violets and held on with a wide cherry-colored ribbon just the shade of the jacket, finished the picture. She obviously knew just how tempting she was.

"Not again," she said. "Still. And this time he won't have to be running around seeing to everything at the estate. They'll both have a whole week of enjoying themselves and getting to know each other better." She slipped her arm through Drew's and snuggled against him. "I'm glad your friends don't mind if we bring them along."

"Old Cummins? Of course he doesn't mind. The more the merrier, that's his motto. His wife's a bit quieter, but I'm sure you'll like her. They're both perfectly grand. A bit Victorian, mind you, yet not stuffy. Oh, Tal and his fiancée will be there, as well. He and Nick and I will have a chance to catch up. Haven't seen him since Oxford."

"What's he like?" Madeline asked, resting her head on his shoulder.

"He's a good chap. Good at history and languages, though no head for figures at all. He'd have punked out in mathematics if Nick hadn't pulled him through. Can't tell you I was much better. Oh, I say!"

The Rolls-Royce crested a hill, giving them a glorious view of Winteroak House, the Cummins estate. It gleamed white in the lush sea of green grass surrounding it, a grand manor house in the Georgian style, three floors high and at least fifteen windows wide. The entrance was grander still with columns and a marble bas-relief of the family coat of arms above the doorway. No matter if the family belonging to the coat of arms happened to have sold the house decades before.

"I've always thought it a nice view of the Solent," Drew said, and she frowned.

"What's that?"

"The Solent? It's right there, between this shore and the Isle of Wight over there. We used to go bathing in the water every day when we came down here. And we'd dig fossils on the beach and in the old caves. It was grand."

Madeline sat up, eyes shining as she looked down on it all. "How long has it been since you've been here?"

"Oh, several years now. I'd forgotten how nice it is. Tal had Nick and me down from school during the hols a few times. That is when we weren't up at Farthering Place. I think my parents spent some time here with Mr. and Mrs. Cummins when they were first married, but mostly the Cumminses came up to visit us."

"I hope Nick won't be late," she said, looking back at the road behind them. "Carrie's ship was supposed to be in at two-ten."

"Don't worry, darling. There's no chance he'll miss that ship. Not since he knows Carrie's on it. Once they get in, though, they'll all have to change into the right togs before they come out here. And you know how girls are about taking forever to dress."

She pursed her lips. "And you swore it was worth the wait."

"I said *you* were worth the wait." He squeezed her a little closer to him. "And I'll stand by that statement, but I can't answer for anyone else. I suppose they could have gotten here before us, but we won't know till we get inside."

By then they were at the park gates. A bewigged and liveried servant bowed deeply as Drew brought the Rolls to a stop.

"Good afternoon, sir."

He held out his hand, and Drew gave him their invitation.

"Welcome to Winteroak House, Mr. and Mrs. Farthering." He opened Madeline's door and handed her out as another servant swung open the gates. "If you would go through, madam, sir, Dryden will drive you down to the house."

Dryden, standing beside a vintage barouche pulled by perfectly matched bays, tipped his hat.

Drew frowned and got out of the car. "Wouldn't it be easier if we drove to the house? I mean, I wouldn't want anyone to have to bother with the Rolls and all that."

"Beg pardon, sir," said the first man, "but Mr. Cummins is very particular on this point. He says we're not to allow anything less than a hundred years old past the gates. Guests excepted, of course. Jimmy here will see to your car and have your luggage brought up nice as you please."

Drew glanced at the boy, who couldn't have been older than sixteen, then at the Rolls, and then pleadingly at Madeline. Eyes twinkling, she took his arm and drew him toward the barouche.

"It'll be fine, darling," she murmured as the boy handed Drew his beaver hat and walking stick and then hopped behind the wheel.

"Not to worry, gov," said the boy as he revved the engine. "I'll treat 'er better than me own gran."

Then with a spatter of gravel he and the Rolls were gone.

Drew looked longingly after them and sighed. "All right, Mrs. Farthering, shall we?"

She made a brief curtsy, head modestly lowered. "Thank you, sir."

Before they reached the barouche, another car came over the rise and pulled up to the gates. It was Nick in the Daimler, with Carrie Holland in the front seat beside him. Drew didn't recognize the young man, perhaps sixteen or seventeen years old, who sat in the back.

"Madeline!" Carrie called, waving a white lace handkerchief.

Nick pulled up to the gate and handed over the appropriate invitation. Before the servant could get around to open the door for Carrie, she let herself out. With a squeal she ran to Madeline, and the two girls embraced.

"Oh, it's good to be back in England," Carrie said. "You've got to tell me everything about your honeymoon. Paris and Berlin and Venice, too. How utterly romantic!"

"You'll have to see my album," Madeline told her. "We have so many lovely pictures, don't we, Drew?"

"Now, now, none of that," Drew pretended to scold. "You know there were no photographs during the Regency. You two will have to talk about something else."

Madeline wrinkled her nose at him. "Well, Paris and Berlin and Venice were there, at any rate. We can talk about them."

"Certainly, just no photographs. Though I would have to say Miss Holland is certainly a picture in her own right."

Carrie laughed and blushed just the slightest bit. "And you're still a flatterer."

Nick smoothed down his tousled sandy hair, scrambled in the front seat for his tall hat and buff gloves, then came up beside her, taking her arm. "The truth is never flattery."

She was dressed in white muslin, just as Madeline was, but instead of a Spencer jacket and straw hat, she had on a moss-colored pelisse coat and a scoop-shaped capote hat trimmed with crocheted lace. One strawberry-blond curl fell artlessly down the side of her neck. Judging from Nick's rather smitten expression, the effect was not lost on him.

Madeline gave Drew a discreet elbow in the ribs, and with a cough he wiped the knowing grin from his face.

"It's lovely to see you again." He bowed over Carrie's hand, just brushing it with his lips in fine Regency style. "And who have you brought along?"

"This is my brother, Billy." She waved the boy over. "Daddy's got some important business matters to see to and couldn't get away. He wouldn't let me come alone, so we thought Billy would do just as well. I hope it won't be any trouble."

She gave Drew an appealing smile, and he shook his head. "Not in the least, I'm sure. Our hosts are expecting a number of guests this week. I daresay, in a house this size, one more will be no problem. Billy, good to meet you."

The boy was considerably taller than his diminutive older sister and had hair that was rather chestnut in color and eyes the same. All in all, he seemed rather typically American, sturdy and capable looking and, even though it wasn't too obvious just now, of a naturally cheerful disposition. He looked almost swallowed up in his frothy cravat and too-large green tailcoat with brass buttons, but he was clearly doing his best to carry off the look with dignity.

Drew held out his hand, and the boy shook it, frowning slightly.

"It's William," he said, his South Carolina drawl very like Carrie's. "My sister'd have you all think I was some hick from the backwoods."

"William," Drew amended. "Will?"

The boy finally cracked a smile. "Yeah. Will would do."

"Will it is." Drew gave him a friendly swat on the shoulder. "Best come along now. Nick, old man, you'll have to leave the Daimler here. I'm told nothing newer than 1833, though preferably not later than 1820, is allowed past the gates until the week is up, and no exceptions. Ladies, our carriage awaits."

They all piled into the barouche and piled out again at the door of Winteroak House. Mr. and Mrs. Cummins were waiting for them, she in a lace mobcap and shawl, and he in buskins and an amber velvet smoking jacket.

"Ah, young Farthering!" He stepped onto the drive, his sturdy hands outstretched and his craggy face softened with a wide smile. "Come in, come in. And the lovely bride. Welcome!"

He gave a hand to each of them and leaned down to kiss Madeline's cheek. "You must forgive us for not being able to come to the wedding, my dear, but perhaps we can make it up to you here, eh? And who have you brought along with you? I remember that young scoundrel there. Running Farthering Place these days, I hear. Always thought you'd come to a bad end."

Nick grinned and shook hands with him. "Mr. Cummins. Very good to see you again, sir." He made a slight bow to the lady of the house. "Ma'am."

She positively beamed at them all. "Dear Drew and Nick. Whatever has happened to my young lads? Oh, it's been far too long."

"This is Miss Carrie Holland, Mrs. Farthering's friend from the States, and her brother, Will," Drew said. "Carrie and Will, our hosts, Mr. and Mrs. Cummins." He, too, bowed to the lady of the house and then kissed her cheek. "Very good of you to have us all, ma'am."

Mrs. Cummins looked at him fondly. "Do come in. All of you. Some of the guests have begun to arrive already. Beddows will show you all to your rooms. Your valet and Mrs. Farthering's maid came with your things about an hour ago,

13

Drew dear, and I suppose the rest of you will have to fend for yourselves." She patted Drew's hand. "I've put you next to Tibby. I thought you'd all like to be together."

"Mother, must you?" Talbot Cummins hurried down the steps, tall and lanky as ever, exasperated but smiling. "I suppose some pet names can never be got away from."

His mother put her hand over her mouth. "Oh, dear, I've done it again, haven't I? You must all forgive me even if my son can't. Old habits, you know."

"Come along now, Margaret," Mr. Cummins said. "Perhaps we ought to see to our other guests and let the boys catch up a bit. All of you, make yourselves at home."

Tal chuckled once his parents had gone inside. "She's an old dear, even if she does forget I've been out of the nursery some while."

Drew shook his hand. "Tal, old man, good to see you. Has Bunny got here yet?"

"Come and gone," Tal said with a chuckle.

"What's that?"

"Got his dates mixed. He showed up in full Regency kit Monday last, inexpressibles and all. When we told him the party wasn't for another week, he said that was all right because he suspected he was meant to be in the Argentine before the weekend anyway. And so off he went."

Nick shook his head. "He never got to the church when Madeline and Drew were married, you know. Got lost in Basingstoke somehow."

"Sorry you missed the wedding, Tal," Drew said, "but you absolutely mustn't miss the bride."

"That'll teach me to spend a year on the Continent. Last I heard, that Daphne Pomphrey-Hughes had set her cap at you. Looks as if you made a fortuitous escape." Tal bent over Madeline's hand. "Best wishes, Mrs. Farthering."

"Call me Madeline, please," she told him, "and I promise I won't call you Tibby."

"It's a bargain, Madeline. Nick, how are you?" Tal and Nick shook hands. "And who's this you've got with you?"

"This is Miss Carrie Holland," Nick said, "and her brother, Billy."

Carrie curtsied. "Thanks for having us, Mr. Cummins."

"Will, if you don't mind," Will said, glaring at Nick as he and Tal shook hands. "You're not the only one who's outgrown his nickname."

"Don't be silly," Carrie said, and she smiled at Tal. "He's been Billy all his life."

"Well, come along," Tal said, leading them into the grand foyer, where the tall windows spilled sunlight onto the pale marble floor. "Get settled in. Tea will be served in about half an hour. After that, I thought we of the younger set might enjoy—"

"Tal! There you are at last!"

A sylph of a girl, pale and wispily blond, glided partway down the stairs in ballet flats and a perfectly ordinary blue frock.

"What are you doing, Alice?" Tal called up to her, only half scolding. "You'd best not let Father catch you out of uniform, as it were. But come down and meet some people now that you're here." He turned back to his guests. "I suppose it's rather silly, but you know how the old governor can be. If we're to have a Regency house party, then we shall certainly do it up right, and no cheating."

The girl came to his side, her blue eyes enormous and darkly shadowed. He slipped his arm around her waist.

"Drew and Madeline Farthering, Nick Dennison, Miss Carrie Holland and her brother, Will, darling. Everyone, this is my fiancée, Alice Henley."

There were hearty congratulations and best wishes all around.

"So you see, Drew," Tal said, fond eyes on Alice, "you're not the only one who's decided to take the matrimonial plunge."

"I can't wish anything better for you than that you both will be as happy as Madeline and I are."

"Thank you," Alice said softly, looking from Drew to Madeline and then up at Tal. "We . . . we need to talk."

He furrowed his brow and shook his head almost imperceptibly.

"Tal," she pressed. "I need you to—"

He managed a bit of a smile. "Go and get your party things on, darling. We're all supposed to be enjoying ourselves this week. Leave the serious bits for afterwards. How'd that be?"

She nodded, wilting a bit, a shy apology in her expression. "Sorry I'm a bit out of sorts just now. It really is lovely to meet you all."

Before anyone could make a proper reply, she scurried back up the stairs and was gone.

"Don't mind her," Tal said. "She's generally steady as a stone, but this past week or two she's been rather on edge. I'm hoping the party will take her mind off things for a while."

"She seems quite a nice girl, Tal," Drew said. "Everything all right?"

Tal glanced at the rest of the group and then shrugged lazily. "You know how girls are, old man, especially the engaged ones. We'll work it out. Now come along. I'll show you all where you'll be staying."

Drew and Madeline found themselves situated in a room

16

with an enormous four-poster hung with airy white linen bed curtains, a match to the ones that fluttered at the high windows. The room itself was rather heavy, paneled and floored in oak and softened with a Persian rug in creams and tans.

"Oh, it's a lovely room," Madeline said. "Nice and sunny like ours at home."

"Splendid." Drew scanned the titles on the well-stocked shelf built into the window seat. "I'm glad we have this."

"I'm glad we have *this*," she replied, peeping into the adjoining bathroom. "How many people do you think will be here this week?"

"Thirty or forty, I expect." He came over to her, wrapping his arms around her from behind and nuzzling her neck. "I didn't think you'd want to spend our anniversary with a whole crowd of people."

She turned to face him, her periwinkle eyes sparkling. "Well, as you said, it's not a proper anniversary."

"So long as we're properly husband and wife," he said, touching his lips to hers, "I don't care about the anniversary."

"I am glad we came, though. It's going to be such fun. I didn't expect Mr. Cummins to be so strict, though. Not really."

"It was printed right on the invitation. 'Regency dress required at all times.'"

"Funny that your friend's fiancée wasn't dressed yet," she mused. "What do you suppose she wanted to talk to him about?"

"Something that's none of our business, I'm certain." He tapped her nose with one finger. "And we aren't going to make it our business."

She pulled away from him with a laugh. "I'm not the one who finds sinister plots at every turn."

"I'm well aware of the sinister plot you have in mind for this week. Step carefully, my girl, or you'll very likely spoil something that's progressing quite nicely all on its own."

"You've seen it, too." She threw herself against him again, arms around his neck. "Nick and Carrie are perfect together, don't you think?"

He smiled into her eyes. "Darcy come to woo Miss Elizabeth Bennet, eh? Well, she will probably have at least one opportunity to fling herself into Nick's arms and burst into tears on his chest."

"I hope so, as long as it's not because of anything too bad. But they're more like Jane and Mr. Bingley, I'd say. Everything sweet and uncomplicated and both of them easy to get along with. He'd never be the brooding Mr. Darcy type. Not like you."

He laughed. "Me? I don't brood. I don't stand about at parties and look cross, and I certainly wasn't as slow as he was to realize the very great pleasure which a pair of fine eyes in the face of a pretty woman can bestow. Of course, he hadn't the glorious inspiration I have."

"Carrie's right," she said, just a hint of a blush coming into her cheeks. "You *are* a flatterer."

"Oh no. The truth is never flattery. Didn't you hear Nick earlier? He got that one from me, you know."

She feathered her fingers through the hair at the back of his neck. "I believe, sir, that you are one of those fellows who, when he is alone, amuses himself with making up compliments he might spring upon unwitting young ladies who would suppose them extemporaneous."

"Well, you truly must make up your mind, darling. Am I meant to be Mr. Collins or Mr. Darcy? Shall I flatter or shall I brood?"

She pursed her lips, her blue eyes twinkling. "I think you shall flatter me outrageously when I am with you and brood when I am not."

He considered for a moment and then nodded. "Fair enough."

Without warning he dipped her backward, making her squeal.

"My dear Mrs. Farthering," he breathed, his eyes fixed on hers, "you must allow me to tell you how ardently I admire and love you."

She giggled, though her breath was a little bit faster than usual. "You, sir, are a plagiarist."

He brought his lips close to hers and then, with a grin, gave her a smacking kiss and set her upright again. "The truth is never plagiarism. And it is true, even if that Darcy chappie said it first."

She sighed and put her still-gloved hand to his cheek. "No wonder Miss Bennet wasn't able to resist him for long. I hope Nick is as familiar with Austen's works as you are."

"Oh, very nice. All the while I'm kissing you, you're thinking of Nick."

"I was just thinking how it might help him with Carrie. Besides, it wasn't a proper kiss anyway."

"Not a proper kiss? I see."

He gave her a smoldering glance, eyes focused on her lips that turned up a little at the corners, and kissed her most thoroughly.

"Better?" he murmured against her ear as she melted against him.

"Scoundrel," she breathed. "You know it's almost teatime and we'll be expected."

"Yes, I know."

With the tiniest hint of a smirk he stepped back from her and adjusted his cravat. Then he offered her his arm and escorted her downstairs.

They found most of the guests already gathered in the library, a spacious room with floor-to-ceiling bookshelves and tall windows that let the June sunshine pour through.

Madeline paused as they stepped inside. "It's like going back a hundred years. Isn't it pretty?"

"Apart from the girl reading that contraband edition of *Silver Screen*, very charming."

The room itself dated well before the Regency, and to see it filled with men in cravats and top boots and ladies in silk slippers and French muslin dresses was quite an experience. There were about twenty people here already. A few were mutual friends of Drew's family and the Cumminses, but most were strangers to Drew himself. Their host was quick to remedy that, situating himself between Drew and Madeline, linking arms with them both, and introducing them here and there. Then his eyes lit.

"You two simply must meet Monsieur Laurent. Rémy!"

Cummins dragged them both to an S-curve love seat elegantly placed in the library's bow-window area. Just as elegantly placed was its occupant, a man of stylish middle age who lounged with a black-lacquer cigarette holder in one hand and a graceful curl of smoke dissipating over his pomaded head, watching his fellow guests with faint amusement.

Seeing Madeline, Laurent tapped his cigarette against the ashtray on the little table at the end of the love seat and rose. "Ah, Sterling, do introduce me to your charming friends." He smiled slyly, adding in a low purr, "*C'est une femme exquis que j'aimerais mieux connaître.*"

"My wife is exquisite indeed," Drew said with a cool smile, "*et je ne m'inquiète jamais des individus qu'elle choisit pour lui tenir compagnie, à condition que ce soit véritablement elle qui les choisisse.*"

"Ah, yes, of course. A lady should always be allowed to choose the company she keeps." Laurent's lips twitched under his thin salt-and-pepper mustache. "Monsieur speaks French like a Frenchman."

Drew inclined his head slightly. "You are too kind. And, in any language, I see my wife is given the respect she deserves."

"An admirable trait. *J'espère que ce n'est pas contagieux.*"

Cummins chuckled. "I really must learn that talk, Rémy. I always feel I'm missing out on the best bits of the conversation."

Madeline pursed her lips. "So do I."

"Your husband and I were just discussing your dazzling loveliness and his good fortune in having met you before I did," he said, the elaborate lace of his sleeve falling just so as he made a courtly bow and kissed her hand. "Madame, I am enchanted."

"This is Mr. and Mrs. Farthering," Cummins said. "They hail from Farthering St. John near Winchester. Drew and Madeline, this is Rémy Laurent. If my collection of wines is the finest in Hampshire, it is solely due to his good counsel and even better contacts on the Continent."

"My family have been in the wine trade for nearly three hundred years," Laurent said, "and Sterling and I have known each other for nearly that long. Since his son was just born, eh?"

"About then, yes." Cummins cleared his throat, looking around the room, and then waved at a fidgeting rotund man unmistakably dressed as the Prince Regent. "Oh, there's old Ploughwright. Looks as though his wife managed to get him into that rig after all. Excuse me, will you? Ploughwright!"

He strode away, hands extended to his long-suffering friend, and Laurent smirked.

"You English. How you love the . . . disguises? No, the costumes. I have done business in your country these twenty-five years now and still sometimes the good English does not come to me."

Madeline gestured to the roomful of people in Regency dress. "Do you also enjoy disguises?"

"Ah, madame, such pretenses are not for me." Laurent ruffled his starched cravat with one hand. "I wear this because my friend he asks, but for me?" He shrugged. "I take a sip of claret and all the world knows whether or not it is a good year, and I need not speak a word. I see a beautiful woman?" He gave her a sly smile. "I cannot help that the husband grows angry when I am politeness itself."

"You are misunderstood then." Her expression was all gentle sweetness. "I am certain we will have no misunderstandings between us, seeing each other as clearly as we do."

The Frenchman bowed in resignation. "Madame is most eloquent. I have often thought—" He broke off with a smile. "Do excuse me, both of you. My fool of a valet seems intent on interrupting. Yes, Adkins?"

He waved over a stocky young man with a sullen face, who had been lurking near the door.

"Beg pardon, sir," Adkins said in a broad northern accent, "but I'm told it's urgent you come to the telephone. Business, sir."

"Ah." Laurent bowed once more to Madeline. "It seems I am not to have even a holiday to myself. *Quel dommage,* madame, but I am certain we shall meet again." With a subtle smile he slipped out of the room, his valet scurrying behind him.

"I see Dad has introduced you to his pet wine expert," Tal said, coming up to Drew and Madeline. "Have you met everybody else?"

Drew looked around the room. "Not strictly everybody. I suppose we'll get to know them all over the course of the week. As Miss Austen says in *Emma*, 'One cannot have too large a party.'"

"My Alice tends rather to agree with her Mrs. Elton. 'There is nothing like staying home for real comfort.'"

Madeline scanned the room. "Drew and I were talking about *Pride and Prejudice* earlier. Is that Mr. Collins there?"

A stolid-looking young man somewhere between the age of twenty-five and thirty sat on the end of a sofa, talking to an elderly lady wearing a turban of orange and violet silk with an egg-sized ruby in front. The man himself wore a suit of somber black and a very plain white cravat, and on his lap was a broad-brimmed black hat.

Tal grinned. "That's our vicar, Philip Broadhurst, and his mother. Come meet them."

The vicar stood as Tal introduced him and bowed, hat over his heart. "Very good to meet you both. Tal has mentioned you before, Mr. Farthering. I wondered if you were the same Farthering we've read about in the papers the past few months."

"I fear so," Drew admitted, shaking the man's hand. "But I assure you their accounts are often highly romanticized."

"Here in Armitage Landing," the vicar said, his fondness for the place obvious, "it's unlikely you'll have to deduce much more than which cards to play at loo." He bowed to

Madeline. "Best wishes, Mrs. Farthering, on your marriage. I pray it will be a blessed one."

Mrs. Broadhurst patted the sofa beside her. "Come sit down, my dear, and tell me about yourself. You are newly married?"

Madeline did as she was bidden. "A little more than six months now. I suppose that makes us newlyweds still."

The older lady's eyes were kind. "I was married to Philip's father for thirty-two years, and all that time he kept surprising me with things I didn't know about him yet. I never had a chance to get bored."

There was a mischievous twinkle in Madeline's eye. "My husband is always looking for crimes to solve. I think after another year or so, I'll be glad not to be surprised."

Drew cleared his throat. "Will you both be staying the week, Mr. Broadhurst?"

"Call me Philip," the vicar replied. "Anyway, I realize we're supposed to be back in Regency days and all that, but we're not so formal here most of the time."

Drew smiled, liking him already. "Philip then. Do call me Drew. I suppose your wife is about somewhere?"

"Actually, I haven't got one."

His mother lifted her eyes to the heavens but said nothing.

Broadhurst lowered his voice to a stage whisper. "I fear Mother agrees with that truth universally acknowledged. But since I have no fortune—good, bad, or indifferent—I fail to see how it applies to me." He shook his head when his mother sighed. "I tell you, Mother, I will know the right girl when I meet her." He turned again to Drew. "Be glad you're already married."

Drew chuckled. "But where is your bride-to-be, Tal? Madeline and I would love to get to know her better."

"I suppose I ought to send out a search party," Tal said with a sigh. "I don't know what's got into the girl. She's not usually like this. Of course, she's been helping Mother with all the arrangements for the party, so they're both a bit out of sorts."

"And what all is planned for the week?"

"Oh, they've got it all set out. Every day we're to do something from the Regency period. Dinner and cards most evenings, though we're on our honor to play nothing but faro, whist, loo, macao and rouge-et-noir. That's all we have on for tonight, so everyone should have a chance to get settled in and meet everyone else. Tomorrow night, Mother's arranged for charades or a pantomime of some sort, and if the weather stays fine we're to cruise up to Beaulieu on Wednesday on Monsieur Laurent's yacht."

"Oooh," Madeline said. "That sounds lovely."

"The river's the private property of Lord Montagu," Tal said, "but we'll try not to do it any permanent damage. There's the Palace House and the Abbey Church to see, too. We rather thought our American contingent would enjoy visiting our modest local sights."

"Ah, excellent," Drew said. "Should be fun."

"And there's to be riding and a picnic on Thursday," Tal added. "A small troupe of actors is to come perform on Friday evening—can't remember the name of the play—and on Saturday we'll end with a grand ball. And if you're not thoroughly sick of playing dress-up by Sunday morning, that's your own lookout."

Madeline smiled up at him. "It all sounds delicious. This is my anniversary present," she said to Mrs. Broadhurst, "so my husband isn't allowed to complain about the clothes or the dancing."

"Oh, about that." Tal glanced at Drew and coughed. "About the dancing."

Drew noticed that Madeline was taking great care not to look his way. "Yes?"

Tal shrugged a bit. "Well, I'm afraid Mother has arranged for all of us to have—"

"I'm not taking dancing lessons!"

— Two —

Everyone turned to see Will Holland storm into the library with Nick and Carrie right behind him.

"Billy," Carrie hissed, "behave yourself."

He stopped in his tracks, turned lobster red and made a brief bow to the room. "I beg your pardon."

Seeing Drew and Madeline, Nick took Carrie's arm and then Will's and towed them over to the group.

"Let me introduce you all," Tal said.

Once everyone had acknowledged everyone else, Drew turned back to Tal, not liking the way he was trying not to laugh. Surely Carrie's brother had been talking about something else.

"What were you saying your mother had arranged for us?"

"Did you tell them, Tibby?" Mrs. Cummins hurried up to them, the lace on her mobcap fluttering after her. "Won't it be just delightful?"

"I was telling them about it, Mother, but perhaps you would rather."

She took Drew's arm, looking girlish and rosy with

excitement. "Would you believe it? I've had the great good fortune to be able to engage Mr. Pomfret to teach us all to dance. He's to come every morning from ten until noon to instruct us. Then all the guests who come just for the ball on Saturday will be quite amazed to see us performing the most authentic dances of the Regency era. Won't it be lovely?"

Drew glared at Madeline, but she was still sitting with her head modestly lowered, smirking no doubt.

"Charming," he told Mrs. Cummins, then softened his expression at the hopefulness in hers. "It will be great fun, won't it, Nick?"

"Rather!" Nick smiled at Carrie, who was beaming up at him, positively no help at all.

Will fidgeted and frowned. "Do I have to?"

"No, young man," said their hostess, "not if you don't—"

"Billy Holland, yes, you do!" Carrie gave her brother a withering look and then turned to Mrs. Cummins. "Excuse me, ma'am, I didn't mean to be rude, interrupting like that, but I know you're not likely to have partners enough for all the ladies who want to learn these dances, and Billy can at least be polite and oblige you in such a little thing. You've been so nice to let him come and stay when he didn't even have a proper invitation."

"It's no trouble at all, my dear." She gave Will the warm, motherly smile Drew remembered from his own youth. "You may find you enjoy the lessons, young man. I have it on very good authority that young ladies are always very fond of nice young men who don't tread on their toes. You'll join our little troupe in the morning, won't you?"

He nodded meekly.

"Wonderful. You know what they say. 'To be fond of dancing is a certain step toward falling in love.'" She didn't seem to notice the boy's painful blush. "Now, do any of you need anything? Are your rooms to your liking?"

They all assured her they were.

"Well, you young people go on with your chat. I have some things to see to. I still haven't decided where we're going to have the play. It's Mrs. Inchbald's *Lovers' Vows*. You know, from *Mansfield Park*. We really could have nothing more suited, don't you think?"

"I'm sure it will be just perfect," Madeline said.

Drew gave her a private glower. She was definitely smirking.

"I do hope so." Mrs. Cummins turned to the vicar. "I haven't forgotten the box I promised you, Vicar. What with everyone staying the week, I got a bit behind on packing things up, but not to worry."

"Very good of you as always, ma'am," Broadhurst said. "I don't know how I'd carry on without you."

Mrs. Cummins looked flustered. "There's little enough each of us can do, but if we each do something, it adds up, doesn't it?"

"It does. And I don't doubt all your efforts will be given their due reward."

"You haven't seen Alice anywhere about, have you, Mother?" Tal asked.

"She was seeing to some things in the kitchen, I believe." Mrs. Cummins frowned. "Shall I go look for her?"

"Here I am." Alice came up to Tal's side and put her arm through his. "Sorry, everyone. From here on out I shall do nothing but enjoy myself."

She was dressed now in a prim muslin gown, her close-fitting jacket as blue as her small velvet slippers and the silk band around the fair hair piled in Grecian ringlets on top of her head. She was quite pretty in a waifish sort of way, though her eyes were almost too big for her heart-shaped little face.

Tal slipped his arm around her waist. "Good. That's what you're meant to do, you know."

"But after the party, after the ball on Saturday night, I think you ought to start helping your mother more. She has so much to do all the time."

Mrs. Cummins patted her arm. "You're a dear, Alice, but you know Tibby . . . er, I mean Talbot isn't interested in that sort of thing. His father's always good about helping me, though, especially with the charity things, but I'd say he's the exception rather than the rule where men are concerned."

"Do you need my help, Mother?" Tal asked. "All you need do is ask."

"No, no, love. Leave me to my puttering about. You'll have enough to see to once you and Alice are married."

"That doesn't mean I can't help with your charity piles."

"Nonsense," Cummins blustered as he joined them. "Woman's work!"

The vicar cleared his throat. "Steady on now."

"No offense, Padre," Cummins said good-naturedly. "Still, the boy's got company and all. No need for him to worry over such things, eh?"

"No, no," Broadhurst said. "Nothing he need worry over at all. I'll see it's all taken care of as usual."

"But Tal . . ." Alice began, a little pucker between her fine brows.

"No more worry about the workaday world," Cummins said. "Tal will have enough to do just showing you off to our guests this week. And I'm certain our vicar will see to the needs of the flock." Cummins gave Broadhurst a nod and turned to his wife. "Time for tea, old girl?"

"Yes, I believe it is." Mrs. Cummins raised her voice just slightly. "Shall we all go in to tea, ladies and gentlemen?"

After dinner, when most everyone was playing cards, Drew sauntered over to where Will was slouching against the library's grand marble fireplace, watching Nick and Carrie as they sat on the love seat looking at a collection of Byron's poems.

"It's not so sickening when it's you who's in love," Drew told him. "Wait and see."

The boy wrinkled his nose. The lovebirds had their heads together, almost cheek to cheek. There might have been no one else in the room.

"What is it you really object to about Nick?" Drew asked. "He really is a capital fellow, you know. I couldn't do without him, especially when it comes to solving crimes."

Will grinned abruptly. "Carrie told me about that. Too bad she and that Muriel Brower left before any of the good stuff happened last year. You must be pretty keen to have figured that all out. And those other murders, too."

"Sometimes one stumbles upon a clue and puts two and two together."

"I read all about it," Will said, a bright eagerness in his eyes. "Carrie made Dad send for the newspapers from over here so she could read about it firsthand. How come that cop who was on all the cases didn't throw you out on your ear? The guy with the funny name."

"You mean Birdsong?" Drew asked. "Well, don't tell anyone, but the chief inspector is a very practical man and appreciates free labor when he can get it. But you know, Nick's been in on most of it right with me. And my Madeline, of course."

Again Will frowned. "And then she moved over here to stay. Why couldn't you have moved back over to the States?"

"I couldn't very well leave my estate," Drew said. "And her family home had been sold off ages ago. She likes it over here. It's not so very horrid a place, is it?"

"It's all right, I guess." Will gave a grudging shrug and looked down at the cravat that stuck out under his chin. "I didn't think I'd have to take dancing lessons or wear this silly stuff. I wanted to see the castles and where the battles were fought and all that. Carrie says we will before we have to go home, but I don't know when since we have to waste a week here."

"I understand this isn't a pleasure trip for you," Drew said, looking over at Nick and Carrie. "Very important business, chaperoning."

Will immediately turned his attention to them, his expression fierce. "I guess I've got better things to do than look at old castles anyway."

"Look here, old man, I'll make you a bargain. You let your sister enjoy herself this week and don't be too strict, and I'll make sure you both get the grand tour of Winchester Castle where they've got King Arthur's Round Table and Winchester Cathedral to boot." Drew tugged the boy's lapel. "And no dress-up required."

Will glanced toward the lovebirds again. "I don't know—"

"I've known old Nick since we were both in the nursery. If I had a sister of my own, I wouldn't think twice about letting her spend time with him. He's not one of these Lothario johnnies you can't turn your back on."

"Maybe not, but you know how girls are. They get all googly-eyed over a silly accent."

Drew chuckled. "Well, she seems sufficiently level-headed,

and if she's not, Nick is. I can tell you, it was good to have him with me when we were looking into those killings at Farthering Place."

"I guess so. I'd sure like to hear more about how you did that."

Drew shook his head. "Couldn't have done it without old Nick, you know. Just ask him."

"Ask me what?" Nick sauntered up to them and helped himself to a piece of cake and a cup of punch from the trolley nearby. "Would you like to know about sheep, drains, or repairing thatch on cottage roofs?"

Will scowled again. "How do I know you weren't just talking big when you wrote to Carrie about solving those murders?"

Nick grinned. "If I told her anything, it was that Drew here was the mastermind and I only his dim-but-loyal minion. I can't possibly be responsible for what she may have told you in consequence."

"Where is she anyway?" Will asked, scanning the room again.

"Oh, she and Mrs. Farthering went to the powder room or something. You know how ladies are. Always something to touch up or adjust or see to."

Will frowned, looking him over for a moment. "All right, since they're out of the way for a minute, I want to know what your plans are for my sister. She's a lady, and don't you think anything else."

Nick held up both hands. "I haven't the slightest doubt of that. A lady and a fine one, as well."

The boy narrowed his eyes and gave a grudging nod. "All right. Just don't forget it."

"Friends then?" Nick held out his hand, but Will only

glowered at it. "Well, shake it or snap at it, old man. Either way we'll know where we stand."

Will's lips twitched, and a little snort of a laugh escaped him as he shook Nick's hand. "I guess you're all right enough. But I'll be keeping my eye on you all the same."

"Sounds fair. And in return I'll tell you all about the body in the greenhouse. How's that?"

The boy glanced at Drew. "Really? That'd be keen."

Drew nodded over Will's shoulder. "Some other time, though. I think the ladies would prefer not to hear it."

Madeline and Carrie were headed toward them, and Will gulped. "She's got that 'what have you been up to' look on her face. I'd better go tame her down." He darted over to his sister.

Drew laughed. "A narrow escape that, Nick, my lad."

"I quite like him," Nick said. "Takes his chaperoning seriously."

Drew considered for a moment. "What do you think, old man, shall we show him how it's done?" He made sure the boy was still talking to his sister and to Madeline. "Firsthand and all?"

"What do you mean?"

"I mean he seems rather keen on the mysteries we've been involved in. Say we were to provide one for him to help us with. One where you could play the hero and win the lad's admiration and acceptance into the family."

"Family? I don't—"

"Don't deny it. I've seen how the girl looks at you. And being the renowned amateur sleuth I am, I know how many beans make five."

Nick shrugged, obviously trying not to look too pleased. "That's not so much to go on."

"That and the tone of her voice when she talks about you

are fairly conclusive. With that kind of evidence, Chief Inspector Birdsong would feel confident in making an arrest."

One corner of Nick's mouth twitched. "Well, suppose you're right. Will is obviously not having any of it. Do you really think we can change his mind? We can't exactly arrange a murder or something vulgar like that."

"No, but perhaps a minor theft is in order." Drew thought for a moment. "The Mystery of the Bride's Pearls?"

Nick nodded wisely. "So you've decided to have Madeline strangle you as you sleep?"

"Not to worry. She'll be in on it from the start, and I daresay glad to help. And the Farthering pearls will be returned to her without a scratch."

Madeline came to Drew's side and took his arm. "What did you say about my pearls?"

"He knows how many beans make five," Nick told her, sounding rather proud.

"All right," Madeline said, "I'll bite. How many beans make five?"

Drew grinned. "One bean, two beans, a bean and a half, and half a bean."

Madeline pursed her lips. "I'm afraid I find that singularly unhelpful. What does that have to do with my pearls?"

He filled her in on the scheme they had in mind. "What do you think, darling? Shall we give it a go? We'll make rather a fuss about the pearls being missing, and then after Will's had a chance to help us question suspects and that sort of thing, we'll help him deduce they fell behind the bureau or something. He and Nick can become great friends in the process, and by the time the necklace is safely back in your jewel case, he'll have forgotten he ever had any objections to having an English brother-in-law."

She gave him that particular arch look that told him she was trying not to smile. "But you'd better not tell Carrie it's a setup. She's always been terrible at carrying off this kind of thing, and she'd give us away in the first five minutes."

Nick's mouth turned down. "I rather thought she'd be in it with us."

Madeline patted his arm. "Don't you worry. It'll be fun for her, too. And she won't mind when we tell her we made it up. Especially if you and Will become friends because of it."

"He might not like being deceived, and then what will happen to our hard-won amity?"

Drew thought for a moment. "All right, so we tell them both it's a game."

"Better yet," Madeline said, eyes shining, "Carrie and I will hide the pearls, and you and Nick and Billy can see who finds them first."

Drew frowned. "I'm not sure that actually helps, darling. We want Will and Nick to be friends, not rivals."

"All right. Nick and Billy can work together to outwit the famous amateur sleuth. He's got to love that. What do you think?"

"You and Carrie, eh? Feel up to it, old man?"

Nick snickered. "You know they'll likely hand us our hats."

"I say let them try." Drew looked at Madeline. "All right, darling, you and Carrie get a few others to be in on it with you, and we'll make a lark of it. But the tricky bit will be we fellows won't know who's in on it and who isn't. So whatever investigating we do, we'll have to do it rather on the quiet so our hosts don't get wind of it and think something's really wrong. Now, how shall we carry it off?"

Madeline took his arm, still with that glint in her eye.

36

"Don't you worry. Carrie and I will cook up a story of a lover scorned and a father bankrupt and a lady's dark revenge."

"Perfect," Drew said. "I think even Miss Austen would approve."

The next morning they began dancing lessons, and it was evident that by the end of the week they would all be, if not proficient, at least competent in the country dance, the quadrille, and the cotillion, the most popular dances of the Regency era.

Drew had quickly realized he didn't actually care for passing Madeline off to Laurent, even in the figure of a dance, and more than once that first day he weighed the social risks of striking a guest in another man's home against the immense satisfaction such a blow would bring him. But in the end he lighted on the more moderate course of merely keeping an eye on the man. Madeline didn't seem to take offense to the Frenchman's insistence on being seated next to her at dinner or even notice his appreciative glances, and she did seem to be enjoying herself a great deal. It would be a pity to make a scene, though if Drew hadn't known how much his wife wanted to be here, he wouldn't have much minded being told to pack his things and go home.

By the time they were ready to retire that night, he was determined to settle the matter. If she was genuinely annoyed by the man, Drew would certainly put a stop to it.

He puttered about in the bathroom until he was certain Beryl had finished helping Madeline out of her gown of pale gold with fine burgundy stripes and taken down her hair. He heard Madeline bid the girl good-night, followed by the soft click of the door shutting. Then he came into the bedroom.

"I want you to teach me French," Madeline said as she sat at the dressing table in her muslin chemise and looked through the earrings in her jewelry case. "I'm tired of missing the best part of the conversation."

He came to sit beside her in front of the mirror, still feeling more than awkward in the billowing nightshirt he was told was *de rigueur* for a gentleman of the Regency, but giving her a smile all the same. "Very well, repeat after me. *La plume de ma tante est sur le bureau de mon oncle.*"

She wrinkled her nose at him. "Even I know that one. And I don't think I'll have many occasions for telling anyone about my aunt's pen or my uncle's bureau."

"Oh, very well. But you must tell me why you want to learn it so I'll know what to teach you."

She frowned. "Monsieur Laurent is always talking to me in French, especially during dancing lessons. I just want to know exactly what he's saying."

Drew's mouth tightened. "I knew I should have punched his nose."

"It might be perfectly harmless," she admitted, "but it doesn't feel that way. He gets a rather slimy expression on his face. I suppose it's meant to be suave and debonair, but I can't say I find it at all enticing."

"Tell him '*Vous êtes un crapaud dégoûtant.*'"

She raised one delicate eyebrow. "Do I even want to know what that means?"

"It's merely a fine way of telling him he is a loathsome toad."

"It does sound much prettier in French, doesn't it?" She sighed. "Somehow I don't think he'll take the hint, even in French."

"I've already warned him off in French and in English."

"Maybe he'd respect you more if you told him you *are* French. You are, you know."

He laughed. "Technically, I suppose, even if I did leave Paris when I was only a few days old. I had a French nurse, though, and a number of French tutors. I expect my father thought it would be an asset for me in doing business on the Continent."

"I hadn't thought of that."

"It is terribly helpful for reading menus. And," he said, leaning close to her ear, "for telling my wife how irresistible she looks."

She put her arms around his neck. "You don't really mind dressing this way, do you, Drew?"

"Not if it pleases you, darling." He kissed her lips. "Are you enjoying your house party?"

"Very much. Are you enjoying the mystery Carrie and I made for you?"

"Nobody will tell me anything." He lifted an eyebrow. "You do know where the pearls are, don't you?"

"Of course."

He scowled at her. "I'm going to find them, never you mind that, and before Nick and Will, too."

"I'm sure you will." She chuckled to herself. "In time."

He gave her a severe look, and she tried to look contrite.

"Tal's parents are awfully nice."

"I've always liked them," he said. "I didn't realize Mr. Cummins had grown so serious about his wine collection. Mrs. Cummins hasn't changed a bit, though. Still everyone's mum."

"She seems like she'd be more at home in a little row house and walking to the market every day. Not that she isn't absolutely lovely and perfectly dressed, but she doesn't seem as if any of it matters except for Tal and his father. I think if they're happy, she's happy."

"She doesn't come from money, not like her husband. I believe her father was a greengrocer in Otterbourne. She made quite a step up in her marriage, but I don't think she's forgotten where she came from. Mr. Cummins is well known for his charity work in London, but it's Mrs. Cummins who gets really involved in the local parish. Knitting and cooking and visiting, all the things that involve more than writing a check."

Madeline looked down at her nails and began filing down some infinitesimal snag. "I wonder what she thinks of Monsieur Laurent."

"No more of him now, darling." Drew stood. "It's well past our bedtime."

"I'm serious. I want to learn French."

He gave her a sly grin and came back to the dressing table, slipping his arms around her as his eyes met hers in the mirror. "Shall we begin at once?"

Her dark lashes swept to her cheeks, which had turned a fetching shade of pink. "If you like."

"Very well, repeat after me. *Tu es divine.*"

"Tu es divine."

"Very good," he murmured, nuzzling her ear. "*Je t'adore.*"

"Je t'adore." Eyes still closed, she leaned her head to one side so he could trace his lips along her neck. "Je t'adore."

"*J't'aime,*" he whispered and reached over to switch off the light. "J't'aime. J't'aime. J't'aime."

A long stripe of sunlight fell across Drew's closed eyes. He frowned, squinting, and turned his face more into the pillow to escape it. He could feel Madeline next to him, nestled under his arm, and a familiar warm weight between his shoulder blades.

"All right, Mr. Chambers," he muttered, trying to reach back with his free arm. "Time to get up." The weight did not respond, and Drew continued to flail. "Come on, Chambers, old man, I need to turn over. If you would be good enough—"

He broke off, just then remembering he wasn't in his own bed at Farthering Place, and his own cat, Mr. Chambers, was not here at Winteroak House. He opened one eye, winced in the morning light, and looked over his shoulder once more. Staring back at him was a sleek little tuxedo cat, her white legs tucked under her, her white chest and muzzle a stylish contrast to the shiny black of the rest of her. She didn't seem the least bit afraid or even faintly curious about why there were strangers in what he suspected was the bed she had appropriated.

"Ah. Good morning," he whispered. "Uh, Drew Farthering here. Don't wake her, but that's my wife, Madeline. And you are?"

Her dark green eyes looked back at him with serene unconcern.

"If you'll pardon me, miss, I'd very much like to get up now. Plumfield will be coming to draw my bath any moment, I expect, and then Beryl will want to attend to Madeline's and there's bound to be a lot of commotion. After that, we'll likely clear out for the day, and you can have your bed back. Fair enough?"

The cat gave a slow blink and then yawned. With a nearly soundless chuckle, Drew twisted until he could reach her and pull her around against his chest as he turned to his side. Even this did not disturb her equanimity.

"What are you doing?" Madeline turned over beside him, nestling now against his back and peering over his shoulder. "What have you got?"

Drew turned so she could kiss his cheek. "I'm not entirely sure. But I think we're in her bed. Uninvited, mind you, which is pretty bad form."

"Oh, dear," Madeline said with a sleepy laugh. "Do you think she'll forgive us?"

"I'm not sure she minds one way or the other."

Drew found it comfortingly homelike to carry out his morning ablutions under a placid feline gaze and was in a cheery mood when he and Madeline boarded Monsieur Laurent's yacht, the *Onde Blanc*. She was a stylish craft, spacious and beautifully fitted, down to the stylized emblem of a white wave repeated on everything from cabinet knobs to table linens to signify her name. Laurent was unabashedly proud of her and seemed delighted to show his guests around as they set sail toward the Beaulieu River.

Drew lagged behind a bit while their host led a small group from the aft deck to the lounge, curious about the marks on the otherwise pristine planks. He traced them with the toe of his boot: little crescent-shaped discolorations in the teak, less than a quarter inch wide and nearly invisible except in the crevices between the planks. He almost hadn't noticed them, for they were only faintly lighter than the rest of the deck. Despite the luxurious bed and table linens, he couldn't imagine the crew did the ship's laundry aboard, but he wondered if someone had perhaps spilled bleach in this part of the hold. No, that would have lightened all of the deck there, not just the crevices. Of course, there might—

"What are you scowling at now?" Madeline said, her voice low as she took his arm and smiled up into his eyes.

"You are displeased with my charming lady?" Laurent said, coming back to them, his eyes, as always, on Madeline.

"Displeased?" Drew narrowed his eyes and put his arm around Madeline's waist, though he kept his voice light and pleasant.

"I mean my lovely *Onde Blanc*, of course."

"Oh, no," Drew said, moving forward so his top boots covered the little marks he'd been studying. "She is perfection in every way and a credit to your success in your trade. You must do very well."

"Monsieur is too kind," Laurent said, bowing deeply. "But she serves me both in business and pleasure, so you see I am an economical fellow after all. But, eh, what is that? Today there is no business and no economy. We shall enjoy the river, no?"

They sailed around a long, thin finger of land that separated the Beaulieu River from the Solent, and then they were on the river itself, rolling along past the tree-lined banks, lulled by the motion of the boat and the sound of the water. Much to the amusement of the local residents, they disembarked at Beaulieu in their period finery and paraded down Palace Lane to luncheon at a charming seventeenth-century country house turned hotel. Afterward they saw the opulent Beaulieu Palace House and the neighboring Abbey Church.

The return trip was rather more sedate than the trip out. Most of the party had broken up into smaller groups of three or four, chatting and watching the scenery slide by. But as they rounded the bend at Buckler's Hard, Alice came to stand at the railing, leaning over a bit to get a better view of the Georgian houses, once again solemn and preoccupied.

"Poor thing," Madeline said, leaning closer to Drew. "She looks as if she would welcome a friendly ear just now."

"Girl talk, eh? Just leave me out of it."

"You," she said, making a face at him, "were not invited."

She went to stand next to Alice. With a chuckle, Drew leaned back in his deck chair and closed his eyes.

Their conversation was low and earnest, muffled by the hum of the engine and the rush of the river, and Drew nearly dozed in the warm sunshine. Then he heard the thump of boots and barely lifted one eyelid to see who was there.

"Alice." Tal came up beside the two girls, his coat over one arm and his cravat hanging loose around his neck. "Gossiping, are we?"

Alice took his arm, bright-eyed and smiling. "We were just trying to decide what to do with the naughty little boys we're meant to be minding."

"Naughty?" Tal protested. "I categorically deny any and all charges. Of course, I can't vouch for that lout there."

He walked over to where Drew was dozing and gave the leg of his deck chair a sturdy kick.

Drew opened both eyes. "That was a decidedly rude awakening."

"We'll be at the house before long," Tal told him. "Better enjoy the view while you can."

Drew managed to struggle to his feet and make his way to the railing with the others. "Oh, I say, Tal, there's a little black-and-white cat in our room. She must have come in through the window sometime last night and made herself at home."

"Not to worry. That's just Eddie."

"Tal thought she was a tom," Alice said, giving him a saucy grin.

"We were *told* she was a tom," Tal said firmly. "By the time it became obvious she wasn't, the name stuck. Call her Edwina, if you like."

"Oh, no. Eddie's rather sporty, don't you think?" Drew said. "It suits her somehow. She seems awfully friendly. For a cat, you know."

Tal chuckled. "She's a funny little thing. Obviously she knows when she's admired."

"A lady, a ship, or a cat?" Nick asked as he and Carrie joined them. "Which are we talking about?"

"A cat this time," Tal told him. "It seems ours has attached herself to Farthering here."

"Cats are like that," Nick observed. "They have a way of honing in on the person most likely to spoil them."

"Where's your watchdog, Nick, old man?" Tal asked.

Nick glanced at Carrie. "I convinced him Miss Dornford was one of the chief suspects in the case of the missing pearls, so now he's trying to find out just what she's been up to."

"I'm afraid I put him up to it," Carrie admitted. "That was mean, I know, but it'll be good for Billy. He should make some of his own friends instead of just tagging after me."

"One does like a change now and again." Nick looked at Carrie. "Three's a crowd, eh?"

"All in a good cause, Nick. How are you and your chaperone getting on now?" Drew looked toward the aft deck, where Miss Dornford was looking worshipfully up at Will, who was decidedly not looking worshipfully back. "Have the two of you made any progress in the great pearl mystery?"

"Nothing yet. Will thinks the pearls were hidden in the kitchen by the groom's gardener, but the cook doesn't seem to want to humor us and let us take a look around. Me, I'm more suspicious of the Australian cousin who may not be exactly what she seems. How about you?"

"I'm afraid I've come up empty, as well," Drew said. "I'm sure the bride's father's solicitor is up to no good, but whether he actually had a hand in the theft remains to be seen."

Madeline gave him a mischievous grin. "Face it, darling, Carrie and I are far too clever for all three of you."

Carrie giggled. "We'll definitely hand it to you if you figure it out before the end of the party."

"But no more extra clues for you," Madeline said, feigning sternness. "You have all the information you need."

"Extra clues?" Drew sputtered. "What extra clues?"

Madeline's only answer was a smug look.

The *Onde Blanc* made her leisurely way back toward Winteroak House. She easily outclassed anything else on the water that day, especially a little fishing boat called *The Gull* that chugged along the shoreline. One of the men on her deck gaped at the yacht as it glided past until finally another man on the smaller ship shoved his shipmate on the shoulder and tossed him an armload of netting.

Drew chuckled. "If that wasn't 'get back to work,' I don't know what is."

"We seem to have made quite an impression during our little outing," Madeline said.

Laurent strolled up to the rail and scowled down at the little *Gull*. "He makes himself insolent. Eh, these vulgar fellows, they should be kept out of sight of reputable people. I trust he did not offend you, Madame Farthering."

Madeline's eyes twinkled. "I couldn't really expect to sail out dressed as Elizabeth Bennet and not attract some attention. But I don't think he was looking at me at all."

"I suppose that is a possibility," Laurent said. "But that would make him more of a fool than I already think him."

Drew put his arm around his wife's waist. "For once, monsieur, I would have to agree with you."

By then *The Gull* and the curious fisherman were out of sight.

— Three —

The next day the whole party picnicked out in a wide, grassy meadow on the estate. A host of liveried servants had gone before them and set out a sumptuous array of roast meats and broiled fish, cheeses and hearty brown bread, boiled eggs and pickles, and a variety of little cakes for afters. Once everyone had eaten and the servants had taken away the remains, the guests chatted and sunned themselves and played charades until the afternoon grew truly hot.

The ladies began talking about going back to the house, so Drew volunteered to go get some cold water from the little brook they had crossed on their way to the meadow. That way they could all bathe their hands and faces and cool off.

"I'll come along." Tal snatched up two more empty wine bottles and followed him over the hill. "Mother hasn't been so pleased about seeing her guests stuff themselves in ages. I see Regency dress hasn't dampened your appetite."

"Not at all," Drew admitted. "And there's much to be said

for this sea air. It not only encourages a healthy appetite, it makes one sleep like a baby. Speaking of sleep, Eddie kept us company again last night. I didn't know she was under the coverlet and nearly laid on her. Madeline and I were thinking perhaps we could put a bell on her. Then at least she wouldn't get stepped on or anything."

"Good idea. We probably should have done that long ago."

"And of course she crept right up behind me when I was shaving this morning. I almost cut my throat trying not to step on her."

Tal grinned. "That must have been quite a sight."

"It amused my wife to no end, I can assure you."

His grin softened. "She's a nice girl, Drew. I'm happy for you."

"Thanks, old man. They say grace is getting blessings we don't deserve, and in my case she's certain proof of it. I hope you'll find it the same with your Alice."

They had walked for a moment in silence before Tal, frowning, turned and said, "When you and Madeline were engaged, I mean, when you were getting close to actually being married, did she seem . . . odd to you?"

Drew smirked. "Odder than usual?"

"I mean it. Did she change?"

"Actually, she did a bit. I think it was nerves mostly, realizing what we were about to do was for keeps. She even called it off once, but we slogged through it all right. I finally made her realize what a wretch I'd be without her, and she took pity on me."

"Yes," Tal deadpanned. "Looks, money, wit—it's a wonder you found anyone who'd take you."

Drew scoffed. "But you say Alice is acting odd. How do you mean exactly?"

"Jittery, I suppose. Always on edge about something, but saying nothing's wrong and then acting too happy."

"I have thought there was something a bit off, but I didn't know if she was always that way. Is this just recent?"

Tal nodded. "Not that she hasn't always been rather vivacious, except there's something different now."

Drew considered for a minute. "Have you just come out and asked her?"

"She says it's nothing, but then she looks at me as if I'm supposed to know that there's something. What's one to do with a creature like that?"

"Admire and enjoy, old man." Drew swatted his shoulder. "Admire and enjoy."

Tal blew out his breath in frustration. "That's hardly any help."

"If I knew the answer, I'd make a tidy sum selling it to husbands everywhere. If you've already asked her, I don't suppose there's much else to do. Perhaps you can tell her that, no matter what she says, you know there's something wrong and you're ready to talk about it whenever she is."

"I told her that already, too."

"Well, you'll just have to be patient until she wants to tell you or it becomes glaringly obvious. And you don't have any clue what it could be?"

Tal shook his head. "She seemed fine until recently. Excited about the party. Particularly eager to meet you and Nick. I know she wants to ask your Madeline about your wedding and honeymoon, all that sort of thing. But she's become more and more unlike herself. Yesterday it was particularly bad."

"What happened yesterday?"

"Nothing I know of." Tal paused, thinking as they walked. "She was helping Mother get things ready for company. Some of the guests arrived. She seemed very happy to have a couple of her own school friends come. The Deane girl, Georgie, and the other one, Violet, both of them hunting husbands, I'll wager, but since Alice is already spoken for, I can't imagine that would bother her."

"You don't think you're blowing this all out of proportion, do you? Grooms have been known to suffer from the jitters, too."

Tal swallowed hard. "It is a big step. What if I'm a complete bust at being a husband?"

"You love her, don't you?"

Tal shrugged and nodded, a little color coming into his face.

"And she loves you?"

"I believe she does."

"Well, there you have it. Just love each other. I'm sure you've heard it before, but a bit of patience, kindness, and humility go a long way. I've found you'll never regret putting each other first, forgetting old hurts, or telling the truth. Love is well worth holding on to, even when you don't feel much like it. Keep that in mind, and you'll both do fine."

"What's this? Trying to do my job, are you, Drew?"

Drew and Tal both started and then turned.

"Didn't see you there, Padre," Tal said.

Broadhurst chuckled as he came up to them, and Drew found it unsettling somehow. The man was soft-footed, if nothing else.

"I'd be a poor substitute, Vicar, believe me. I'm only just learning all this myself."

"From what I've heard, you're doing just fine. Saint Paul gave very nearly the same advice to the Corinthians."

"Well, I certainly didn't think it up all on my own," Drew

admitted, "though I've found it to be extremely practical so far."

"Have you been sent for us, Padre?" Tal asked.

Broadhurst glanced back toward the rest of the party. "I'm afraid I have. The ladies are getting restless."

"Can't have that, can we, Tal?"

They approached the stream, and Tal said, "Claridge Rindle, the coldest, freshest water on the estate. It's always beautifully clear."

Drew stepped closer, meaning to fill the empty bottles, and then frowned. There was a faint trace of white just at the waterline, marking the stones and the earth and even some of the grass that grew low on the bank, even though the water itself appeared to be clear. "I say, Tal . . ."

Tal looked down at the stream and nodded. "I haven't seen it like this before. I haven't been up here in some while, I'll admit."

"Perhaps we'd best go on back," Broadhurst suggested. "It's likely nothing."

Drew cupped his hand, dipped it into the water, and brought it to his mouth. It tasted clean and fresh enough. Still, he walked upstream a few yards, just to have another look. The white residue was there as well, at least until he reached a little clump of trees that shaded the stream. Above that, there was nothing to mark the passage of the water but some mossy stones.

"I think it's a bit clearer up here." Drew filled the bottles and walked back downstream. "I thought it might taste of alkaline or something."

"I don't think there's anything like that round here," Tal said.

"Something left those marks."

Tal frowned as he studied the waterline. "It could be something leeching into the water from a deposit in the stream bed or along the bank."

"Most likely," Broadhurst said. "But maybe you'd best dump that out. Better safe than sorry, eh?"

Drew shook his head. "I tasted it. Sweet and clear."

Broadhurst looked uncertain while Tal filled his own bottles, and then the three of them carried the water back to the others. Soon there were a number of cool, wet handkerchiefs being applied to warm brows and wrists.

Alice stretched languidly and leaned against Tal's shoulder. "Must we go in?"

He laughed. "I thought you wanted to."

"It's turned cooler now," she said, "and I'm too lazy to walk back."

"I'll carry you."

He leapt to his feet and scooped her into his arms, making her squeal and kick over the last of the water, which spilled onto Carrie's shoe.

"I'm terribly sorry." Tal put Alice down and knelt in front of Carrie with his handkerchief. He shook his head. "I'm afraid it's rather too wet to be of much use."

The vicar immediately reached into his own pocket. "Allow me." He pulled out his handkerchief, and a small, square packet tumbled into the grass at his feet.

Drew bent to retrieve it for him, but Broadhurst scrambled to grab it first, his face reddening as he stuffed it back into his pocket. "Clumsy of me." He pressed the handkerchief into Carrie's hand. "I hope you aren't too wet."

"No, not at all," Carrie said, looking puzzled at the quizzical glance Drew and Nick exchanged.

Will had been sprawled on the blanket beside his sister,

but he sat up, narrowing his eyes at the vicar. "Where were you on Tuesday night?"

"What?" Broadhurst blinked, then grinned faintly, obviously recalling the response Madeline had told him to give. "I was ministering," he said with a pious look toward heaven, "to the sick and poor in spirit."

"Then what are those pearls doing in that box in your pocket?"

"Sorry, Will, but they'd never fit in such a small box." Broadhurst dropped his voice to a stage whisper. "And if I did steal them, I'd hide them someplace a bit less obvious."

"And no fair guessing with nothing to go on, Billy," Madeline scolded lightly.

"It's not a guess," Will protested. "It's deduction. He had motive, means, and opportunity. Anybody who has all three of those is a suspect in anybody's book. Besides, I saw him creeping around in the back garden yesterday."

"Creeping?" The vicar made a comic show of hemming and hawing. "Merely taking the air, young man, that's all."

"I'm still not satisfied with your explanation for the shortfall in the church poor box," Drew told him, "but we can discuss that when we're back at the house."

"I'm not sure about that one, either." Will fished a well-worn piece of paper out of his pocket and studied it for a moment. "Hmm, this says the earl's son has gambling debts he must pay before the local crime syndicate makes an example of him. Sounds like somebody who needs money fast. Hey, Tal!"

The vicar chuckled as Tal began protesting his innocence and Carrie playfully squabbled with her brother. "Will's rather keen on mysteries, isn't he?"

Madeline shook her head. "I think my husband's created a monster."

"Not I, madam," Drew said. "I am only trying to keep the boy amused long enough to let you play Cupid."

"Well, you're certainly not making any progress finding my pearls. And you a detective."

He scowled at her. "I'm working on it."

"Ah," Broadhurst said. "So the matchmaking is your doing, is it?"

There was a sudden mischievousness in Madeline's expression. "Carrie and Nick just needed a little nudge."

"Meddler," Drew muttered.

"Take it from me," said the vicar. "Nudging works only when both parties want to be nudged."

"They were already hurtling toward each other at full speed anyway," Drew said.

Madeline shook one finger at him. "And they might have hurtled right past each other if someone hadn't stepped in."

"Don't you know the dangers of matchmaking?" Drew gave her a warning look. "Didn't you read *Emma*?"

Broadhurst sighed. "I have continually brought just that volume to my mother's attention. She tells me it all worked out in the end."

Madeline wrinkled her nose at her husband. "See?"

"All I see," Tal said, pulling Alice to his side, "is that it's time the lot of us went back in."

A flicker of worry passed through the girl's large eyes, but then she smiled and, her fingers twined in his, walked with him back to Winteroak House.

It was definitely worth wearing fussy cravats and shoes that pinch, so long as Madeline was having a good time, but Drew was glad when Saturday came. The day was warm and sunny, and Mrs. Cummins served luncheon out on the lawn. Afterward, hardly anyone seemed inclined to move away from the pleasant venue. A number of foursomes gathered to play cards. While Will did his best to pin down suspects in the pearls mystery, Nick and Carrie slipped over to the gazebo in the middle of the luscious rose garden and curled up in the swing. Drew knew better than to intrude on them even to ask if they knew where Madeline had gone, but he was happy to see Tal coming his way.

"I say, Tal—"

"Have you seen Alice?"

"No." Drew shaded his eyes, looking out toward the water. "I was just going to ask if you'd seen Madeline. She hasn't played fair with the clues about the pearls, I'm sure of it."

Tal grinned. "Just because you haven't figured it out yet, eh? Well, I saw her in the house just a bit ago. She said to tell you she'd be right out."

"Right. Thanks. I'll just—"

"Tal! Tal!"

Drew and Tal both looked up to see a group of bright-eyed girls, all in fresh muslin gowns, standing on the other side of the hedge.

"Tal!" Alice called again, waving a gloved hand. "We're going to play croquet. Won't you both join us?"

"Coming." Tal turned to Drew, lowering his voice. "She wouldn't crack a smile this morning, and now she's in one of her top-of-the-world moods. I suppose I should just do as you say. Admire and enjoy."

"Best for now, I'd say. Only we can't play croquet for another thirty years or so. I believe it wasn't properly invented yet. We'd better call it pall-mall. It's practically the same."

"I'll tell everyone," Tal said. "Just in case my dad's listening in."

It seemed that Alice had summoned nearly everyone to join the game or at least watch. Mrs. Cummins brought out lemonade and some excellent little cakes, and the afternoon passed pleasantly enough. Drew couldn't help keeping an eye on Alice as she played. She did seem rather excitable, but he didn't know her well enough to know if that was out of the ordinary for her. Even taking Tal's word that it was, she seemed no more than bright and vivacious. Her two friends, Georgie and Violet, on the other hand, did make him wonder.

They played enthusiastically, if badly, and it took nothing to make either of them laugh uproariously. They flirted with every unattached man present, a few attached ones, and even poor, flustered Will. He brushed them aside, though, clearly more interested in keeping an eye on his sister anytime she and Nick were within fifty feet of each other.

The day grew warmer, and several of the men shed their coats. Old Ploughwright had removed both coat and waistcoat and still sat mopping his red face in the shade of an oak tree. Miss Dornford had given up on attracting Will's attention and was comforting herself with an overindulgence in cake.

Cummins sat talking to the vicar under the striped awning that shaded part of the terrace. Laurent, evidently having just risen, joined them, a glass of tomato juice in hand. They made an interesting trio, and Drew took a seat beside them.

"I'm not intruding, am I?"

"Not at all," Cummins said. "Just chatting. The padre's collecting again for the needy."

"The same cause Mrs. Cummins collects for?"

"That's right. The old girl likes to feel useful."

Drew helped himself to a macaroon. "I hear you like to lend a hand, as well."

"Ah, well," Cummins sputtered. "When I can. Not that I have much time for it, you know, but when I can."

"And the vicar here distributes it all to the local needy?"

"Only part of it." Broadhurst leaned forward, a light of eagerness in his eyes. "The Good Book says we should 'preach the gospel in Jerusalem, and in all Judea and Samaria, and even to the remotest part of the earth.' I take that to mean we have responsibility to our neighbors and to the world at large, not neglecting either for the other. Not that we've reached those remotest parts yet, but we do send much of what we collect up to London."

"You get in that much?" Drew asked. "I'm impressed."

"Oh, not just from little Armitage Landing, of course," the vicar said. "We have several of our ladies up and down the coast who gather donations in their own villages and package them up for us to distribute. Money when we can get it, but more often foodstuffs, castoff clothing, and household goods. Some of the ladies make some items themselves such as baby clothes, knitted jumpers, that sort of thing."

"You might be interested in helping out, Drew," Cummins suggested.

Broadhurst looked a bit flustered. "Well, we're all off duty here, you know. I'd hate to bother any of your guests—"

"No, he's quite right," Drew said. "It's a worthy cause. It's rather a balance helping close to home and farther away, isn't it? I like that you're doing both. Remind me before the party is over and I'll send you a check."

"Very generous of you, Drew, I'm sure."

"Not at all. I'm rather outrageously blessed. No good keeping it all to myself, eh?"

Broadhurst chuckled. "I wish all of my appeals were so fruitful and with so little effort on my part."

"You might speak to Mrs. Farthering about it, as well," Drew suggested. "If I can manage to keep out of trouble for more than six months at a go, I imagine she'll want something worthwhile to do with her time."

"We'd certainly appreciate the help," Broadhurst said.

"And very charming help it would be, too," Laurent said, making a tomato juice toast as Madeline came out of the house and sat down beside Drew.

"Hullo, darling. I've just pledged you to help Mr. Broadhurst with his charity."

"Oh, may I?" she asked the vicar, her eyes eager. "I don't know if I'll be as good at it as Mrs. Cummins, but I'd love to help."

"Excellent," Broadhurst said. "Once you've gotten a chance to get settled back at home, I'll be in touch. We can sort out what you can do to help in your neck of the woods."

Whatever else he might have said was interrupted by a croquet ball rolling to a stop at his feet. Alice and her two friends hurried over to him.

"Do be careful," Tal said, giving the Marlow girl a disapproving glance.

"Well, I didn't hit it," Violet said. "That's Georgie's ball, isn't it?"

Georgie laughed and swung wildly at it, sending it out of play and perilously close to Mr. Ploughwright's head. He huffed and sputtered in protest.

"Steady on there, young lady!"

Georgie and Violet both shrieked with laughter, and Georgie scampered over to him and planted a smacking kiss on his bald pate, causing him to sputter more and Mrs. Ploughwright to look stern and purse her lips. Apparently both girls found this even more hysterical.

"Oh, Georgie, really!" Alice said, giggling. "Come on now. It's still your turn."

Tal came up beside her, taking her arm. "Perhaps we've had enough for a bit, darling," he said, his voice low. "Isn't it about time you ladies go in and start primping for tonight?"

She set her mouth and lifted her chin. "I'm having fun. I thought that's what all this was for—for us to have some fun before we have to go back to real life tomorrow."

"Alice—"

Her chin quivered, and she pressed her fingers to her lips. Then she gave him a brittle smile. "You're right. It really is getting late. I think I'll start getting ready." She nodded to the wide-eyed onlookers. "Excuse me."

She hurried across the lawn and into the house. Tal started to go after her, but Drew stopped him.

"Give her a little while."

Tal looked as if he might protest, but instead he nodded and sat down again.

"Alice," Georgie whined, "you can't quit now. We haven't finished."

Violet beamed at her. "If she's out, I win the game. Ha ha."

Georgie made a face at her and, with one fierce blow of her mallet, sent Violet's ball sailing over the hedge and out of sight.

"Georgie!"

The two girls stalked off, squabbling furiously, and disappeared into the trees.

"And so ends the match," Laurent observed, downing the last of his tomato juice. "*Quel dommage*, but perhaps Mademoiselle Alice is correct. The hour grows late, and we must prepare for the evening's festivities."

The vicar looked at his wristwatch and got to his feet. "I told Mother I would wake her from her nap when it was time to dress. I'd better see to it, if you will all excuse me."

"Perhaps it would be best if we all went in," Cummins said, looking rather dismayed, and he too stood. "Ladies and gentlemen, you might all wish to go prepare for tonight's ball. Our other guests will be arriving before long, and we want to be ready to greet them in grand style, eh?"

People began strolling back into the house in little knots of two and three.

Madeline took Drew's arm and looked back toward the hedge where Violet and Georgie had gone. "Do you suppose they're all right?"

"I'm sure they'll be in soon," Drew said, starting them walking. "It's a wonder nobody was knocked cold by one of them, though. Well, come along. Tonight's our last night here. We might as well make it a memorable one."

Madeline shook her head once they were in the privacy of their room. "I don't think there have been two such silly girls in England since Kitty and Lydia Bennet."

"In the world," Drew corrected, "not just in England. I suppose I ought to be a little less easy to annoy, but I wish they'd just settle someplace and be still, even for just a minute. They were a bit wild this afternoon."

"A bit?" Madeline huffed. "I was in the powder room earlier, and the two of them were preening in front of the mirror. Giggling as usual of course. I came up next to them, wanting to make sure my hair was still pinned up right, and I noticed Violet had face powder on her nose. You know, not blended in or anything. When I told her, just so she wouldn't be embarrassed to find out after she'd gone back to the party, she only sniffed at me. Not a dainty little sniff of disdain, but a loud vulgar sniff. I'm sure she meant to be offensive. Then the two of them shrieked with laughter and dashed out."

She had thought he would laugh or say something pithy about silly females, including herself, but instead his relaxed expression tightened and there was no more tolerant amusement in his gray eyes.

"Hmmm. Alice wasn't with them, was she?"

"No. Not while I was there. Why?"

"I just hope, for her own sake and for Tal's, she's not as foolish as her friends." He smiled abruptly and kissed her hand. "But I am blessed to have a level-headed and nonetheless charming wife who hardly ever makes a spectacle of herself at society parties."

She raised one eyebrow. "Hardly ever?"

"I seem to recall a time, just a year ago today in fact, when you poured a glass of water down a gentleman's quite admirable shirtfront during a very high-class gathering. I was shocked, I tell you. Shocked."

Her face turned hot, though she was smiling. "In the first place, he was no gentleman. In the second place, I did it only to keep you from punching him in the nose. And in the third place . . ." She paused and gave him a peck on the cheek. "In the third place, I didn't think you'd remember."

He gave her that lazy grin she loved. "How could I forget the day I found the other half of my heart." He slid his arm around her waist, pulling her closer to his side. "How could I resist someone so charming and respectable, with a little streak of wickedness hidden inside like nuts in a bonbon? No, don't tell me it's not there, but not to worry. It'll be our secret."

She laughed and then sobered, remembering her talk with Alice on the *Onde Blanc*. "She's going to hurt him."

Drew raised both eyebrows. "What?"

"I never told you what Alice said when we were sailing the other day. While you were dozing. I didn't think it was important, but now I'm wondering."

"What do you mean?"

"She's got something to tell him, and he's not going to like it."

Drew sat on the bed. "And she didn't give you a clue about what it was?"

"I'm afraid not. There were a couple of times after that when we were talking and I thought she might want to tell me more, but she didn't. She said she'd wait until the party was over before she tells him. I suppose that'll be tomorrow. I really hope it's not as bad as she thinks it is."

He took her hand and drew her close. "I don't know what it is she has on her mind, but it's not uncommon for people to imagine their failings are more devastating than they actually are."

"Not that either of us would ever do that."

He feigned outrage. "Certainly not."

She laughed and then sighed and leaned against him. "She loves him so much. I know she doesn't want to lose him."

"He loves her, too," Drew responded. "I imagine they'll figure out how to deal with whatever it is. Together."

"But if it's very bad . . ." She laughed abruptly and twisted away from him. "No, I'm not going to borrow trouble. They'll have to work it out between them, as you say. All we have to do is get changed. Hurry now."

"Right." He got to his feet and straightened his coat. "I'll be back in just a moment."

She huffed. "Drew, you really must get changed. We need to be there in plenty of time. Mrs. Cummins will expect us to be in the first group of dancers."

"Don't worry, darling. I'll be back before you and Beryl have even gotten started. Anyway, there may not be any dancing tonight after all."

She gaped at him. "What do you mean?"

"I have to go see a man about a dog," he said with a wink. "If anything comes of it, I'll let you know."

Before she could say anything more, he was gone.

— Four —

The good weather held, though there was a steady wind off the water and the evening turned rather cool. True to his earlier edicts, Cummins would not allow automobiles inside the park gates. Instead, he had two barouches ferrying guests down to the house, complete with two liveried torchbearers running ahead to light the road. But the moon hung bright and round as the bottom of a copper kettle in the clear night sky, illuminating the front lawn and making their lights almost superfluous.

Drew stood at the upstairs window overlooking the drive and watched the guests arrive, the ones who hadn't stayed at Winteroak for the week. There were gentlemen in satin knee breeches and long-tailed coats with their flattened opera hats tucked under their arms, and ladies in their finest ball gowns with their hair done up in the classical Grecian style, adorned with jewels and ribbons and feathers.

"And where is your lady fair?"

Drew turned to see Nick coming up beside him, looking particularly dapper in a white satin waistcoat with gold embroidery.

"Madeline and her maid drove me out of our room because I was abominably in the way. They're not used to doing all their preparations in such close quarters. What about Carrie?"

"I told her I'd meet her here and then we could go down to the ballroom together. How many do you think they're having tonight?"

"Oh, it will no doubt be a full house, if I know Cummins."

Drew watched a particularly tall lady in orange silk and ostrich feathers being handed out of the carriage, followed by a man in period regimentals and an elderly gentleman in a powdered wig.

"Old Cummins certainly knows how to throw a proper bash," Nick said. He straightened his shoulders and adjusted the lace at his wrists. "Everything shipshape and Bristol fashion?"

"Very nice. The lovely Miss Holland will be charmed, though I doubt any manner of adornment will have a positive effect on her brother."

"No fear. Every time I think he's decided I'm not Jack the Ripper, he catches me and Carrie together and it sets him off again. Not that he says anything, mind you. I suppose she's warned him off on that, but it's hard to enjoy a nice party when you know someone would rather drown you in the ornamental fountain than have you speak another word to his sister."

Drew stifled a chuckle. "I think he's rather to be congratulated for taking his chaperoning so seriously."

"Yes, I suppose," Nick said, disconsolately. "But it's not as if I've given him any cause for alarm. Carrie and I have done nothing but talk."

"Well, buck up, old man. I don't think he's as set against

you as you think. I know he's had a ripping time with the little mystery of the pearls, and from what he tells me he's perilously close to figuring out our little riddle." Drew made a woebegone face. "Better than I have."

"The girls did make a deuce of a puzzle for us, eh? And Will does seem to be enjoying it. And when his sister's not the topic of conversation, I don't think he minds me too awfully much. Most of the time. He's not a bad kid."

"No. Not a bad detective, either. At least you've been able to spend a bit of time with Carrie while he's sleuthing."

Nick grinned. "Don't think I don't know it was you and the missus who arranged it all by getting Mr. and Mrs. Cummins to invite her."

"We couldn't miss the chance to see you primped up like Beau Brummell for a week."

Nick snorted. "You should talk."

"Well, at least I don't have to suffer alone. And the ladies seem to like it."

The corner of Nick's mouth twitched. "Doesn't hurt, eh?"

Drew glanced over his shoulder and then lowered his voice. "Just between you and me, how are things progressing? May we expect an announcement in the near future?"

Nick looked out over the drive, watching the carriages once more. "No."

Drew blinked, certain he hadn't heard properly. "No? Don't worry, I won't say anything to Madeline, not that she doesn't know already, but you can tell me. I won't even devil you over it."

Drew smiled, but Nick only winced.

"I hadn't thought it all out before she came." He shrugged helplessly. "I suppose I was too much in love to think straight. But what's she going to do with someone like me? Her family has money. Good breeding. All that. I'm just an estate agent. Not even that. I'm an estate agent in training, God help me. What can I offer her but a life halfway round the world from everything she knows and everyone she loves?"

"Perhaps she likes the idea of moving here. Or perhaps she just likes you. As Miss Austen says, 'What have wealth and grandeur to do with happiness?'"

"She also says, 'A large income is the best recipe for happiness I ever heard of.'"

Drew shook his head. "You've been around those 'large incomes' all your life, old man. You and I both know the rich are no happier than anyone else. But why don't you trust Carrie to know her own mind about such things? Every girl in the world isn't a ruthless mercenary."

"But that's just it," Nick said. "She's always had everything she wanted. She doesn't really know what it's like to live a bourgeois sort of life. Suppose she marries me and then decides it's not so romantic to live in a garret after all?"

Drew laughed. "Are your quarters at Farthering Place so bad?"

"No, no, that's not what I mean at all." Nick growled low in his throat. "Oh, blast it all, you know what I mean. How can I possibly marry a girl and ask her to take permanent residence in someone else's home, no matter how grand it is? It's not as if we'd be in service there."

"No, of course not."

Drew considered for a moment. Nick's parents had been butler and maid at Farthering Place. Nick himself had been born there and lived there all his life. But as a married man and likely with children coming eventually, it wasn't quite practical for him to stay where he was. And, yes, Madeline and Carrie were great friends, but there was such a thing as too much closeness, especially for young ladies striving to establish themselves as wives.

Drew smiled. "I know the very thing, old man. When you and Carrie get married, you'll have to leave Farthering Place."

"Yes, I know."

"No, no, there's nothing for it. I'm sorry, but as you say, you can't ask a girl to marry you and then just stuff her into the attic next to the old bureaus."

"I know," Nick repeated, shoulders slumping. "*If* we were to marry. Well, never mind."

"What do you mean never mind? You and Carrie are absolutely dotty about each other, aren't you?"

"I know I am about her."

"Well then, how can you not marry?"

Nick's jaw tightened. "Look here, Drew, you and your family have been good to me all my life. You're more than generous with my salary, especially with providing room and board as well, but you and I both know it's not enough to keep a wife. Not in anyplace Carrie deserves. How's that any way to start a life together?"

"Madeline didn't think Rose Cottage was so terrible," Drew said. "Even her aunt Ruth couldn't find anything much to complain about while she was there."

Nick's brow wrinkled. "Rose Cottage?"

"Madeline and I thought that, if you do actually get married, a life estate in Rose Cottage might not be so shabby a wedding gift. You could run Farthering Place from there, couldn't you?"

Nick turned his head a bit to one side as if he hadn't heard properly. "Rose Cottage?"

Drew nodded. "You know, the quaint little dwelling beyond the back garden? Green door? Roses growing up the walls?

I'm sure you've seen it back there a time or two while you were performing your duties."

"Don't be an idiot. Of course I've seen it. But you're—"

"Madeline tells me it's sweet, but I'll let you and Carrie judge for yourselves."

"You're saying you would give Rose Cottage to us? I couldn't possibly—"

"Purely selfish on my part," Drew interrupted. "Can't have you and the bride moving off to Timbuktu. Once old Padgett retires, who'll manage the estate for me? The whole place would fall to ruin."

Nick laughed half under his breath. "It's more than good of you, Drew, but it's far too much. Dad would bust a garter."

"Denny's your father, not mine, and though he's a top-notch butler, I can't have him taking on airs, can I? No, I really must be my own master in this. Besides, Madeline will be dead vexed with me if I don't make the offer."

"Look here—"

Drew held up his hand. "That's all I have to say on the matter. If a sweet cottage in the Hampshire countryside isn't enough to overcome her objections to you personally, I fear your cause is a hopeless one."

"Well there is that," Nick said. "Best hold off on signing any papers until she and I at least have an understanding."

"Fair enough. I wouldn't have said anything at all yet, but I didn't want you to give up the fight just for want of adequate housing."

Nick chuckled. "I won't hold you to it. I might be wishing on too distant a star as it is."

"Judging by young Will's scowling, you're closer than you think."

Nick started to say something when a light came into his eyes. "There she is. Excuse me."

Carrie stood at the top of the stairs, a vision in an empire-waisted gown of emerald silk and Mechlin lace, with her red-gold curls framing her sweet face. Nick darted up the stairs, seized her hand and pressed it with a fervent kiss. Smiling, he tucked her arm in his and escorted her down to the ball.

"Don't they look wonderful together?"

Drew turned to find Madeline at his side, slipping her arm through his. Instead of the muslin dress and Spencer jacket she wore during the day, she had on a gown of pale blue and ivory-striped silk and long white gloves. Her dark hair was swept up and secured by a gold-and-diamond tiara, and around her graceful neck, in place of her missing pearls, she wore the diamond pendant that had once belonged to his great-grandmother. He was certain she hadn't any idea how perfectly charming she was.

He bowed over her hand and brought it to his lips. "You honor me, madam."

She curtsied, periwinkle eyes sparkling. "And you me, sir. Now, shall we join the others?"

"As my lady pleases."

He escorted her down the grand stairway, but she stopped halfway down.

"Don't stare at me," she whispered, her cheeks turning pink. "Can you see my petticoat or something?"

He put his free hand over the one on his arm. "All I see, my darling, is the most gloriously beautiful and scandalously intoxicating woman in all the world."

She glanced to one side and then the other, then stood tiptoe and touched her lips to his. "You've been up to something."

"Me? Madam, I protest. I am the very ideal of the complete

Regency gentleman, from my exquisitely tied neckcloth to these ridiculous silk stockings and satin knee breeches. Really, the things I do to prove my undying devotion."

"You're *my* ideal of the complete Regency gentleman," she said with another slightly more tantalizing kiss. "And since I'm sure you haven't been gambling, drinking, or womanizing, that means you're up to something else."

He made a low harrúmphing sound as if he were a disgruntled member of Parliament.

"Behave," she whispered when they had reached the ballroom. "Oooh, isn't it glorious?"

It truly was. Over the course of the week they had grown used to seeing people in their period costumes, yet this evening was different. Muslins and buckskins were nowhere to be seen. In their place were silks, satins, embroidered velvets, and rich jewels. Ladies in diamonds and fantastic headdresses walked beside men carrying opera hats, men whose cravats were so high and stiff they could scarcely turn their heads. Liveried servants lined the walls, and a very correct butler in a solemn powdered wig announced the guests as they arrived. In one corner a violin and pianoforte played "The Soldier's Adieu," accompanied by bass fiddle and flute. It reminded Drew of his upcoming fate.

"I don't suppose you'll allow me to excuse myself from the dancing. If there is to be dancing, I mean."

"No mysteries," she said sternly. "Not now. Either tell me where you went earlier or don't talk about it."

"Oh, very well. I don't know what I'm talking about anyway. Could be nothing. But must I really—"

"Yes. You promised. No complaints."

"Yes," he sighed. "Yes, I did."

"You're complaining."

"I was agreeing," he protested.

"While making it clear you don't agree." She looked up at him through her lashes, well knowing that would be more persuasive than a scolding. "You dance so beautifully."

He sniffed. "'Every savage can dance.'"

"Don't be grumpy Mr. Darcy now, Drew. I thought you enjoyed it."

"I do, when it's a proper dance where I can hold my wife close, not all this hopping about in these ridiculous shoes that look like something you should be wearing."

"It's just for one night. Tomorrow you can go back to your regular clothes, which will also look quite ridiculous in another hundred years."

"Not, my dear, if *I* am wearing them."

"Oh, there you are." Mrs. Cummins hurried up to them, the feathers in her headdress bobbing alarmingly. "Forgive my overhearing, but you mustn't fail me now, Drew. You simply mustn't."

He laughed. "Wouldn't dream of it, ma'am," he drawled and then kissed her hand. "Merely deviling the old ball and chain."

Madeline made a face at him.

"Oh, don't tease now," Mrs. Cummins said. "It's really a disaster. Those two friends of Alice's, that Violet and Georgie, what do you think they've done?"

Drew glanced at Madeline. "What have they—?"

"They've left," Mrs. Cummins said with an emphatic and indignant dip of her chin, her lips tightly pursed. "Gone off without so much as a by-your-leave. Sterling said it was for the best and that I mustn't mind, but I'm sure he knows something about it, no matter what he says. A woman can tell these things."

"That's very odd," Madeline said. "Why would they—?"

"Now, darling, it's not as if we were great friends of theirs. They seemed rather more likely than not to make some sort of scene before the evening was over. Forget about them."

"But Drew," Mrs. Cummins moaned. "Now we have only six couples for the dances, and everything's spoilt."

"Now, now." Drew took her arm, giving it a soothing pat as he did. "It's not as bad as all that. We can still do the dances, just four couples at a time. We'll all switch out, and no one will know the difference."

She blinked, her face relaxing. "Do you really think so?"

"I promise it will be fine. And you promised to stand up with me for the country dance. Now don't forget."

That coaxed a smile from her. "I won't. Oh, there's Tibby. I must tell him. Do excuse me." She hurried away to the far side of the room, talking urgently to her son.

Drew made another formal bow. "Shall we, ma'am?"

"Why do you think they went?" Madeline asked, taking his arm again. "They were terribly silly girls, but I didn't think anything would make them leave before the grand ball. They were really looking forward to it."

He shrugged. "I think Mr. Cummins is right, darling. It probably is for the best. Now, shall we go find Nick and Carrie and make sure Will isn't being overwhelmed by the unfortunate Miss Dornford?"

She didn't move when he took a step forward.

"What is it?"

"You knew about this," she said, her voice low. "You knew they were going to leave and that the dancing would be ruined, didn't you?"

"Madeline—"

She gave him a look, and he blew out his breath.

"This isn't the time or place for it, darling. I promise I'll tell you all about it, but not now. It's not exactly suitable for a jolly occasion like this, eh?"

She frowned.

"Trust me on this one. Put Violet and Georgie out of your mind and just enjoy the evening. I will dance as if I were Mr. Bingley himself." He kissed her hand. "In honor of the anniversary of the happiest day of my life."

She smiled. "We did come to have fun, didn't we?"

"And we shall. Look, there's Nick and Carrie." He chuckled. "And Will is trying to hide behind them."

"We'd better tell them the plans have changed."

She steered him over to the French doors that opened onto a terrace. Will stood next to Nick and Carrie, wearing a perfectly correct long-tailed coat of blue superfine, buff knee britches, and a rather wary expression.

"I think you've been given a reprieve, Will," Drew said, taking two cups of limeade from a tray on the sideboard and giving one to Madeline. "Two of our ladies have departed, so Miss Dornford will have to share you with the others."

Will brightened, helping himself to a drink. "Well, that's just too bad."

"It's those two friends of Alice's, isn't it?" Nick said with a shake of his head. "Can't say that I'm sorry."

"Shh," Carrie hissed. "There's Alice and Tal now."

Alice looked particularly pale, and her eyes had the slightest tinge of red as if she had recently been crying. Tal looked more than a bit grim.

"I suppose you've heard," he said. "About Violet and Georgie, I mean."

Drew nodded. "I know your mother's upset, but I told her already that we can carry on, just with four couples at a go."

Alice set her empty limeade cup on the sideboard, rattling the silver tray. "I'll just sit it out, too. I'm not much in the mood for dancing."

"Come now, Alice," Tal begged, setting down his own cup. "You know we're short of ladies as it is. Mother's already upset over it. We can't desert her now. Please, love."

She looked pleadingly at him. "Tal, you just don't under—"

"Please, sweetheart. This is Mother's grand occasion, the highlight of the whole week. Can't we just enjoy tonight and worry about everything else tomorrow? I promise we'll talk about anything you like then, all right? Will you do this for me?"

For a moment she only looked at him. Finally she nodded and, smoothing her skirt, put on a smile. "For you." Her smile suddenly became more genuine as she reached up to caress his cheek. "For you, Tal."

"Good girl. Now," he said, turning back to Madeline and Carrie, "you ladies will have to pitch in especially, since we're down two."

"I won't mind not dancing," Will said.

Carrie gave him a stern look. "You'll take your turn like everybody else. And stop looking like a whipped pup. This *is* a party."

Will took another cup of the limeade and didn't say anything else.

"This is delicious," Carrie told Tal, her expression bright again as she took a sip of her own drink. "I'm a little surprised you're serving it tonight, though. Was it popular during the Regency?"

"Actually, no," Tal replied, "but we thought we ought to offer something for those who don't usually imbibe. Dad was willing to bend a bit, just on that."

"Good evening, everyone." The Reverend Broadhurst made a bow to the ladies and then took a sip of the drink he carried. "I must agree with Tal about his mother's limeade. It's been a local treasure for years now."

Laurent sauntered up to them in a black coat with silver filigree trim. His cravat was exceptionally frothy, and he carried an elegant walking stick. "Good evening, gentlemen." He bowed to the girls, the usual insinuating smirk on his narrow face. "Ladies, I do not know by what means, but you manage somehow to grow lovelier each time we meet." He put one elegant hand up to his bicorne hat. "You make me wish to imitate my great countryman Napoleon and conquer all I see."

"Then I shall have to be Wellington," Drew said solicitously. "Though I'm sure we needn't go as far as Waterloo."

The Frenchman returned an arch nod. "What is it your Kipling says? 'Oh, beware the English when the English grow polite'?"

"Very nearly that," Drew said. "And I've always thought him a very wise man."

Mrs. Cummins bustled back up to them all, looking much more pleased than she had just a few minutes ago. "I've talked to Mr. Cummins, and he said we ought to open the country dances to anyone who wants to join in. It may not be so elegant a display as we had planned, but at least more of the guests can take part. And of course everyone can waltz. I think it might not be so disastrous an evening as I had first thought."

Tal gave her a fond kiss on the cheek. "There, you see? Now, how shall we arrange things to begin?"

"We'll start with the cotillion. You and Alice, your father and I, Mr. and Mrs. Farthering, Nick and Miss Holland.

How would that be? You'll know when they begin the Gallini 'Allemande' and Beddows will announce us. Monsieur Laurent, you don't mind being in the second group, do you?"

"Certainly not, madame." Laurent made an elegant bow. "There are many things to keep me occupied."

"And . . ." She looked faintly embarrassed. "I'm so sorry to mention it, and please don't think me rude, but will you ask your Mr. Adkins to try to be a bit less conspicuous? He seems everywhere all at once."

"Of course," Laurent assured her. "I apologize. The man's an oaf, to be certain, but well, if I did not see to him, who would?"

She squeezed his arm. "Thank you. Now, I must see to Mrs. Hope's little dog. It bites, you know, but she insists on having it with her."

The cotillion went off without a hitch, as did the quadrille that followed, except Alice had seemed uncharacteristically rushed in her steps.

"What was Alice in such a hurry over?" Madeline asked when she and Drew stopped to have another limeade. "She's always such a lovely dancer, but tonight she seems almost . . . forced."

"Perhaps she *is* trying too hard to enjoy herself as she promised Tal she would. Or perhaps she's upset about whatever it is she wants to tell him."

"It doesn't seem very like her, though, does it? To spoil things for him after she said she'd wait?"

"No. From what I've seen of her until now, she seems the type to withdraw if she's hurt or upset rather than putting herself forward." He looked over her shoulder and smiled. "Here they come, darling."

"No, you should," Alice was saying, laughing as she did.

"Madeline, tell Tibby you'll dance with him. He's afraid to ask. You won't mind, Drew, will you? Of course you won't, because you're going to ask me. You wouldn't want to leave me just standing here, would you?"

Her eyes were almost too bright as she clutched Drew's arm, and he looked at Tal with a questioning smile. "What do you say?"

"Uh, of course." Tal bowed to Madeline. "Will you do me the honor, ma'am?"

She curtsied and went with him, looking faintly uneasy.

Alice immediately took Drew's arm. "Now, sir, I believe you owe me a dance."

He bowed gravely. "Ma'am."

With one hand on hers and the other at her slim waist, he guided her into the throng of dancers. At once he realized it was a mistake. She clung to him, again ahead of the music, trying to lead instead of following him. She stepped on his foot more than once, looking alternately mortified and amused, and hung off him so heavily he feared his coat would tear.

Mercifully the music ended. Bowing, Drew offered her his arm. She stumbled a little as she took it and then laughed.

"You're a good dancer. I'm *not* a good dancer. I mean, I can dance, but I don't dance good. I mean, well." She laughed again, hanging on him now, her words coming out far too rapidly. "You're a good dancer. Tal's a good dancer, but he doesn't much like it. But when we're married, I'll get him to like it. I'll get him to dance and dance and dance all the time. And he'll be a good dancer. I like good dancers. You're a good dancer."

"I'm not very good at this sort of dance, I'm afraid." Drew tried to pull his arm away from her, yet she clung even tighter. "Perhaps we ought to sit down for a while and catch our breath."

He finally freed himself, only to have her put both slender arms around his neck and stand tiptoe to whisper in his ear, "I like you, Drew." She inhaled deeply. "You smell nice. You feel nice."

He shrugged out of her embrace. "I think Tal is looking for you."

"Oh, Tal. He's really not a good dancer. You're a good dancer."

She twisted her fingers into the sleeves of his coat, and he tried again to pull away from her, looking over his shoulder to see if he could spot Tal somewhere in the throng of dancers. This was all wrong, and he was afraid he knew why.

At last he saw Tal and Madeline coming through the crowd, each of them with a glass of Mrs. Cummins's limeade.

"Oh, there you are," he called.

Madeline looked up, smiling, but then her expression changed. No doubt she could read the concern in his. She and Tal hurried over to him just as Alice linked her fingers through his and started swinging their hands in a wide arc.

Tal's forehead wrinkled. "Alice? What are you doing, darling?"

Her smile was manic, her eyes wide and far too bright as she grabbed his hand with her free one and began swinging it in time with the other. "Tal, Tal, Tal, won't you dance with us? I so love to dance. Drew's a lovely dancer, isn't he, Madeline? You don't mind if he dances with us, do you?"

Madeline looked at Drew, her concern deepening.

Tal put his free arm around his fiancée, holding her as Drew freed his hand.

"Oh, don't," she whined. "We were just about to dance."

82

"I think you've had quite enough for the evening," Tal said, and he winced. "Sorry about all this, old man. I don't know what's got into her. She's never been much of a one to overindulge."

Drew shook his head. "Tal, I don't think—"

"Tal," Alice singsonged. "Tal, Tal, Tibby."

"Everything quite all right?" the vicar asked as he came to Tal's side.

"It's nothing. I think she's just had a bit too much." Tal gave Alice a reproving look and tried to lead her away, but she only squirmed out of his grasp.

"You don't want to dance with me, do you?" She gave Madeline a poisonous glare. "You want to dance with *her*. You want to get rid of me and dance with her, don't you?"

Her voice was shrill and loud, and the other guests were beginning to stare. Laurent was watching them from the back of the room, his expression unreadable.

"Alice," Tal pled, low and urgent. "Let me take you to your room. I'll get Mother."

He tried to take her arm again, but she shoved him away from her.

"I don't want your mother. You know what, Tal? She makes rotten limeades. She really does. They're thoroughly nasty, and she can't dance." She flung herself against Drew again, looking up at him with wide eyes, her pupils so dilated it was nearly impossible to see the pale blue of the irises. "You'll dance with me, won't you, Drew? You're so awfully nice."

She tugged on the wide lapel of his coat, pulling it askew as she listed sideways.

"Steady on now," he said, catching her under the arms. "She's deuced hot, Tal. Best get your mother after all and then call a doctor. Or perhaps there's one here."

"I said I don't *want* her!"

Alice wrenched away from him, her attempted slap landing with a dull thud on his upper arm. Then she slid to her knees at his feet, laughing again.

"They think I don't know," she said, glancing at Tal and Madeline and then looking up at Drew. "They think I don't know about them, but I do. They made up this whole party just as a cover." She struggled to her feet again, steadying herself against him. "There are things going on, you know. Things *they* won't tell you about. But I know. I've seen them together."

Drew held her by both arms. "Madeline, go and get Mrs. Cummins. Please, and quickly."

Brow furrowed, Madeline looked at the girl one last time before hurrying off. The music and dancing had stopped entirely by now, and everyone was talking in low murmurs, trying not to stare but staring all the same.

Tal looked around the room and then ducked his head, his voice painfully unsteady. "Drew, please, what is it?"

"We'd better get her to her room. Madeline will find us."

Drew tried to shift the girl into Tal's arms, but she beat her fists against him, twisting away, breaking free and bolting toward the open terrace doors like a bird unexpectedly out of its cage.

"Alice!"

Tal bolted after her, catching her as she collapsed at the terrace railing. He gathered her into his arms with her pale skirts billowing around him, clutching her close, breathing her name against her cheek, his tear-filled eyes pleading and desperate, both of them haloed in moonlight. The guests stood in silent shock, staring at the tableau, until Drew took his friend's arm and guided him back into the ballroom and just as quickly out of it.

Nick caught up to them in the hallway. "What is it? What's wrong?"

Drew shook his head. "Stay down here. Look after Carrie and Will. Try to keep everyone calm."

"Right. Let me know if there's anything else I can do."

By the time Drew and Tal reached Alice's room, her fever had spiked even higher and she was babbling deliriously. By the time Madeline came upstairs with Tal's mother, Alice was gasping and convulsing. By the time the doctor arrived, Alice Henley was dead.

— Five —

The doctor, a severe-looking white-bearded man named Fletcher, removed his pince-nez and tucked them into his waistcoat pocket. For a moment he peered at Drew and Madeline, then at Tal, who was kneeling at Alice's side with his face pressed against hers.

"Did you know she used the stuff?" Dr. Fletcher asked, his tone cold.

Madeline turned to Drew. "She was drunk, wasn't she? It was just alcohol."

Drew shook his head, and the doctor pressed his lips into a tight line.

"Alcohol's bad enough, miss." He exhaled and shook his head in disgust. "You young people. You think you can do anything, pour any kind of poison into your systems, and not have it hurt you. How many times must I see this? A perfectly lovely girl, dead now and for a lark."

Mrs. Cummins put a plump hand over her mouth, horrified.

Tal's head shot up. He glared at the doctor with red, swollen eyes. "What do you mean? What are you saying?"

Fletcher glared right back. "Don't be coy with me, Tal Cummins. I've known you far too long for that. A party like this, teeming with spoilt young society pups, and you think I don't know what you get up to? And right under the noses of your fine mother and father. It's a scandal, that's what it is."

"What are you saying?" Tal demanded again, his voice choked and shaking. "What are you saying? That she wasn't drunk? That it was something else?"

Fletcher's expression softened. "All right, son, all right. Perhaps you didn't know. I don't see any marks on her arms, nothing to show she snorted the stuff for any length of time. Maybe it was her first time. Once is too much for some, especially for a wisp of a girl like she was. I'm sorry, but it makes me angry. Waste and foolishness always make me angry."

Tal looked up at Drew, lips quivering. "What is it? Drugs?"

"Tibby, don't," his mother murmured, reaching her hands toward him from the other side of the bed.

Drew bit his lip, wishing there was something else he could say. "Cocaine, isn't it, Doctor?"

Madeline ducked her head against his shoulder. "Oh, Drew, no."

Tal bolted to his feet with his fists clenched. "That's a lie!" He glanced at the slim, bloodless figure on the bed. "Alice wouldn't touch the stuff. Drew, I swear it. It wouldn't have been like her at all. She barely drank! Drew, tell them. Tell them!"

He grabbed Drew by both arms and dropped his head, wrenched with sudden sobs, trembling violently.

Drew put his arm around his shoulders and guided him away from the bed. "Come on, old man."

Tal dropped heavily onto the sofa in the corner, not releasing his hold on Drew's sleeve, and his mother came to sit beside him, looking pitifully dazed.

"It can't be," she said over and over again. "Not in our house. It can't be. Oh, what will your father say?"

"It's not true." Tal made a visible effort to steady himself, mopping his face with the handkerchief Drew offered and pushing his mother's soothing hands away. "No, I'm all right now. I'm all right. But you've got to understand. You've all got to understand. She'd never have taken cocaine."

"Her friend Violet," Drew said. "And Georgie."

Tal nodded. "What about them?"

"Tal, I—"

Tal grabbed Drew's sleeve again. "Tell me!"

"Madeline saw the two of them taking cocaine in the powder room near the terrace earlier today," Drew said, pressing his friend's hand and then gently freeing himself. "One might naturally conclude that's where Alice got it."

The doctor huffed and snapped his black bag shut.

Madeline looked at Drew, round-eyed. "Oh . . ."

He gave her a cautioning glance, and she pressed her lips firmly together.

"I'm sorry there's no more I could do." Dr. Fletcher pulled the coverlet over the dead girl's face. "Such a pity."

Tal covered his face with his hands, shaken with silent sobs. His mother wrapped him in her arms, pulling his head down to her shoulder. For a moment he struggled against her, but then he broke and truly began to cry, clinging to her like a child.

"Come on, darling," Drew said, and he and Madeline followed the doctor out of the room.

"Dr. Fletcher?" Drew stopped him at the top of the stairs.

"I don't suppose . . . that is, I'm wondering if it's possible someone could have given her the stuff without her knowing it. Tal is awfully certain she wouldn't have taken it intentionally."

The doctor scoffed. "Highly unlikely, sir. One can hardly snort or inject a substance and not know it."

"Perhaps in her food?"

Fletcher shook his head. "Stomach acids render cocaine inactive. Such a thing would have required her being given a larger dose than is usual, and that with some kind of alkaline. But I'll leave that to the police."

Drew nodded. "It seems they're already here."

There were several uniformed policemen milling about in the foyer, and two others who had the unmistakable look of a Scotland Yard inspector and his sergeant.

The doctor frowned. "How did they get here so quickly? Perhaps Cummins—"

He broke off as Sterling Cummins stepped into the foyer. His wrists were cuffed, and he was accompanied by two policemen. At least he had been allowed to change out of his Regency costume.

"Here now!" Dr. Fletcher charged down the steps. "What are you doing? How dare you! Do you know who this is?"

The inspector, a youngish man with brilliantined black hair and a bulldog jaw, came forward. "We're well aware, sir. Take him to the car, Fuller."

Cummins looked up, his face grim but stoic. "It's all right, Doctor. We'll have this sorted out soon. Just look after Tal, will you? He's had a shock. The wife too."

"Shall I fetch them, sir?" Drew asked. "At least Mrs. Cummins. Before you go and all?"

"Thanks all the same," Cummins said, looking down.

"It will be easier if I just go." He lifted his head. "Tell them what's happened. Look after them, eh?"

"I'll do that, sir." Drew glanced at the inspector and then back at Cummins. "I know a chief inspector of police, sir. Shall I ring him up? He might be able to clear this up more quickly for you."

"I know a few chief inspectors myself, sir." The inspector present stepped between Drew and Cummins. "And I can assure you Mr. Cummins will be introduced to a number of them shortly."

"What precisely are the charges?" Drew asked.

"Contributing to the girl's death," the inspector said, "as well as trafficking in illegal drugs."

Madeline gave a little gasp.

Drew looked at Cummins, a sudden queasiness in his stomach. "Sir, that can't be."

Cummins glanced at him and instantly looked away. He denied nothing. There was nothing but shame in his expression.

The inspector nodded to the constable holding on to Cummins's arm. "Go on, Fuller."

The uniformed officers escorted Cummins out, and there was a moment of taut silence. Drew could only watch them leave. Sterling Cummins trafficking in cocaine? Sterling Cummins, captain of industry, known for absolute integrity in his business dealings? Sterling Cummins the philanthropist who had contributed millions to charity for the past two decades? Sterling Cummins, friend of Drew's father, someone Drew had admired and endeavored to emulate since he was a boy?

The doctor cleared his throat. "I demand to know just who you are, Officer, and what all this is about. Sterling Cummins—"

"Endicott. Scotland Yard." The inspector handed the doctor his card and nodded toward the colorless little man at his side. "This is Sergeant Dane. And I presume you are Dr. . . . ."

"Fletcher," Dane supplied, looking at his notebook. "Called about an hour ago to see to the girl."

Fletcher frowned, and Endicott turned to Drew and Madeline. "And you are?"

"Drew Farthering. This is my wife, Madeline."

Madeline nodded. "Inspector."

Endicott's eyebrows went up. "American, eh? And what brings you here?"

"I wanted to be near my husband."

The inspector pursed his lips. "I mean here to Winteroak House." Endicott looked them up and down. "Both here for the house party?"

"That's right," Drew said. "We've been here since Monday. We were to go home in the morning."

"And home would be where?"

"Farthering Place. In Farthering St. John, just a few miles north of here."

"You're that Farthering, are you?" Endicott sniffed. "Fancy yourself a detective, eh? Scotland Yard will see to things, I can assure you."

Drew gave him a very slight bow, one hand pressed to the fine lace of his shirtfront. "Quite."

"We will be questioning all the witnesses as quickly as we are able," the inspector added. "If you and Mrs. Farthering will be so good as to wait."

"Yes, of course."

"If that's all for the moment," Dr. Fletcher said, "I'd like to take the body. I will, of course, forward you a copy of my complete report."

"We'd best leave that to the coroner and the undertaker," the inspector said with a ghost of a smile. "Thanks all the same."

Dr. Fletcher drew himself up to his full not-very-impressive height. "I serve both of those functions locally."

The smile vanished. "I see. Very well. The sooner you can get the report to us, the better."

"Naturally."

"We will need a full statement from you," Endicott said. "And then we'll need to talk to young Mr. Cummins."

The doctor's face was coldly professional. "The boy's had quite a shock. Could this possibly wait until tomorrow at least?"

"Is Tal a suspect?" Drew asked.

Endicott stuck out his bottom lip. "No, Mr. Farthering, we don't have anything against him as yet. Yes, Doctor, tomorrow will be satisfactory. And no, we don't have anything against Mrs. Cummins, either. But we will have men on guard here until we complete our interviews, guests and all."

He looked Madeline and Drew over once again, his lip curled. "A whole week of playing dress-up, eh? And I ended up working for a living."

Sergeant Dane snickered almost silently.

Drew forced a smile. "Always happy to keep the constabulary amused. But, if we are dismissed, I think we'd like to see how Tal and his mother are doing. I've no doubt you have plenty to busy yourselves with for now."

"Just don't try to leave the house, Mr. Farthering."

"Wouldn't dream of it." Drew took Madeline's arm again. "Come along, darling."

He was surprised when, in answer to his knock, Tal opened the door himself. He looked absolutely wretched, red eyes swollen, face blotched and bloodless, clothes and hair disheveled. He stepped back to let Drew and Madeline come in and then shut the door behind them.

"What is it? Where did my father go?" He went to stand beside the shrouded figure on the bed. "We saw him out the window. He left with the police. Was it about . . . about arrangements? She hasn't got any family. I'll see to everything for her."

His mother sat there looking as if nothing that had happened made the least bit of sense. "Please come sit down, dear. Please."

"Mother—"

"It might be best, old man." Drew took him by the arm and led him to the sofa by his mother. "I have something to tell you."

He looked pleadingly at Madeline, and she gave him the kindest of her smiles. "Please do, Tal."

Bewildered, he did as she said.

Drew pulled up a chair next to him. "Your dad wanted me to tell you both what's happened. I know he wouldn't want either of you to worry."

Tal glanced at his round-eyed mother. "What is it?" He scrubbed one hand over his face. "What else has happened?"

Drew took a deep breath. "Very well, here it is. He's been arrested for smuggling cocaine into the country and for contributing to Alice's death."

Mrs. Cummins's soft cry was muffled by the plump hands she pressed to her mouth.

Tal shook his head. "That's insane. That's . . ." He put his head into his hands and started to laugh. "Absolutely stark staring mad. My father, cocaine?" His laughter turned harsh, shaking him until his mother reached over and took his hand. With a shuddering sob, he quieted. "All right, what else?"

"Evidently they've been watching your father for some time now," Drew told him. "Their theory is that he's having the stuff brought into the country through here and then he takes it up to his warehouse in London to parcel it out all over England."

"Here?" Mrs. Cummins breathed. "In our house? No. I would have known, wouldn't I? We would have known."

"I don't want either of you to worry." Drew patted their clasped hands. "I know someone with the police. He'll help sort things out, I'm sure."

"This isn't just a matter for the local bobby, you know." Tal's lips trembled. "This is drugs and murder and Scotland Yard."

"I know, Tal. I know. I don't know what else to tell you, but I'll see what I can do, what I can find out. I probably can't get in touch with my chief inspector till morning, but I'll try."

It was already past midnight, but Drew went ahead and rang up Birdsong's office. The chief inspector had gone home hours earlier, but the officer who took the call said he had already been told about the situation and was on his way to Winteroak House. Dr. Fletcher took Alice's body away at a quarter to one. By one-twenty, Chief Inspector Birdsong had arrived. Drew was waiting for him in Mr. Cummins's study.

"Detective Farthering. I should have known you'd be involved," Birdsong grumbled as they shook hands. "And the bride?"

"She's upstairs doing her best to look after Cummins's wife and son."

The chief inspector took a quick survey of Drew's Regency eveningwear. "A bit sporty given what's happened here, wouldn't you say?"

"We were to stay in costume for the full week. Mr. Cummins wouldn't allow anyone to cross his threshold wearing anything modern. I've sent my man Plumfield back up to Farthering Place to fetch all of us some regular clothes."

Birdsong raised an eyebrow.

"I already cleared it with Scotland Yard."

Birdsong looked uncharacteristically impressed. "Endicott is usually impossible to shift once he's made a proclamation as to what will and will not take place during one of his investigations."

"I think having the lot of us cavorting about as if we'd just stepped out of *Pride and Prejudice* was rather wearing on him. And it seemed quite awkward carrying on the charade in front of Tal and Mrs. Cummins."

"Very true, I suppose. And I'm not the least bit surprised to find you here. Is there any mischief about that you're not in the middle of?"

"Merely an innocent bystander," Drew said. "But I think your Scotland Yard friends have made a rather silly mistake."

"They have, have they?"

"They've arrested Sterling Cummins for trafficking in drugs. I just don't see how that could be."

"Friend of yours, is he?"

"He and my father were friends for years. I went to school with his son. He's a good businessman and a good fellow all the way round. He couldn't possibly be mixed up in something like this. Murder as well? I don't believe it."

"They told me. Well then, who was this girl?"

"Alice Henley." Drew exhaled and sat down on the sofa. "She was engaged to Cummins's son, Talbot."

"Family?"

Drew shrugged. "My wife tells me Alice shared rooms in

96

Buckler's Hard with an elderly aunt of hers, all the family she had. When the aunt passed on this past March, Alice and Tal moved their wedding up to next month."

"And Cummins supposedly killed the girl? Why?"

"Inspector Endicott doesn't think it was intentional. She took an overdose of cocaine. They're holding Mr. Cummins responsible for providing it for her." Drew shook his head, laughing. "Granted, you don't know him, but surely you know *of* him. Who in Hampshire doesn't? But imagining he's a drug smuggler? The whole thing's ridiculous, don't you think?"

Drew waited for Birdsong to make some sour remark about the incompetence of Scotland Yard in dealing with local matters, but no such remark came. The chief inspector sat there looking grim, but that wasn't as unsettling as the bit of regret in his expression.

"Don't you?" Drew prompted, his stomach queasy at the thought.

Birdsong pursed his lips, making his heavy mustache shift to one side. "Yes, I've heard of Mr. Sterling Cummins of Winteroak House. For some while now, in fact, but not, I'm sorry to say, for his business acumen or his benevolent works. Scotland Yard have had a rather intense focus on him for a number of months now, with evidence pointing to his being the center of the drug trade in some quarters of London."

Drew thought of the bewildered incredulity on Mrs. Cummins's face, the anger and utter disbelief on Tal's. How could they all have been so deceived? How could Drew?

"I . . ." Drew shook his head. "It's just not possible."

"It's true."

"But Alice—"

"I suppose he didn't mean that to happen. Likely she asked him for it, and he thought nothing of it."

"No." Drew stood up, unable to sit still any longer. "I don't think he gave it to her at all. If she did take it intentionally, and Tal says she never would, I think she got it from one of the other guests."

The chief inspector's eyes narrowed. "Why's that?"

"Madeline saw a couple of girls using cocaine in the powder room earlier today. She didn't realize at the time that it was cocaine, but I knew it by her description. They'd been showing signs of it all week. I thought Mr. Cummins ought to know about it, in his own home and all, and he asked them to leave. If Alice Henley got it from anyone, I'm almost certain it was from those two girls."

"Not from her fiancé?"

"Tal? Good heavens, no. Mr. Cummins gave us both a lecture before we went to university about what that sort of stuff does to a chap. Sad to say, we did see more than a bit of it at Oxford, too. Neither of us thought the opportunity to make fools of ourselves was worth the risk of turning our brains to blood pudding."

"It's been a while since you were at university, either of you. I understand you haven't kept in touch."

"No," Drew conceded, "but it just wouldn't be like Tal. He and Nick and I ran cross-country, rowing, everything like that. We none of us dabbled in this sort of thing at all, and I haven't seen any indication of it in Tal all the time we've been here. Not in Alice either. Not until tonight."

Again Birdsong pursed his lips. "And you didn't find it rather strange that a man like Cummins would know enough about drugs to warn you about what they would do to you? About cocaine in particular?"

Drew frowned, remembering the urgency on Mr. Cummins's face, in his voice, as he made Drew and Tal both promise to leave the stuff strictly alone.

"I . . . I expect he'd come across it in the charity work he and Mrs. Cummins sponsor. I mean, drugs and alcohol are often the reason people end up needing charity, am I right?"

Birdsong frowned. "I wish I could say it weren't the case."

"Then how does that translate into Mr. Cummins being the head of some elaborate smuggling operation?"

"It's rather an old tale, I'm afraid," the chief inspector said. "There's money to be made, and so long as people insist on killing themselves with the stuff, what does it matter who sells it to them? Likely a man like Cummins figures he's only supplying what the market demands. So long as he doesn't actually force it on anyone, he doesn't see the harm."

"But it *is* harm!" Drew gritted his teeth, forcing himself to lower his voice to a more appropriate level. "And he knows it is. Why would he have warned me and Tal off the stuff years ago if he didn't know full well what it does to a person? If he didn't know the death he was peddling?"

"I've seen it too many times before," Birdsong said. "They see business as business and not something that affects them as people. It's the only way they can live with themselves."

"It's a wretched way to live, if you ask me," Drew muttered.

Birdsong shrugged. "And then you have poor tomnoddies like me who have to make sure they're stopped."

"And their families, people like Tal and his mother, who are torn to bits when you stop them."

"Has to be done," Birdsong said, his face hard.

"I know, and you fellows can't be blamed for what the families go through. They're victims of the criminal as much as anyone else, whether or not that's what he intended."

"I've had to remind myself of that more times than you might expect." The chief inspector paused, then cleared his throat. "Regardless, it doesn't surprise me that Cummins would warn off his son and anyone else he cared for."

"But that's just it," Drew said. "If he felt that way, why wouldn't he have done the same for Alice? Tal was dotty about the girl and his father knew it. Why would Cummins give her cocaine?"

"That is rather an interesting question, I must admit."

"That's why I think she must have gotten it from her friends, Georgie and Violet. Don't recall the surnames."

"Deane and Marlow," Birdsong said. "We'll be having a little chat with them, I'm sure. Scotland Yard will, as well. Anything you'd like to add? Any observations that might be helpful?"

Drew could only shake his head.

— Six —

Birdsong gave Drew the standard warning about keeping out of trouble and then shuffled off to talk to the men from Scotland Yard. Drew stood for some time where he was, simply looking at the office of the man he had long admired, the man he thought he knew. He'd been in here a few times before, but now they seemed to close in on him, these walls full of plaques and awards and newspaper clippings.

And photographs. Cummins with the Lord Mayor of London. With Queen Mary. With the Archbishop of Canterbury. With film stars and captains of industry. Breaking ground for a charity hospital. Cutting the ribbon on a new orphan asylum. Handing over the keys to a free clinic in London's worst slum. In all of them, the man seemed humble and kindly, genuinely happy to give, to ease the burdens of others, to share those blessings he had with those who had nothing.

Drew's stomach twisted and roiled inside him. The man was a rotter through and through, and Drew had never seen it. Never suspected it. Everything in him balked at the idea.

Not Mr. Cummins. Not Tal's old governor. There had to be some mix-up, no matter what Birdsong said. He couldn't . . .

No. There was no getting round it. Drew had seen the man's face. Shame. A touch of fear. Perhaps wary resignation. No protestations of innocence. No cries for help. No pleas for Drew to uncover the truth. Cummins had simply and quietly surrendered.

He sighed, trying to rub the tightness out of the back of his neck. If he felt dumbfounded and betrayed, how must Tal be feeling? And poor Mrs. Cummins? He ought to go up and see if there was anything he could do for them. At the very least he should see how Madeline was getting along. After all, Tal and his mother were his friends, not hers.

He trudged up the stairs, determined to be as comforting and supportive as he could manage, but when he reached Alice's room, Madeline was coming out. Seeing him, she put one finger to her lips and drew the door shut behind her.

"He's just now fallen asleep," she told Drew. "The doctor left him something, but he wouldn't take it. His mother had to slip it into his water."

He put one arm around her, and they walked toward their own room. "Poor old girl, how is she?"

"Trying to carry on. I don't think she's totally taken in what's happened with Mr. Cummins. She keeps saying it will all be straightened out by morning."

Drew huffed. "He's got no business doing this to them. None at all."

Madeline shushed him. "Wait until we get into our room."

Neither of them said anything more until they were in their own quarters with the door firmly shut. Then Madeline pulled him down onto the sofa beside her, her blue eyes wide.

"Was it really cocaine? When I saw those girls in the powder room?"

"I'm afraid so, darling. It seemed pretty obvious from the way they were acting that some sort of drug was involved. And when you told me about one of them having powder around her nose, I thought it must be cocaine. After Cummins sent them off, I thought that would be the end of it. I had no idea it would come to this."

"And now poor Alice is dead." Madeline bit her lip. "Oh, Drew, what if she did get it from them? And I could have stopped them?"

"It still wouldn't be your fault, sweetheart." He pulled her into his arms. "But I don't think she took the stuff herself. I don't think she knew she had taken anything."

"But who would give it to her deliberately? You know Mr. Cummins. Would he have done such a thing?"

He shrugged. "I shouldn't think so, but then again, I would have sworn blue that he'd never be involved in anything shady." He put his head in his hands. "What kind of nitwit am I?"

"What do you mean?"

He shook his head, not looking up. "Here I fancy myself some sort of sleuth, able to see through the most accomplished liar, capable of discerning the most obscure motive, and I'm a drooling idiot."

"Of course you're not." She ran gentle fingers through the back of his hair. "How could you have known? He's been deceiving people for decades."

Again he shook his head. "Not just Cummins. There have been others. People I thought I knew. People I would have vouched for. Sworn by. Someone so easily fooled has no business trying to solve crimes."

"Even his own family didn't know. You're not a mind reader. You hadn't even seen the man in several years."

"But I should have known something was wrong. I mean, I did know. Or thought I knew, but I didn't figure out what it was. What good is it to be meant to help people when you do nothing but stand by and let them die anyway?"

"Come on," she said, and she helped him out of his tailcoat and the satin waistcoat beneath. "Now sit down." She guided him a few steps backward until he felt the bed against his legs and sat down. Then she knelt at his feet and began tugging at his shoe.

"Here now, I can do that."

"I know," she said. "And so can I." She struggled with the first and then the second, but soon both shoes were tossed at the foot of the bed and she was sitting beside him on it, her arms around his waist and her head nestled against his shoulder. "Better now?"

He dredged up a smile. "Truly, a man who finds himself a wife finds a good thing."

She said nothing for a long while, and he thought perhaps she had fallen asleep. Then she pressed a little closer to him, breathing warm against his neck.

"I don't know how to answer your questions, Drew. I'm not wise enough to see things as God sees them, and neither are you. But I don't think we're responsible for outcomes, just for doing what we're called to do. And even then, we'll never do it perfectly. But I believe He'll use us anyway, if we let Him."

"And if, in our stumbling, we do more harm than good?"

She nuzzled his neck, tightening her hold on him. "None of this is your fault, darling. But you're willing to do all you can to help. For Tal and for his poor mother. I think that's ministry as much as standing in a pulpit or feeding the poor. Doing what you're made to do the best you can do it, even if it's not the usual thing, glorifies God more than pushing yourself into a role you're not suited for."

"I suppose," he said, and then he surprised himself with a yawn. "I don't think I can think about this any more tonight."

She leaned up to kiss his cheek. "Tomorrow will be soon enough."

The night passed wretchedly. Drew had lain awake until the sky lightened again with the coming day and then he finally fell into a fitful sleep. He woke to find Eddie lying across his neck and sound asleep, with Madeline at the door asking Plumfield to bring them breakfast in bed.

They went through the usual morning routine until, shortly after ten, Beddows informed Drew that Chief Inspector Birdsong was in Mr. Cummins's office waiting to see him.

Birdsong sat behind Cummins's desk, clearly having commandeered the room for his headquarters while he was investigating Alice's death. Evidently, Endicott had done the same in the small sitting room across the corridor.

"Do sit down, Mr. Farthering," Birdsong said, and Drew complied.

"I take it our Scotland Yard chaps have been keeping an eye on the house for some little while."

"They have," the chief inspector said. "They've been trying to pin down Cummins on trafficking charges for several months now, but they haven't been able to figure out how he gets the stuff into the country and up to his warehouse in London. They're sure this French wine fellow is involved, but they've never been able to find anything on him. When the girl died, they decided they'd better make an arrest."

"They got here rather quickly last night," Drew said. "How'd they know something had happened?"

Birdsong shrugged. "Endicott told me they got a telephone call from one of their men. However it was, they want to stop the drugs coming into London. I want to stop them coming into Hampshire and, on top of that, I have to find out if Cummins had anything to do with Alice Henley's death."

"Right," Drew said. "I don't know how much help I can offer, but I'll certainly do my best."

"Fair enough. There is a small matter you might be able to clear up for me to begin with." Birdsong reached into his coat pocket and drew out a long string of pearls with a diamond clasp. "I believe these belong to your wife."

"They do." Frowning, Drew took them from him, only just then remembering the fabricated mystery had never been solved. *Quite the detective, eh, Farthering?* "Might I ask how you came by them?"

"Bring him in, Griffiths."

The constable at the door nodded and disappeared into the corridor. A moment later, he brought in Laurent's valet.

The chief inspector smiled coolly. "One Mr. Edmund Adkins, gentleman's gentleman. Seems he was in the process of 'returning' them, but was interrupted when we happened to bring him in for questioning."

"It's true," Adkins said, a fierce scowl on his freckled pug-nosed face. "I didn't want nobody else to take 'em off. If I hadn't meant to hand 'em in, why'd I have 'em in so daft a place as my own pocket? With all the bother about the girl and Mr. Cummins, I might've stashed 'em anywhere." He glared at Birdsong. "But don't mind me. I know you lot.

Never mind the swells when you can haul in a poor working-class bloke for anything that goes missing."

Drew studied him for a moment, keeping his expression mild. "And might I ask how you came by them?"

Birdsong pursed his lips, and Adkins's glare turned even fiercer. "I found 'em in the back of the mantel clock in the library, and I put 'em in my coat pocket for safekeeping. With all the fuss since last night, I never had the chance to give them back."

So that was why Madeline and Carrie had giggled every time they said "face" or "hands" or anything to do with time. Yes, he was a brilliant sleuth. Just deuced brilliant.

"Ah. Well, good of you to finally get round to it." Drew slipped the pearls into his own pocket. "Thank you. We hadn't even thought to miss them yet."

Birdsong narrowed his eyes. "You don't seem very surprised to hear where he found them. Was that your wife's usual place to keep them?"

Drew gave him a weary grin. "We were playing a game, a little mystery for Mrs. Farthering's friend, Will Holland. Evidently Mr. Adkins found them first." He turned again to the valet. "May I ask why you were looking in the back of the mantel clock in the library? I can't imagine it's one of your regular duties."

"I . . ." Adkins tugged at his collar as if it were suddenly too tight. "Well, I heard the clock chime, only it didn't sound quite the thing, you know? I wondered if there might be something wrong with it. So when everyone had gone into dinner, I went and looked, and there they were. The pearls, I mean. I thought maybe someone was smuggling 'em out. Mrs. Farthering, she's a nice lady. I didn't want her to be unhappy at losing her necklace and all."

"Very considerate of you, I'm sure," Drew said.

Adkins snorted. "That'll teach me to try to do a good turn. I'm just saying."

"That's all, Griffiths," Birdsong said. "You can take him out again."

P.C. Griffiths took the suspect by one arm. "All right, Sonny Jim, this way."

"Do you think he's telling the truth?" Drew asked when they had gone.

"I can't say one way or the other," Birdsong said, "but I've been asked to see if you would like to press charges in the matter."

"You've been asked?"

Birdsong nodded.

"I, uh, well . . . no, I suppose not. Now that we have the pearls back, I don't see the point. But isn't this sort of thing your province, as it were? Why didn't you just ask me?"

The chief inspector's mouth tightened. "I'd've had him the minute they found the goods on him. But it seems he is a . . . person of interest in a larger investigation."

"I see. Scotland Yard wants you to let him go about his business until they figure out exactly what his business is."

"Got it in one." Birdsong leaned in, lowering his voice. "Seems he has a history, and not just in service to the gentry."

Drew nodded. "Good of our Monsieur Laurent to give the man a second chance, eh?"

"The good monsoor seems to find it in his heart to employ many who have taken a false step earlier in their lives. According to Endicott, almost all of his associates have been under investigation for one thing or another."

"And Laurent himself?"

"Now there's a puzzle." Birdsong settled himself on the

corner of the desk and crossed his arms over his chest. "Family in the wine trade time out of mind. Before the Revolution, if I remember right. If anyone had the means and opportunity to smuggle anything into the country, he would be the one."

"And?"

The chief inspector shook his head. "Not a sausage. The French government have had leads from a number of suppliers that seem to indicate he's a major player in drug traffic, though they never seem to catch him with anything. We've done our own investigations—I should say the Yard have—and still came up with nothing. Every cask, every bottle, every keg is declared and the duty properly paid."

Drew could see the smug look on Laurent's face as he invited the police aboard his yacht and granted them permission to inspect whatever they pleased. "It would seem rather a coincidence that, thick as proverbial thieves, Cummins and Laurent aren't somehow working together."

"Exactly. But how the stuff gets from Laurent's warehouse in France to Cummins's in London we have yet to figure out."

"I don't think it comes through here," Drew said. "The family don't know anything about what Mr. Cummins was doing. He wouldn't want them to. Surely he gets it up to London some other way."

"It seems rather a stretch of the imagination to think Monsoor Rémy Laurent, long-suspected trafficker in cocaine, comes back and forth from the Continent with cargo and docks here at the home of Mr. Sterling Cummins, long-suspected trafficker in cocaine, and the goods are transferred somewhere else? I suppose it's possible."

Drew sighed. "Possible, but not very likely. Well, Scotland Yard can sort that out, can't they? I'm more concerned about what happened to Alice Henley."

"We know precious little about that except she died from an overdose of cocaine. Your mate Talbot Cummins says someone had to give it to her on the sly, because she'd never have taken it on her own. Those two girls, Marlow and Deane, claim they never gave her any, nor ever saw her taking it. Sterling Cummins says he never gave her anything of the sort and would never have, but I'll tell you a little story about that." Birdsong leaned forward on the desk. "It seems more than likely she saw or heard something she shouldn't have, and Cummins had to keep her from talking."

"What do you think she saw?"

"Well, what would it be but proof of his involvement with the smuggling and how they're bringing in the cocaine?"

"And what does Mr. Cummins say to that?"

Birdsong blew out his breath. "What would he say but that he did no such thing?"

"It seems you have very little to go on. Is it really enough to make an arrest? What hard evidence do you have?"

"Technically, we're only questioning him on that at present, though it seems unlikely he wasn't involved given the rest of his business venture."

"But he's not denying the smuggling?"

"No, he seems resigned on that point. But he says he won't stand for being called a murderer."

"Well, a man must have his standards, eh?" Drew shook his head. "At least he'll be able to tell you how the stuff was being brought into the country. And he can tell you how our Monsieur Laurent is involved, if he is."

"Oh, no," said Birdsong. "That's the fun bit. He says he won't deny any of the smuggling charges. He doesn't want a solicitor, though he'll have to have one all the same. But he won't say a word in his own defense, and he won't tell us anything we don't already know."

"Really?"

"He's afraid what will happen to his wife and son if he implicates anyone else now."

"I don't suppose we can much blame him for that," Drew said. "Some of these smugglers won't stick at anything, and they don't like to be betrayed by one of their own."

Birdsong scowled. "If he'd just tell us what we need to know, then we could make some arrests. And there wouldn't be anyone on the outside left to make mischief for his family."

"I don't suppose your lads can make one hundred percent sure of that, eh? Whatever he's done, I can't rightly blame Mr. Cummins for holding his tongue, if that's his fear."

"He's a determined cove," Birdsong said. "I'll give him that."

"You must have some fairly conclusive evidence against him on the smuggling."

"It's something Scotland Yard have been working on for some time now. He has a warehouse in London, and there's definite proof the contraband is coming out of there. How it gets in there before then is an entirely different question."

"Have you discovered anything helpful since the arrest?"

"I interviewed Miss Henley's friends, Georgie Deane and Violet Marlow, this morning. Separately, mind you. Miss Deane denied everything, even when I told her she'd been seen taking cocaine. She swore blue no one she knew would ever stoop to such a thing, certainly not Alice Henley."

"And Miss Marlow?" Drew asked.

"She was a bit more helpful, once she calmed down enough to actually answer in complete sentences." Birdsong looked faintly disgusted. "She admitted she and Miss Deane had been taking cocaine off and on all week, just for sport, but she said Miss Henley was afraid of the stuff and wouldn't even get close to it. In fact, Miss Henley asked them not to use it while they were at Winteroak House, just as a favor to her. She didn't want to upset Mr. and Mrs. Cummins."

"At least that agrees with what Tal said about her not taking the stuff. Did either of the girls say where they got the cocaine? Was it from Cummins, after all?"

The chief inspector shook his head. "According to Miss Marlow, Miss Deane got it from a young man who's been calling on her for the past few weeks."

"Fine fellow."

"We'll have a word with him about this, never you mind. As far as the rest of the guests go, we were able to dismiss most of them late last night. We can't see that any of them has any connection to the case."

"Most?" Drew asked.

"Laurent, of course, has been given the option of staying here or joining us down at the station. I believe he's elected the former."

"A wise man."

"The rest of Cummins's guests have given their names and addresses and gone home." Birdsong looked mildly annoyed. "And then there's you lot."

"We'll do our best to stay out from under foot, but I don't feel right leaving Tal and his mother to deal with all this alone."

"No, I suppose they could use a bit of support. Just don't interfere with my men doing their jobs, eh?"

Drew nodded. "They're doing quite a thorough job of it from what I can see, from the box room to the wine cellar. The cook's in high dudgeon over the state of her cupboards and pantry, and Mr. Beddows has been fussing about, trying to put things back in order everywhere else. I just hope you've left Tal and his mother alone."

"We had to question them, of course." Birdsong scowled at the look Drew gave him. "I promise you, we kept it as brief as possible."

"And your Scotland Yard friends? I don't fancy they were too concerned with Tal's grief or Mrs. Cummins's."

Birdsong's expression darkened even further. "They haven't got time for the niceties, so Endicott tells me. Results are what he needs, and results are what he'll get."

They didn't deserve this, Tal and his mother, neither of them, but Endicott and Birdsong weren't really to blame. It all went back to Cummins himself and the greed that had ultimately devastated those he should have done everything to protect. Well, Drew couldn't bring Alice back, he couldn't return Mrs. Cummins to the pleasant, sheltered world she had always known, and he couldn't mend Tal's shattered heart. Evidently, he couldn't even find a string of pearls his wife had hidden for a lark. But he could at least help his friends get through the unpleasantness that was still to come.

"Could Tal or his mother tell you anything?"

Birdsong shook his head. "Evidently our Mr. Cummins was quite good at leading his double life. Mrs. Cummins still doesn't quite believe he was involved in any of this, I think, though she was cooperative with us. Your mate, young Cummins, not so much."

"He has had rather a blow, you know."

"Yes, I realize that. That's why he's still here and not down at the station with his father. But we haven't found anything to show he knew what was going on either here or in London."

Drew opened his mouth and then shut it again. *I'd know*

if he did, he wanted to say, but then he remembered how utterly wrong he'd been about Mr. Cummins. Did he know Tal, really know him, anymore? They'd been close at school, he and Tal and Nick, but that had been half a dozen years ago now. They'd all lost touch. . . .

"I'll talk to him, too," Drew said at last. "Maybe there's something he's seen or heard that he doesn't even realize has to do with the case."

"Could be."

Drew stood. "Either way, I'm not going to leave him and his mother to deal with all this alone."

"Fair enough," Birdsong said, studying him with dour eyes. "But you might want to send the bride and her friends back to Farthering Place. Alice Henley's death might very well be murder, and if someone other than Sterling Cummins is to blame, you wouldn't want to find yourself a widower before you've had much chance to be a husband."

— Seven —

Just as Drew expected, Madeline and the others had no
interest in going home yet. Madeline didn't want Drew
to stay at Winteroak House without her, and she didn't
want to leave Mrs. Cummins without another woman to talk
to. Carrie said she didn't want to leave if Madeline wasn't
going to, though her eyes were on Nick the whole time she
was saying it. Nick wanted to help out Tal if he could, but he
made no bones about not budging if Carrie was staying. Will,
Drew did not doubt, just wanted to solve a real murder case.

Two days after the grand ball, the day of Alice's funeral,
the police finished searching the house and grounds. Will had
been forbidden to accompany them as they carried out their
tasks, but now that they were gone, he was doing his best to
follow in their footsteps on his own, certain he would find
something they had missed.

After the service was over, Tal had made himself scarce,
clearly wanting to be left alone. Carrie and Nick volunteered
to go into the village to get some headache powders for
Mrs. Cummins while Madeline sat at the older woman's

bedside, reading quietly to her as she lay with a cool cloth over her forehead. Restless and tired of seeking and finding nothing, Drew took a walk through the trees and all the way down to the narrow beach. It was a clear afternoon, and he could see the Isle of Wight with its low chalk cliffs and green fields.

He looked up into the nearly cloudless sky, blue and untroubled, fresh with the smell of the sea and the sounds of the birds. He knew God was beneath his feet and at all sides of him as much as up in His heaven, but it seemed natural to look into that endless blue in search of Him. There were too many questions racing through Drew's thoughts, too many for him to be able to catch hold of only one and fashion it into speech, but surely the one who fashioned both thought and speech knew what was in his mind and heart. He merely stood there, soaking in the heat of the sun and letting his heartbeat slow to the soothing rhythm of the water, listening for that still voice that would tell him what to do.

"Might I have a word, old man?"

Drew turned to see Tal standing beside him at the edge of the water, still in the dark suit he'd worn to Alice's funeral, still with his collar buttoned to the top and his tie pulled so snug, Drew wondered that it didn't strangle him.

"Anytime, of course. How are you?"

Tal looked perfectly wretched, which was no surprise. He'd hardly eaten or slept since the grand banquet on Saturday night. He'd barely spoken.

"Jolly," he said, his mouth a tight line. "Couldn't be better."

Drew looked out over the Solent, waiting for him to go on.

"I went to see him this afternoon."

Drew didn't have to ask who he meant. "How is he?"

Tal shrugged. "All right enough, I suppose. Says he wants me to 'understand.'"

"Understand?"

"About what he's been doing all this time. About why. I suppose he thinks that'll make it all right."

Drew studied him for a moment. "And does it?"

"I . . ." His lips trembled. "I just don't know. He's my dad, right? I mean, he's always been good to me, right? And now I don't even know him."

Drew had no answer to that. He felt the same. Deceived. Hurt. Foolish. How much more so must Tal feel when Cummins was his own father? "What are you going to do?"

Tal kicked at the grass and then picked up the stone half buried there, squeezing it in his hand. "I haven't anything that wasn't bought with dirty money. I don't know where Mother and I are supposed to live, but we can't stay in the house. Not now." He drew back and flung the stone into the water.

"The police can hardly turn you out of your own home."

"We can't stay here." Tal picked up another stone and then another, hurling them in succession into the river. "There's no one in the parish who'll speak politely to us now."

"You had nothing to do with any of this."

"They might not blame us, but they'll talk about us and pity us and treat us as if they don't know us."

"Not everyone, surely," Drew said, knowing he was more than likely right. "Your friends, your true friends, won't be that way. Mr. Broadhurst seems a good chap. He wouldn't turn away from you."

Tal shrugged and threw another stone, not so violently this time. "Maybe not. Mother's done charity work with him for ages now. He's all right enough."

"I've had my share of scandal," Drew said, "but I've found

there's always a new scorcher to take attention away from the old ones. As far as I've ever seen, there's no one can shame you but yourself, and you've done nothing to be ashamed of."

Drew turned to face him, wanting to know Tal had truly heard that last. Tal only shrugged again.

"I could have seen what was happening. I could have . . ." He covered his face with both hands and then raked his fingers through his hair. "I could have listened when Alice tried to tell me something was wrong. Now she's dead."

"Your father did his smuggling out of his warehouse in London. Did you spend time there?"

Tal shook his head.

"Did Alice tell you anything specific you could have told the police?"

Again Tal shook his head. "But she knew something was going on. Why didn't I find out what it was?" He scanned the ground for more stones, but there didn't seem to be any more. He kept his eyes down anyway. "I came to ask you a favor, Drew."

"Certainly. What is it?"

"I have to know who killed Alice."

"Tal—"

"No, don't tell me it was my father." Tal looked at Drew, his eyes fierce and rimmed with red. "I don't believe it. I'll never believe it. Even with everything that's happened, it's just not true. And don't tell me Alice took the cocaine herself. Someone killed her."

It seemed unlikely Cummins and Alice both were living double lives.

"If it wasn't your father, who would have done it? Who else would have wanted her dead?"

"I don't know. Nobody." Tal stopped for a moment, his

breath coming hard. "I don't like how Laurent used to look at her. Typical foul-minded Frenchman."

"If he's in on the smuggling, it's more than the police have been able to find. They've watched him even longer than they watched your father. Not a bit of evidence connects him to anything to do with drugs. Just wine, and every bit of it declared and properly imported."

Tal frowned. "Maybe it had nothing to do with the drugs. Maybe he just didn't like that she turned him down."

"Did she?"

Tal glared at him, and Drew quickly shook his head.

"I mean, did he go as far as making that sort of proposition to her? Right in front of you, as it were?"

"Not that she told me, no. And I think she would have." Tal looked faintly disgusted. "But he was that way with all the girls, the old lech."

"Yes, I know." Drew gave him a rueful smile. "If he'd been the one murdered, I could easily understand why."

"I think your Madeline stands up for herself rather well." Tal cracked a weak smile and added, "Women like her aren't easy to come by."

His voice broke a little at the end, and Drew knew he was thinking of Alice again.

"I'll do my best to hang on to her," Drew assured him. "And believe me, I know there aren't many like her. Alice, she was a lovely girl. I'm . . ." He shook his head, knowing the right words were beyond him. "I'm sorry."

Tal took a deep breath. "So will you? Will you find out who killed her?"

"I don't know, Tal."

Tal grabbed his arm. "Don't put me off, Drew. I'm begging you. I have to know, for her sake and—" he looked up at the cloudless sky, blinking back tears—"for my dad. I have to know he's telling me the truth about something." Abruptly, he dropped his hold and looked out at the water again. "Please."

"All right, old man," Drew said at last. "I'll try."

Tal answered with a curt nod, and the two of them stood in silence for a minute or two. Then Drew handed him another stone.

Drew stood watching the Solent long after Tal had gone back into the house, watching the boats cruise up and down the waterway, wondering about how Laurent could be bringing contraband into the country without it being found in his possession when he docked. There were certainly plenty of boats passing by. It seemed unlikely the police could search them all.

He watched as one chugged along near the bank, a trig little craft compared to the others used by the local fishermen, and evidently new. He realized it was the boat he and Madeline had seen when they sailed up the Beaulieu River.

It went round a bend and disappeared from his sight. He watched for a while, waiting for it to come back into view, but for the longest time it didn't. Just as he was about to go down to see where it had gone, it came sailing along again and docked just below the village. Three men clambered out, spoke to the old man smoking and loitering on the weathered old dock, and the four of them headed up the rocky path. The last Drew saw of them, they were going into the pub, The Knight and Lady.

Intrigued, he took the path leading to the beach and then toward the docks. There was the boat he'd been watching:

The Gull. Chuckling at the irony of the name for a boat bringing in contraband, he climbed the stone steps leading from the narrow beach to the boardwalk, thankful to see the windows of the pub faced toward the town rather than the docks. With one more look round, he hopped aboard.

There didn't seem to be much to see. Nets, coils of rope, a pair of rusty buckets, a kerosene can. Either the fishing that day had been particularly bad or they had been out on some other errand. There wasn't a fish to be seen, and they hadn't unloaded any. But the deck was wet, as if something had been brought aboard. Whatever it was, it wasn't on board now.

Finding nothing of interest, he was about to walk back to the house when he noticed something light in color stuck in a crevice in the deck. It looked like it had been scraped off of something else. He bent down and picked up the little scrap.

"What you lookin' at?"

Seeing the three men who had gone into the pub coming down the dock toward him, Drew used one swift motion to slip the scrap inside his pocket watch. Then he straightened and turned, giving them a friendly smile.

"Just wondering if this boat might be for hire."

"You see a sign on it?" the one on the left said, his bushy red beard wagging in indignation.

Drew made a slight bow. "No harm meant. Good afternoon."

"Hang on there!" A tall boy with bony wrists poking out of his too-short sleeves moved toward Drew. "Turn out your pockets."

"I beg your pardon?"

"He took something," the boy said to the others, his attempt to look fierce foiled by the adolescent whine in his voice. "I saw him."

121

The man with the beard held out a weathered hand. "I'll have that."

"I can assure you gentlemen I have nothing much of any value. Upon my honor."

"Hear that," said the third man, his grin showing a missing front tooth. "Lord Coxcomb swears upon his honor."

The other two laughed.

"We'll have a look all the same," the bearded one said, again holding out his hand. "Turn 'em out."

Drew gave him a taut smile. "Seeing that you asked so nicely."

In truth, he didn't have much on him: wallet, keys, handkerchief, a few coins. The bearded man rummaged through it, looking unimpressed.

"Not much here for a toff, eh?"

He tugged at Drew's watch chain, pulling the watch into plain sight along with the silver sixpence that hung from the same chain, dangling them before his face.

"Careful there," Drew said. "That was my grandfather's."

With a sneer, the bearded man put the watch back. "What'd he take, Tom?"

"Dunno." The young one glared at Drew. "He put something in his waistcoat pocket."

Drew reached into the suspect pocket and turned it inside out and then held up his hands. "As I said, I've got nothing much of value. I simply wanted a look at the boat. It seems ideal for bringing things in from the sea."

The bearded one narrowed his eyes. "What 'things'?"

"Fish, of course." Drew lowered his hands, keeping his movements slow and unthreatening. "I don't know of anything else of value floating about out there, do you?"

The one with a missing front tooth gave him a sly grin.

"Had some nosy gent end up facedown in the Solent a few months ago." He stuffed the lining back into Drew's waistcoat pocket with two thick fingers. "'Course, there weren't much value in him by the time he were brought in."

"Oh, no doubt," Drew said. "No doubt."

"A wise man don't get himself in a position to have unfortunate accidents, I always say." He displayed his gap-toothed grin again. "He stays out of places he don't belong and then there's no need to put the local police to the trouble of dragging for him. Just by way of being thoughtful, you know?"

"I do indeed," Drew said. "No need to burden them when they already have so much to see to."

"Right. You're absolutely right. Ain't he right?"

The bearded man's smile had disappeared. "We wouldn't like to bother them about folk taking liberties with our private property either, seeing as they are so busy."

"I wouldn't like that a bit," Drew said. "No. So I expect I should toddle along now. The wife'll be worrying. You know how women are."

He tipped his hat and strolled not too quickly down the dock and out of their sight. They were up to no good, those three. Whether it had anything to do with Cummins's business operation remained to be seen.

He found everyone except Mrs. Cummins in the library at Winteroak House, all having tea and biscuits.

"Where have you been?" Madeline asked, hurrying to him. "Look at you."

She smoothed back his hair and straightened his tie, then pushed his watch chain and the sixpence deeper into his waistcoat pocket.

He gave her a wink. "I've just had a nice chat with some

local fishermen. They did not offer their names, and they most emphatically do not hire out their boat."

He gave them a brief account of his conversation with the fishermen, and afterward Tal frowned.

"Sounds like Bill Rinne and Bert and Tom Kimlin. I've known Bert and Tom since I was born. Rough lads but no worse than most, at least not until they hooked up with Rinnie. Even their own father, when he was partners with Rinnie, didn't want them around him much. But they're a trifling lot, big lads at the local pub but nowhere else."

"You're lucky you didn't get your head bashed in," Nick said, "going without me. And Mrs. Farthering would not at all be pleased if you were suddenly missing your front teeth."

Madeline shook her head emphatically. "Not at all."

Drew squeezed her hand. "Nonsense. They were perfectly charming fellows and quite concerned for my safety."

Nick scoffed. "Right."

"And if we're totting up how many beans make five just now and our host was one bean, I'd wager your new putter that these fellows are our two beans. They fit in here somewhere. And, wittingly or not, they were kind enough to leave this behind."

He opened his watch case, took out the little scrap, and saw it was a strip from a label—most of it too faded to make out. All that was clear was most of a capital letter and some decorative scrollwork.

"What's D?" Will asked, studying it.

Drew looked it over again. "Any ideas, Nick? Tal? Is this something local?"

Tal shook his head. "Nothing I've ever seen. Looks like an advert of some kind. Maybe a label from a can or a box."

"That's what I thought."

"We should go look in the pantry," Will suggested. "I'll go."

"You just hold your horses," Carrie said. "This isn't play-acting anymore. I don't want you getting into trouble while we're here."

"I've been all over the place," he said with a bit of a swagger. "Nobody's even noticed."

"Billy!"

"Not a good idea, old man," Drew said mildly. "After what's happened."

"I can take care of myself."

Carrie glared at him. "If you don't behave, we'll just have to go back home. I mean it."

"Aw, c'mon, sis. It's just the pantry, not some dockside opium den."

"She's right," Drew said. "Nick and I get in enough trouble for poking our noses in where they don't belong. Old Birdsong's used to us by now, but he might not be so lenient with you."

Will snorted at that but made no further objections.

"Do you think your mother would mind if we had a look in the kitchen?" Drew asked Tal. "Not that I think this came from the house, but I suppose there's a chance it came from the local grocer and perhaps your cook bought the same thing."

"Mother won't mind," Tal said. "But you might have to get round Mrs. Ruggles. She rules the kitchen with an iron fist and doesn't care for intruders."

"What won't I mind, dear?" Mrs. Cummins came into the room, her pale forehead creased with worry, yet she gave them all a determined smile.

Standing just out of her line of sight, Drew gave a slight shake of his head, a warning to the others not to trouble her with the matter they were discussing. Then he put his arm around her narrow shoulders. "I was just thinking it would be nice to have some more of that apple cake we had last week. Might cheer us all up."

Her smile softened. "I'll ask the cook to make another one." She turned to Madeline. "Speaking of staff, my dear, I hate to ask it of you, but our Josephine was feeling ill so I sent her to bed."

"I hope it's nothing serious," Madeline said, looking rather puzzled. "Is there something I can do to help?"

Mrs. Cummins held up both hands. "Oh, forgive me, I've got everything back to front as usual. I should have asked you first if your maid has ever served at table."

"Beryl's served at Farthering Place several times, and I'm sure she wouldn't mind helping you. She's always been happy to do whatever I've asked."

"Oh, lovely." Mrs. Cummins squeezed Madeline's hand, looking as if she might weep in relief. "Things have been so difficult since . . ." She glanced at Tal. "Well, since everything, you know, but I don't want things to fall to pieces here while it's all being straightened out. I could have Cook serve, but well, she's not the most graceful thing and she does tend to spill. She makes the loveliest meals, mind you, but she was never meant for the formal occasion, if you understand me. Anyway, she thought perhaps your girl would be willing to help."

"I'll speak to Beryl right away," Madeline said. "Please, don't worry any more about it."

Drew didn't like to broach the subject, not with Tal in the room, but he couldn't help wondering. Was it a mere

126

coincidence that this girl Josephine should fall ill just now? Had the murderer tried to do away with her too, or was this just another instance where the celebrated amateur detective had gotten everything utterly wrong?

He'd keep quiet until he knew more.

— Eight —

That evening there was only quiet in the library of Winteroak House. Pleading another headache, Mrs. Cummins had retired shortly after dinner. Tal had made no excuses and shut himself in his room not much later. Nick had taken Carrie and Will to the cinema in Southampton, leaving Drew and Madeline alone together.

"You should have gone with them," Drew said. "Take your mind off all this."

"Not if you wouldn't go. I didn't care to see the picture anyway."

"No, of course not." He put an arm around her. "Never mind it's got that Cary Grant fellow in it and you've demanded to see everything he's been in since I've known you."

"I just wasn't in the mood to see a picture about war and death, even with Cary Grant." She shrugged. "I just thought it would be nice to have an evening to ourselves. After all that's happened." She paused, looking at him, then traced her fingers along his jawline. "I didn't want to leave you here alone."

He caught her hand and pressed it to his lips. "I don't much feel like being alone, though I don't much feel like being with anyone but you either. And I was wondering too—"

"About the maid."

"Exactly that. Perhaps Alice wasn't the only one who'd seen something she wasn't meant to. If the murderer put something in Alice's drink, why shouldn't he do the same for this Josephine?"

"You don't think it's as serious as all that, do you? Mrs. Cummins didn't seem worried about more than having decent service at her table."

He relaxed, if just slightly. She was probably right and no doubt much more perceptive than he could ever hope to be. "What do you think then, darling? Perhaps some coffee and a chat about something other than this wretched case?"

"That would be wonderful," she replied.

Drew rang the bell and requested coffee. A few minutes later, a rather rotund little woman, red-faced and with her hair done up under a cap, waddled into the room and thumped down two cups, sloshing coffee on the end table.

"Beg pardon, sir. Madam." She wiped up the spill with her apron, her expression taut. "Can I get you anything else?"

"You must be Mrs. Ruggles," Drew said. "I've been meaning to send you my compliments this whole week. Your apple cake ought to be classified as a national treasure."

The hostility in the woman's expression softened into a mixture of embarrassment and grudging pleasure. "You're very kind, sir, I'm sure."

"We didn't expect you to have to bring the coffee yourself."

"Oh, it's no trouble, sir. It's just . . . well, I've been cook here nigh on to thirty years. I think I know my job, if you'll pardon me."

"I'm certain you do," he said. "The meals this week have been perfection."

"I can't say that much of my own cooking, sir, though I thank you. But food poisoning? In my kitchen? No, sir. That I will not have."

"I can hardly blame you. Who would make such an infamous accusation?"

"Dr. Fletcher. He says there's no doubt of it. Oh, pardon me, it's Josephine, our maid. She's took to her bed. That's why I had to bring your coffee." The cook ducked her head. "Not that it ain't a pleasure, sir, I'm sure, but I'm that mortified for anyone to hear something bad came from my kitchen. A baby could eat off that floor and no worry, and that's the floor, mind. There's not a bit of the whole kitchen not kept scrubbed and shined day in and day out, and all the food bought fresh, too. Nothing in tins. Where's the food poisoning in that?"

"I certainly can't see where you'd be to blame," he said, taking an appreciative sip of the coffee.

"But how we're to keep things in good order with so many people staying, I don't know, sir, and that's the good Lord's truth. It's not so much the guests, mind you, but there's hardly one of them doesn't bring his own people along, and I'm the one as has to keep them out of mischief."

Madeline's eyebrows went up. "I hope our—"

"Oh, no, madam. Not to worry on that account. Beryl's a love and always willing to help. And your Mr. Plumfield, sir, well he's rather quiet, but never a bit of trouble. Not like some as I could mention."

Drew nodded encouragingly. "I can see that you'd have a lot to manage."

Mrs. Ruggles frowned. "You take that Mr. Adkins, who

sees to Mr. Laurent when they're in town. Why, I wouldn't trust him with the jam spoon, telling you the truth. He's got a look about him I just don't like. Do you know, sir, that I found him in my pantry yesterday?"

Drew made his expression appropriately horrified. "No."

"Yes. Bold as brass he was. I'd been out to the garden to get some of the mint Mrs. Cummins grows. I came back in, and there he was poking about with who knows what. I should have made him turn out his pockets then and there, but I thought the master might not care for it, seeing as he and the French gentleman are such good friends."

"And what do you suppose he wanted in the pantry? Mr. Adkins, I mean."

The cook snorted. "He says he was looking for headache powders. Headache powders? In with the flour and sugar? Doesn't seem quite right, does it?"

"Doesn't seem right at all," Drew said.

"Did he take anything?" Madeline asked.

"I didn't give him a chance," said Mrs. Ruggles, pursing her lips. "I caught him before he could take anything more than a look round. Don't think I didn't send him off quicker than he came and count the teaspoons afterwards!"

"I trust they were all safe," Drew said.

"They were, sir, and they are, but I'll keep my eyes open all the same. And now there's this business of food poisoning, which is utter nonsense. I think I know my own cooking, thank you very much."

"Could it have been something bad from the butcher?" Madeline suggested.

"No, madam," she said, her china-blue eyes snapping. "I've bought from Mr. Gibbons nearly as long as I've been in this house. He knows better than to give me anything that's turned, and I know good meat from spoilt. Besides, if that were the case, wouldn't we all of us got sick?"

"Very true," said Drew.

"That Dr. Fletcher, I say he don't know food poison from a case of the mumps, that's what I say."

"And I hope Josephine will recover soon," Madeline said.

The cook beamed at her. "Oh, yes, madam. The poor dear weren't but half dead. I expect she'll be back at work sooner than later. Anyway, sir, if I can get you anything else, you just send word. I don't mind."

"That's very good of you, Mrs. Ruggles." Drew took another sip of his coffee. "And if anyone brings up the subject of food poisoning in my hearing, I'll be certain to set him straight."

She ducked her head. "I'm obliged, to be sure, sir."

Drew glanced at Madeline and then turned again to the cook. "I say, Mrs. Ruggles, do you buy all the food for the house?"

She stuck out her lower lip. "I tell you there weren't anything gone bad in my kitchen. I know absolutely there couldn't—"

"No, no, I'm sure you're right. No doubt of it." He took the scrap of label out of his waistcoat pocket. "I was just wondering if you recognized this."

She wiped both hands on her apron and took it from him, studying it for a moment. "Can't say as I do, sir. D. Hmmm. There's Dovecote Wholemill Flour and Dunning Flavoured Coffee Beans we buy regular, but neither of them has a label like this."

"Could it possibly be soap or some kind of cleaner?" Madeline asked.

"Not as I've seen, madam. I could ask Mrs. Brogan, who

sees to that sort of thing. Is it something you'd like us to get for you?"

"No," Drew assured her, reclaiming the tattered label. "Just wondering where this might have come from. But if you'd check with Mrs. Brogan for us, it would be much appreciated."

"I'll do that, sir. Leave it to me. Will there be anything else?"

"Not tonight, thank you. You've been more than helpful."

"Only too happy, sir. Madam."

She waddled out of the room, head held higher than when she had waddled into it.

Madeline took the scrap from him. "Could it be from a medicine of some sort?"

"Or tooth powder or motor oil or furniture polish." He shook his head. "Any number of things. Maybe a bit of a circus poster or an advert for a new automobile."

"Well, I won't try to tell Mrs. Ruggles her own business."

"Not more than once, I suspect," Drew said.

Madeline grinned. "I think I'll have a look in the pantry myself after breakfast tomorrow. Maybe I'll see something she's forgotten."

"Fair enough, darling. And I'll see what I can find out at the grocer's."

She nodded. "Do you want me to come with you?"

"Best let me see to this on my own. People seem to be a bit less on their guard with one person rather than two."

She gave him a knowing nod. "Especially the women."

"Now, now, darling, don't make assumptions. The only one behind the grocer's counter may very well be old Mr. Worrywart with a bushy beard down to his belly, jelly-jar spectacles, and an ear trumpet. He's not likely to be won over by my boyish charms."

"And it's as likely to be young Miss Worrywart with big brown eyes, bobbed hair, and a flask of gin tucked into her garter."

"If it is, I promise I'll tattle to her mother about the gin."

She laughed and snuggled against him on the couch. "Bargain."

Drew and Madeline went up to their room a couple of hours later. Madeline stepped into the bathroom to get ready for bed while Drew moved to the bed, where Eddie was lounging.

"Hello, love." Drew took off his coat and put it over the back of a chair and then began scratching the cat between the ears. "I thought I left my book just where you've settled. What have you done with it, minx?" He raised his voice so Madeline could hear him from the bathroom. "Darling, have you seen my book? Darling?"

The water shut off, and Madeline came back into the bedroom. "What was that?"

"Have you seen my book? Or did Eddie carry it off somewhere?"

"It's on the table by the bed."

Drew picked up the book and put it down again. "This is *Lord Edgeware*. I finished it yesterday. I was looking for that new one by Allingham I started last night. *Sweet Danger*."

She rolled her eyes. "You had it in the morning room and out in the garden. If it's not in one of those places, I don't know."

"Right. Back in a jiff."

Still in his shirtsleeves, he made his way down the stairs and into the morning room. It was dark, but there was enough moonlight for him to locate the book on the sofa. He snatched it up and tucked it under his arm and then turned to find someone blocking the doorway back into the corridor.

He squinted into the darkness and smiled faintly. "Hullo there. Is there something I can do for you?"

Laurent's valet stepped into the rectangle of moonlight that fell from the morning room window and spilled onto the floor. "I'd say there's something I can do for you, Mr. Farthering, seeing as you were good enough to understand about Mrs. Farthering's pearls and not have me put in chokey for something I didn't do."

Drew raised one eyebrow. "Go on."

"That American kid, he'd do better to keep himself to himself, if you know what I mean. I'm sure you've heard about curiosity and cats and all that. I told him already he ought to let things alone, but maybe he'd be more apt to listen to you than me."

"I see. And just which things has he not been letting alone?"

Adkins lifted his pugnacious jaw. "Just never you mind what things, Mr. Farthering. I'm just saying, friendly like and for his own good, he ought to let things alone. You wouldn't do so very badly yourself to stay out of it as well. As I said before, Mrs. Farthering's a nice lady. I shouldn't like to see her a widow."

"I don't fancy that much myself."

Drew heard the sound of a car engine and glanced over his shoulder to see Nick had pulled into the drive in the Daimler. He and Carrie and Will would be coming into the house soon. Adkins saw them, too.

"Just a word to the wise, Mr. Farthering. Just as a favor for a favor."

Drew narrowed his eyes. "Does your master know you're warning me off like this?"

The valet glanced toward the door and moistened his dry lips. "Monsieur Laurent's a busy man. I don't like to trouble him with trifles."

Drew heard the latchkey in the front door. Tal had given it to Nick so he and Carrie and Will could let themselves in without waking the house. Adkins looked back toward the sound, then gave a little nod.

"A favor for a favor, eh?"

He was gone before Nick and the others were inside.

Drew tucked his book under his arm and went to meet them in the hallway. "How was the cinema?"

Carrie sighed, "That Cary Grant is awful nice-looking."

Nick made a piteous face. "How's a chap supposed to compete with that, I'd like to know?"

Carrie took his arm, smiling up at him. "He couldn't possibly be sweeter than you, Nicky."

Drew chuckled. "You see, Nick old man? Miss Austen was right. 'There is no charm equal to tenderness of heart.'"

Will rolled his eyes. "Spare me the hearts and flowers, will you?"

"And what have you been up to, Will?" Drew asked. "I understand you had a bit of a run-in with Mr. Laurent's valet."

"Aww, him." Will made a face. "He's nobody. I'm not afraid of that stooge."

"Billy!" Carrie scolded. "What have you been doing? How did you find out, Drew?"

Drew held up *Sweet Danger*. "I'd just come down for this, and Adkins told me I'd ought to have a word with young Master Holland about his ill-considered ways."

"It was nothing, sis," Will said, his voice overly earnest.

"I was just poking around the house, and he was all high-and-mighty and told me to stay out of the way."

Carrie shook her head in disgust." And you couldn't possibly have listened."

"I didn't hurt anything." He grinned at Drew. "I got into that pantry and out again without the cook even noticing."

"Billy!" Carrie turned to Nick, eyes blazing. "Did you know about this?"

"Not until now," Nick said. "But I'd say you ought to take Mr. Adkins's advice to heart, Will."

Will wrinkled his nose. "You're not my dad." He glanced at Carrie. "Or my brother."

Carrie shook her finger in his face. "You be nice, Billy Holland, or I swear this is the last time I take you with me anyplace. I mean it. And I don't care what Daddy says."

"All right, all right." Will gave Nick a sullen apology. "I don't know why you guys get to have all the fun."

"You listen to your sister, Will," Drew said. "I know this seems quite exciting at the moment, but it's serious business and not something to trifle with."

"I was just watching the police investigate. The fellow doing the fingerprinting was pretty nice about letting me tag along with him, but then that inspector guy told me to clear off."

Drew chuckled. "He's told us that a time or two, in point of fact, eh, Nick?"

"And neither of you ever listened to him, either." Carrie shook her head, lips pursed. "Boys."

Nick squeezed her hand. "Will you forgive us if we promise to lead blameless lives evermore?"

"I guess there's no harm done." Fighting a smile, Carrie stood on tiptoe to give Nick a peck on the cheek. "You two

behave yourselves. Come on, Billy, it's past your bedtime."
She took Will's arm, tugging him toward the stairs. "You
boys can play detective in the morning."

"I'd like a private word with you, Will," Drew said. "If
you and your sister don't mind. Nick, perhaps you could
escort the ladies upstairs."

Carrie put her arm through Madeline's. "Come on. I'll tell
you about the picture we just saw. Oooh, that Cary Grant."

Drew waited until they were out of hearing before he
turned to Will. "I'm serious about what I told you. This isn't
a game anymore."

Will huffed. "All right, I get it. I just don't know why you
let that Nick in on everything and not me."

"I thought you two were getting along nicely now."

Will was silent for a moment, and then he huffed again.
"Why does he have to be after my sister all the time?"

Drew fought a smile. "She doesn't seem to mind, does
she?"

"Aw, her head's full of rocks. She doesn't even think about
things. I mean, it's just me and her and Dad as it is, and I'm
going off to college in the fall. Then what's Dad going to do
all by himself? And what's she going to do if she's not home
where he can look after her?"

"You had to expect she'd leave home sometime. I can't
imagine the fellows over on your side of the pond haven't
noticed her."

"Well, sure. I don't expect her to stay an old maid or anything. But she can't come all the way over here and live. We'd
never see her! Besides, she's supposed to marry Kip Moran."

Surely Nick didn't know about this.

Drew kept his expression mild. "Who's this Moran fellow?"

Will beamed at him. "He was the captain of the varsity

football team at the college. His dad's a state representative, and he drives one of those new MG Midgets, orange with tiger stripes and everything."

Drew refrained from rolling his eyes. "And he and your sister are engaged?"

"Heck no. They went out some. Carrie says he's a swell fellow and all, but I don't think he ever proposed." Will scowled again. "Now she'll hardly give him the time of day."

Drew exhaled mentally. "I see. And was this recently? This spring?"

"Nah. About a year ago, I guess. Right after she was over here the first time."

After she'd met Nick, then. That was definitely a good sign.

"Well, Nick's a good fellow, you know, even without a tiger-striped car. And ladies' preferences must be taken into consideration."

"I guess so, but would it hurt her to marry someone keen?"

Drew gave Will a searching look. "You do realize Nick's the reason she's come, don't you?"

"Yeah, I guess," Will said, looking as if he'd just agreed to take a dose of castor oil. "I just don't know why she can't get together with Kip Moran."

"Suppose your sister decided to choose someone for you," Drew said, trying not to smirk. "You wouldn't stand for it for a moment."

Will's eyes widened. "Well, I . . . I mean, uh, I guess people ought to pick for themselves." He sighed, shoulders drooping. "But that MG is awful swell."

"Buck up, Will," Drew said, clapping him on the back. "Maybe you'll have one of your own someday, and you won't have to trade your sister for it."

Will grinned. "Maybe I will. Besides, if Dad found out I wanted her to marry a guy just so I could drive his car, he'd probably take my license away." Just then he saw Nick coming back down the stairs and went to him, hand extended. "Sorry I've been such a pill, Nick. You're a good guy, and if Carrie likes you, I guess that's okay with me."

He shook Nick's hand and then hurried up the stairs and out of sight.

Nick watched him, dumbfounded. "Whatever did you say to him?"

"Oh, not much. I just told him to stay out of trouble and that Carrie ought to be the one to choose between you and your rival."

"Rival?" Nick frowned. "Who?"

"Not here. Back in America. Will tells me his sister has been pursued by a star of American university football, who just happens to drive a rather natty tiger-striped car."

Nick huffed.

"It probably plays the school fight song when one presses the horn as well," Drew added.

Nick glared. "Yes, that's all very well, I'm sure. And why haven't you told me this before now?"

"Just found it out a minute ago."

Nick glanced up the stairs, a flicker of hurt in his eyes. "I would never have known it by the way she acts."

Drew chuckled, and the hurt became more than just a flicker.

"No, no, Nick, old man, no need to fall on your sword quite yet. Will tells me that since she came back from her first trip over here, she won't give the football chap the time of day."

Nick exhaled. "And if Carrie's made up her mind, woe betide young Will if he tries to change it."

"Those fiery redheads." Drew shook his head. "Are you sure you know what you're letting yourself in for?"

"Not exactly," Nick said with a grin, "but I'm eager to find out."

"It'll be good for you, I daresay. Keep you on your toes." Drew tucked his book under his arm once more. "I'd better toddle along myself. Mrs. Farthering will think I've stopped to read this one rather than just coming down to fetch it."

Nick's expression turned serious. "I came back to ask you about Adkins. He had a little word with you, did he?"

"He didn't say much, only that Will ought to leave things be, and my wife, being so nice a lady, shouldn't be left a widow."

"Something you ought to let our chief inspector know about?" Nick asked, frowning.

"I dunno, old man. Evidently Birdsong's been told to leave Mr. Adkins to heaven, as it were. Scotland Yard would rather he be allowed to mature his felonious little plans, or rather abet Laurent's, until they can finally decide what the two of them are actually up to."

"He threatened you," Nick protested.

"I'm not so sure about that." Drew thought back on the valet's words, wondering if he should have noticed something more about them than he had. "He did seem grateful for our not pressing charges about the necklace. Maybe, rough as it was, it was just as he said—a friendly warning for my own good."

"Conveniently putting you out of the way while he goes about his business, as well." Nick scoffed. "Very nice. I suppose there's plenty of time to tell Birdsong about it after we've found you facedown in the Solent, eh?"

"All right. If you feel it's that important, I'll tell him about it when I see him next. It's not as if he and Scotland Yard aren't keeping an eye on the fellow as it is."

"A rather lax eye, if you ask me." Once more, Nick glanced toward the stairs. "I wish Carrie and Will had gone back to Farthering Place. And Madeline too, if you want the truth."

"Don't think I don't agree with you. At least here we can look after them."

"If they'll let us," Nick said, "I ought to go stand in front of Carrie's door and keep watch all night."

"I'm sure she'd admire your chivalry, but it's probably enough for tonight for her to lock her door. That's not a bad idea for all of us, actually. At least until we figure out what's going on here."

"Right. Well, come on then. If there are any more sinister valets lurking in the shadows, we can fend them off together."

— Nine —

As planned, Drew made a visit to the local greengrocer, a little shop across the high street from The Knight and Lady. A plump woman in a flowered dress and apron was halfway up a ladder, stocking the shelves behind the counter. She turned at the jingle of the bell.

"Oh, good morning, sir. Just half a moment." She scurried down the ladder with surprising agility, quickly dusted off her hands, and turned to him with a smile. "Now then."

Drew removed his hat. "Good morning. I was wondering if you have any cat collars."

"Cat collars?"

"The kind with bells."

The woman shook her head. "Don't have much call for that sort of thing. We did have some collars for small dogs." She began rummaging in a box on the shelf behind her. "I suppose they're all gone now. Nothing with bells, I'm afraid."

"Ah, well, bad luck then, eh?" Drew leaned on the counter with a touch of a confidential smile. "I don't suppose you could help me with something else."

"I'll certainly try, sir."

"I fancy you see a lot of labels in your line of work." He opened his pocket watch and took out the sea-washed scrap of a label he'd found in the bottom of *The Gull*. "Do you recognize this one?"

She took it from him, squinted, and then put on the glasses that were hanging from a chain around her neck. "Hmm . . . D. D."

She turned to scan the shelves behind her, and Drew did the same.

"Dabney and Sons Jams?" She glanced again at the paper and then shook her head. "No. Daugherty Potted Meats? It's close, but no."

She considered a can of Denton's Delish Fish, which featured a drawing of an eager-eyed salmon complete with knife and fork and a napkin round its neck. "Not quite the same, and the background is green, not yellow."

"Right." Drew gave her his most appealing and hopeful smile. "Might I come back there and look as well?

"Well," she said, stretching the word out like a cat's wheedling meow, "I'm really not supposed to, you know."

"Just a quick look, then I pop back to my side and no harm done, eh?"

She grinned, her freckled nose wrinkling and girlish. "Oh, all right. But if anyone comes in, you go, agreed?"

"Agreed."

He slipped behind the counter before she could change her mind and started searching the lower shelves, the ones he couldn't see from the customers' side of the store, looking for anything that would be a less-faded shade of yellow than the paper he had found. Anything with a large letter *D*.

"Have you lived in Armitage Landing long, er . . . forgive

me, and allow me to introduce myself. I'm Drew Farthering. I come from Farthering—"

"Farthering Place! Oooh, is that you then?" She clasped her hands over her heart. "Have you come here on a case? It's the goings-on at Winteroak, isn't it? Oh, poor, sweet Miss Henley. He used to bring her in here, you know. Not often, I suppose, but now and again for the *Times* and that. Such a charming young lady and him so sweet on her. He must be brokenhearted. And Mr. Cummins! Why, who'd've thought it? Next you'll tell me old Mrs. Nesbitt who has the shop next door has poisoned someone."

"I'm afraid I wouldn't know about that."

"Of course not," the woman went on cheerfully. "What with her gout, she couldn't get properly about even to buy the poison."

Drew managed an understanding nod. "I suppose you've lived here some while, Mrs. . . ."

"It's Marsrow." She bobbed a curtsy. "And yes, all my life. The shop's called Camworth's. I was born a Camworth, you know, but with five sisters and all of 'em married, well, there wasn't much chance of us passing down the name. Still, me and my Harold do all right for ourselves here. Did you have something you wanted to ask?"

Drew blinked in the sudden absence of chatter. "Uh, not actually, no."

"Oh." Her mouth went down in a pout. "And here I thought you'd come down to Armitage Landing to investigate about poor Miss Henley."

"Actually, I came for the party at Winteroak House."

"Oooh, I fancy it was ever so lovely. My friend Myrtle, she's Mrs. Smythe-Brandon's maid, she said it was just like stepping back a hundred years into one of those storybooks, all the ladies and gents in their fancy duds and dancing and all. Did you dance, Mr. Farthering? I mean those dances they did back then?"

Drew cleared his throat. "As little as my wife would allow me to get by with."

Mrs. Marsrow chuckled. "It's a wise husband who humors his wife when and how he can."

"So I've been told and well believe it. And does your husband humor you?"

She smirked. "If he knows what's good for him."

"And what does he do when he's not at his job?" Drew shifted a few boxes of washing powder to one side, seeing if he could find a match for the label while watching the woman from the corner of his eye. "I'm wondering if he could tell me about the fishing in the area."

"No, not Harold. Can't abide fish, my Harold. They give him a rash."

"Oh, that's a pity." Drew moved some jars of salmon paste. "It's just I saw some men in a little boat a while back coming in with their catch, and I thought it looked rather jolly. With everything that's gone on at the Cumminses' house, I thought perhaps I'd take some friends and go out on the river and get away for a while."

"Probably Bert and Tom Kimlin and Bill Rinnie. Was one of them a great tall fellow with a red beard?"

Drew nodded and pretended to be interested in comparing the *D* on a can of fruit to the one he'd brought with him. "I believe that's who it was, yes. They pulled into the cove just east of here, below Winteroak House."

"Precisely." Her face lost its cheeriness. "I don't like to talk out of turn, sir, but I wouldn't recommend you speak to them about their boat. They're quite particular about it. I suppose it being their livelihood and all, they would be, but there's no need to be so hard about it, is there? I mean, we all have to earn our bread."

Drew nodded and then knelt down to inspect a lower shelf, still eyeing her covertly. "And how do they do—Bert, Tom, and Bill? Make a good living at their fishing, do they?"

"Nah." She wrinkled her nose. "It's a hard job, that's what it is. My sister's first husband was a fisherman till the sea took him, and they never had two beans. Aw, but they were happy as ducks, they were. Now with Mr. Burnside, she's got more and wants more, if you ask me. Money's no replacement, I say, but what's a lone woman to do when her man's left her nothing but a broken heart?"

"It is rather a thorny problem, isn't it? But I suppose everyone has his struggles. Look at our three fishermen. They have mouths to feed as well, I suppose."

She laughed. "Only their own. Not that Bert wasn't keeping company with Mary Elizabeth Lyles a year or two ago, though nothing came of it. Poor Mary Elizabeth, and now she's married to—"

"No doubt. Still, it's rather a trig little boat for poor fishermen. I naturally assumed . . ." He gave her a look that invited her to take him into her confidence, and she seemed delighted to oblige.

"Well, I won't say there wasn't a pother when they started going about in that instead of the old tub they had. And Bill was ever so tetchy if anyone asked about the new. But, well, his old gran did pass over not long before, and we just naturally assumed she left him a bit of something when she did."

"And they've been partners some while, have they?"

Mrs. Marsrow frowned, thinking. "Five or six years now, I'd say. Of course, it was just Bill with Tom and Burt's dad well before then. But when old Mr. Kimlin went, the boys naturally took up for him."

By that time, Drew had looked over most everything on the shelves. "Well, I'm afraid to say I haven't found anything the least like my little sample here, but I am most grateful for your assistance."

"Oh, dear," she said, looking genuinely distressed, "and I did want to help. I'm sorry to have been so useless."

"No, not at all." He took her hand, bowing formally over it. "You've been very kind, Mrs. Marsrow, and I'm terribly grateful. If you happen to see anything that puts you in mind of this label . . ."

"Oh, I'll let you know at once, Mr. Farthering. I'd be quite pleased, I'm sure. Is there's anything else I can do for you?"

He walked around to the customer side of the counter and picked up a newspaper, the same one he'd read over breakfast that morning. "Just this, thank you." He gave her a half crown, and she smiled.

"I'll just get your change."

"You keep it," he said, and with a wink he put on his hat and stepped outside.

Madeline pushed open the kitchen door and found Mrs. Ruggles sitting at the table peeling potatoes. Seeing Madeline, the cook wiped her hands and got to her feet.

"Is there something you'd like, madam?"

Her tone was cordial enough, but she didn't look at all pleased to see that Madeline had come uninvited into her kitchen.

"I was just wondering what we're having for lunch," Madeline said. "Everything you make is always so delicious."

"Baked chicken and potatoes and some boiled vegetables. I didn't think Mrs. Cummins or Mr. Talbot would want anything fussy."

"No, of course not."

There were peas and carrots laid out on the counter next to a pan that held two plump chickens.

"I meant to tell you how much we enjoyed the chicken we had during the party. What do you do to them to make them so tender?"

Mrs. Ruggles pursed her lips. "I don't like to say, madam. It's been our family secret some while now."

"I understand." Madeline put her hands behind her back like a scolded child. "You mustn't mind me. I'm afraid I'm not much of a cook myself, but now that I'm married I think I ought to remedy that."

The cook nodded. "Wouldn't want to poison your young husband the first year out, I'd think."

"Not if I can help it."

Mrs. Ruggles nudged Madeline with one reddened elbow. "Wait till the second, eh?" Her lined face crinkled into a grin.

Madeline couldn't help giggling. "Maybe the third."

"Well then," said Mrs. Ruggles, "perhaps I'd better tell you my little secret anyway. I put the chickens in honey brine the night before and then truss them up so they cook nice and even. Easy as winking and you won't have any husband, young or old, not asking for more."

"I'll make sure and try it sometime. Thank you. I was wondering . . ."

"Yes, madam?"

"That label my husband asked you about, the one with the *D* on it."

Mrs. Ruggles nodded.

"I was wondering if you had remembered anything like that."

"No, dear, I'm sorry. I just can't think of anything that would be what Mr. Farthering was asking after. And Mrs. Brogan couldn't place it, either."

"That's too bad." Madeline glanced toward the pantry door. "Do you think it would be all right if I looked in there myself? Sometimes people see the same things so often they don't really see them anymore."

The cook's expression grew cool again. "I think I know what's in my own pantry, begging your pardon, madam."

"Oh, no," Madeline said, laying a hand on her arm. "I didn't mean to say you don't. I just thought I might look around and—"

A high-pitched little mew came from behind the pantry door, and a white paw shot out from underneath it.

"Eddie!" Madeline pushed open the door. Eddie was crouched down, blinking at her. "What are you doing in here?"

Eddie tilted her head to one side and began grooming her paw, no longer interested in leaving the pantry.

"Well, come on."

The cook scowled. "That little devil, she's always sneaking in there when I have my back turned. Go on! Shoo!"

Madeline scooped the cat into her arms. "My husband and I were thinking she ought to have a bell or something. Just to keep her out of mischief. But with everything that's happened, I guess we forgot about it." With a sidelong glance at Mrs. Ruggles, Madeline turned to Eddie. "What were you doing in here?"

She strolled into the pantry, glancing at the cans and boxes stacked on the shelves. There seemed to be an enormous variety of things piled into the back section, not just food but clothing and blankets and household items in no particular order.

"That's Mrs. Cummins's charity pile." Mrs. Ruggles sniffed. "Not that it isn't grand of her to collect it all and send it over to the vicar, but it does make bedlam of my pantry. I'm afraid it's stacked up a bit since, well, since the master and all, and the police did us no favors rummaging through it. I suppose the missus will put it all to rights when she's feeling up to it, poor thing."

Madeline cuddled the cat closer, still studying the shelves. "Maybe my friend Miss Holland and I can help her with it before we have to go."

The cook huffed. "Just as you say, madam. I don't know how I'm to keep the house fed with great crowds of people in my pantry, mind you, but that's not for me to say."

She stood at the pantry door, looking expectantly at Madeline until she and the cat were safely back in the kitchen, and then she waddled back to the table and her potatoes.

"Will there be anything else, madam? Would you like me to put the cat out?"

Eddie, lying like a baby in Madeline's arms, looked unconcerned.

"I'll take her. Maybe we'll see if we can find a collar for her. Do you think they'd have one in the village?"

Mrs. Ruggles snorted. "There's not much in Armitage Landing but the post office, the greengrocer, and the pub. You'd best try Lymington for your collar."

Madeline thanked her and carried the cat out of the kitchen and into the garden. Drew was just coming up the path.

She waved to him. "Any luck?"

He kissed her cheek, looking distracted. "Not much. Mrs. Marsrow at the greengrocer didn't recognize the label. Yet she did know that Bill Rinnie's gran died and that's why he has a new boat, and he most definitely doesn't hire it out. How about you?"

"I'm afraid I didn't do much better. Mrs. Ruggles doesn't care for visitors in her kitchen, she knows what is and isn't in her pantry thank you very much, and there's nothing like that label you showed her. Oh, and she thinks I shouldn't poison you until we've been married at least two years."

He nodded thoughtfully. "Sound advice. And did you manage to have a look in the pantry yourself?"

"It was pretty quick, but yes, I did. The only thing of interest in there was Eddie."

Drew chuckled. "Somehow I'm not at all surprised. I did ask about a collar for her, by the way, but they hadn't any."

"Mrs. Ruggles says Lymington's the place to go for that."

"All right. We'll have a look there when we have time. Do you know where Will was off to just now?"

"What do you mean?" Madeline cradled Eddie against her shoulder. "He's inside with Carrie and Nick."

"Actually," Drew said, "I saw him just a bit ago walking toward the beach."

"What's he doing down there? I know Carrie told him not to leave the house."

"Evidently he didn't care to comply."

"Oh, there you are." Madeline turned to see Mrs. Cummins coming from around the side of the house with Tal beside her.

"Everyone seems out of place at the moment, though I suspect Nick and Miss Holland must have found some trysting place away from her brother." There was an indulgent twinkle in her eyes as she sat down in the sun. "It's good to see some sweetness left in this old world."

Madeline put Eddie down to let her investigate the butterfly that had caught her attention and then sat down next to Mrs. Cummins.

"How are you today?" She glanced up at Tal. "How are you both?"

"All right," Tal said, but it was clear he was not.

A shadow passed across Mrs. Cummins face, and she sighed. "Poor Josephine is still ill, so Cook went herself to see Mr. Gibbons about the joint for dinner. She simply wouldn't trust it to anyone else, even your Beryl, if you don't mind my saying so. I don't know why one of the other girls couldn't go, but she insisted. She is very particular, yet you couldn't ask for anyone more loyal. I think there's hardly anything she wouldn't do for us. Then again she's been with the family for ages. Before I came to Winteroak House as a bride."

"Our Mrs. Devon is like that," Drew said. "I don't know how we'd manage without her."

"I'd have to do the cooking, then." Madeline laughed. "And it would be you who had the food poisoning most of the time."

Drew wagged his finger at her. "Naughty."

"Isn't it a nice sunny morning?" Mrs. Cummins asked, looking a bit brighter. "I haven't seen such a long stretch of good weather in ages."

"It's glorious," Madeline agreed.

Mrs. Cummins shaded her eyes against the sun. "I was afraid we'd have rain and it would spoil the party. Before everyone came, I told Mr. Cummins, I said . . . I mean, that was before I—" She broke off, her cheeks reddening. "Oh, dear. What have I said now?"

Tal was paler than before. "It doesn't matter, Mother.

Why don't you sit here for a while and enjoy the weather until lunchtime?"

"That's a lovely idea," Drew said. He pulled up a chair for himself. "No use letting it all go to waste."

Mrs. Cummins's lips trembled into a smile. "It is such a comfort to have you here, Drew. Especially for Tal." She looked at Madeline, pleading in her eyes. "The boys were always such good friends. It's a shame their reunion had to be so horribly spoilt, but at least they're here to help him through." She took her son's hand. "Don't you think so, dear?"

"Of course, Mother."

His voice was low and grim, and there was a touch of fresh worry in her eyes. Tal must have seen it there, because he drew a deep breath and then forced a smile.

"We'll have it all sorted before long. I don't want you to worry."

Her eyes filled with tears as she turned to Madeline again. "Goodness knows, he tries to shield me from everything unpleasant, even when his own poor heart is breaking."

"All right, Mother," Tal said. "No need to bore everyone with sentiment."

She flinched almost imperceptibly at the coldness in his voice and fished a handkerchief out of the pocket of her dress. "Oh, I'm sorry. Do forgive my silliness, all of you. It's been rather a difficult few days."

"Of course it has," Madeline said, giving Tal a reproving look. "And you've been very brave all this time."

"Mother, I . . ." He covered his eyes with one hand. "I didn't mean . . . Please excuse me."

In a few long strides he disappeared around the side of the house.

Mrs. Cummins breathed a nearly inaudible "oh" and started to stand when Drew stopped her.

"Maybe I should see to him," he said.

Her lower lip trembled. "I never meant to be a bore."

"And you never were," he assured her. "He's just on edge. You mustn't take that sort of thing to heart. He doesn't mean it."

"No, of course not. Losing poor Alice and everything with his father." She patted his hand. "He doesn't mean it."

Madeline met Drew's eyes out of Mrs. Cummins's line of sight, and he nodded in return.

"Excuse me a moment, will you, ladies?"

— Ten —

Drew went into the garden after Tal, who was grieving and so didn't mean what he'd just said. Still, there was no need to make a bad situation worse. He found Tal pacing the grass, sometimes steering clear of the carefully tended flower beds and sometimes not.

"Look here, Tal—"

"Have you come to tell me what a beast I am?"

Drew shook his head. "We all understand what a rough go you've had of it. But she has too, you know."

"I know." Tal sank down onto a marble bench beneath the weeping willow and put his head in his hands. "All this is hard enough without seeing what it's done to her."

"We've all been rather on edge, but perhaps she's had it the worst, what with finding out about your father and you losing Alice that way. I think most mothers would rather be hurt themselves than have to bear the hurt of their children." Drew shoved his hands into his pockets. "She'd make it all better for you if she could."

Tal looked up at the cloudless sky with a groan. "Don't

you think I know that? Don't you think I feel an absolute swine for snapping at her? She thinks she can fix everything with a jam bun and a cup of tea. I know she means well, but it's not enough. Some things just can't be fixed."

The fierceness in his expression faded as quickly as it had come, and he put his head in his hands once again. "You saw her at dinner last night, nearly falling to pieces over a bent fork and a cracked plate."

"I'm sorry. It's always the little things, isn't it?"

"Doesn't help that I can't manage to be civil, either."

Drew shrugged. "She seems a bit lost these days. Without your father to lean on and all. I expect you feel the same way, but maybe the two of you could lean on each other now."

"We're all we have left, aren't we? And you know how Mum is. Even when the world is coming down around my ears, I know she's there for me."

"It's a good thing to know."

Tal managed a crooked smile. "It is that."

Drew clapped him on the back. "Maybe you ought to tell her so."

Tal said nothing for a moment, and then he nodded. "I suppose I ought. Thanks, old man."

Drew got to his feet. "Ready to go back?"

Tal made a wry face and stood, too. "You don't have a healthy portion of humble pie on you by any chance, do you?"

Drew chuckled. "Sorry, no. But you tell her anyway. See if it doesn't help."

They walked back toward the terrace, but Tal stopped before they reached it. "No."

Drew stopped beside him and studied his wan face. "What is it, Tal?"

"I can't do this, Drew. I can't keep pretending things are

160

all right, that they're ever going to be all right." He caught a quivering breath. "I can't go tell my mother I'll help her get through this when I don't know if I can even get through it myself. I feel as if I'll go mad caged up here, knowing my father had help doing what he did and not know who's in it with him or what lengths he'll go to stay hidden."

Drew couldn't say he didn't have the same fears, especially with Madeline and Carrie staying at Winteroak, but he wasn't going to let those fears make him turn tail and let a murderer go free. For now, though, he just wanted to help Tal make it through the morning.

"Maybe you ought to get away from the house for a bit. I don't mean leave the country or anything, but maybe just take a drive or a walk. Clear your head. You should have gone to the cinema with the others last night. Would have done you good. Better than shutting yourself up as you have. I haven't seen you all morning. Not until now."

Tal shrugged. "Don't know where I'd go. Everything seems so . . . useless."

"We're going to find out who killed her, Tal." Drew took hold of his shoulders, looking steadily into his pain-dulled eyes. "We're going to find out what happened and who was helping your father. It's going to stop, do you hear me? You just have to hold on. Your mother needs you."

Tal said nothing, and Drew began to wonder if he'd even heard.

Then Tal took in a deep, strengthening breath of the fresh salt air and nodded. "Yes. Of course she does. Come on."

Carrie and Nick had joined Madeline and Mrs. Cummins on the terrace by the time Drew and Tal came around to the back of the house once again.

Tal leaned over and kissed his mother's cheek and murmured

a swift apology. Mrs. Cummins's worried face suddenly bloomed, and she patted his hand. That was all, but it was clearly enough. Tal seemed more at ease afterward.

"We've just had a wonderful idea," Madeline said, pulling Drew down onto the bench beside her. "What do you think, Tal? We were just talking about the Little Abbey. I hear it's very pretty this time of year."

"Is it very old?" Carrie asked.

"I, uh, yes." Tal cleared his throat. "It was built in 1123 and then dissolved and abandoned in Henry VIII's time. They took the roof off for the lead, and the locals used the stones for their houses, so there's not all that much left of it. But it's a pretty place. There are still three walls, some steps, and nice stone tracery, and the walk through the forest up to it is rather pretty, too."

"May we go see it?" Carrie asked. "It's not too far to go, is it?"

"Perhaps a half-hour's walk is all. A bit more if you take the path round by Claridge Rindle. It's quite lovely, in fact."

Madeline glanced at Drew, then turned a warm smile on Tal. "We were thinking, if you'd like, that it might be nice to go see it."

"There you go, Tal," Drew said. "It'd make a welcome change, wouldn't it? You can be our tour guide and point out all the sights, and I daresay we'll be back just in time for lunch. What do you think?"

"Well, I . . ." Tal hesitated, catching the hopeful look on his mother's face, and then managed a small smile. "It might not be a bad idea, after all." He squeezed his mother's hand. "Provided we *all* go."

Mrs. Cummins beamed at him. "Oh, yes! But really, we ought to invite Mr. Laurent to come, too."

"Mother," Tal protested.

"Now, yes, we should. The police haven't found that he's done anything wrong, and there's really no reason you shouldn't be friends with him. He's our guest, and it's not right him being left out."

"Actually, ma'am," Drew said, "I believe he went down to his yacht earlier this morning. I heard his valet telling the cook he wouldn't be in for lunch."

"Oh." A little pucker formed between Mrs. Cummins's brows. "I suppose that's all right, then. Perhaps that's the way they do it in France. Well, never mind. I'll just go put on my walking shoes and won't be a minute." She hurried away.

Madeline frowned. "He might have let her know himself." She sighed and looked down at her own shoes. "I suppose these will do for a half-hour walk. How about yours, Carrie?"

"They're fine," Carrie said, half distracted as she looked around the garden and out toward the beach. "You two haven't seen Billy, have you? I told him if he was late coming to lunch again today, he'd just have to do without. I don't know why everyone should have to wait for him to show up every day."

"Oh, he's all right," Nick told her. "At least he's been keeping himself busy and not staring at us every minute."

"I saw him earlier," Drew said. "He looked as if he was headed down to the beach, and he seemed rather pleased with himself."

"Did he tell you where he was going?" Carrie asked. "At least he wasn't searching the house again."

"He didn't say anything to me," said Drew. "He and the vicar were having a talk. Then Will just grinned at me and hurried off."

Carrie rolled her eyes. "He's driving me crazy with this detective business."

"Shall I go down and fetch him?" Nick asked, and she frowned.

"No, it's all right. He'll be in when he feels like it."

A moment later, Mrs. Cummins came back onto the terrace wearing what were no doubt her most sensible shoes. "I think this walk will be just what we all need. Everyone ready?"

Beddows appeared in the doorway and made a bow. "Beg pardon, madam. The Reverend Mr. Broadhurst is here to see you."

Mrs. Cummins bit her lip. "Oh, dear. He did say he was coming today. I completely forgot. I hope you will all excuse me."

"Couldn't you see him another time, Mother?" Tal asked.

"He could come along with us," Madeline suggested.

"You'd all better go along," Mrs. Cummins said. "I know he has several calls to make today, and I don't want to keep him too long. Just enjoy yourselves and be back in plenty of time for lunch."

The walk up to Little Abbey and back was a pleasant one, and by the time they returned to Winteroak House, everyone was in better spirits. Even Tal was eager for lunch. But when they all trooped into the dining room, Mrs. Cummins told them they would have to wait.

"Miss Holland's brother hasn't come back from his walk yet," she said. "We really shouldn't start without him."

They sat down at the table anyway and told Mrs. Cummins about their visit to the abbey. Drew tried to ignore the tantalizing smell of roast chicken and vegetables coming from the kitchen and hoped his stomach wouldn't decide to growl.

"How is Mr. Broadhurst?" Madeline asked after a while.

"I wish he could have come with us. I wanted to talk to him about his charities."

Mrs. Cummins smiled fondly. "He couldn't stay long, I'm afraid. But he only came by to see how we were doing. He was so pleased to know you were all out getting some fresh air and sunshine. He takes such good care of his flock." There was a lull in the conversation, and she looked worriedly at the clock above the fireplace.

"I'm sorry my brother's being so inconsiderate," Carrie said, looking at her wristwatch. "Why don't we go ahead and eat? There's really no need for everyone to wait for him."

"I suppose it would be all right," Mrs. Cummins said. "If you're sure he won't mind."

She rang the bell, and Beryl came into the dining room wearing a cap and apron that clearly belonged to someone else.

"Yes, madam?"

"We will begin now, thank you," Mrs. Cummins told her. "And please tell Cook to put something by for when Mr. Holland comes in."

"Yes, madam. Right away."

She curtsied, beaming when Madeline gave her a subtle nod of approval, and then hurried back into the kitchen. A moment later, she was back.

"I beg your pardon, madam, but the cook says to tell you she wouldn't be surprised if the chicken is dry as last week, having to keep it warm so long and all." She glanced at Madeline and made another curtsy. "I beg your pardon."

Drew chuckled when she was gone. "At least we'll know why."

"Oh, dear," Mrs. Cummins said. "You must all forgive me. If it's overcooked, then certainly we shall have something else."

She reached for the bell, but Tal stopped her.

"Don't be silly, Mother. No matter how late we sit down, have you ever known Mrs. Ruggles's chicken to be anything but delicious?"

She chuckled softly. "I suppose you're right. Well, I'm just not going to worry. At the worst, we can all eat the cake she made this morning."

Drew and Nick exchanged glances at the mention of cake.

"Did you happen to notice what variety of cake she made?" Drew asked.

"Chocolate." She smiled at her son. "Tal's favorite."

That won a faint smile from Tal in return. "I'd as soon start with that as chicken."

"Now, Tibby—" She broke off at a muffled thud and then a clatter from the direction of the kitchen and was immediately on her feet. "If Cook has broken another of my serving platters!"

Her threat unfinished, she scurried out of the dining room, leaving her puzzled guests behind.

"That didn't much sound like a serving platter," Drew said. "A serving platter would be more of a crash than a thud. That was—"

A shriek pierced the air.

Tal shoved his chair back and leapt to his feet. "What in the world—?"

Drew was immediately beside him, not liking the profound horror in the sound. "We'd best go see. Nick, look after things here."

Tal was already out of the dining room and into the kitchen before Drew caught up to him. The cook was standing at the open pantry door, rolling pin at the ready, wide-eyed and determined to take on whatever had dared invade her hallowed domain. Beryl fled up the stairs, almost running the two men down.

"Oh, sir! Mr. Drew! It's horrid! Down—down there! Oh, hurry! Please, please, hurry!"

By then several of the other servants were peeping into the pantry, gawking and murmuring among themselves.

"See to her," Drew called back to the cook as he scrambled down after Tal.

The wine cellar was lit by a single shaded bulb overhead, a bulb that illuminated Mrs. Cummins's bloodless face and bloodied hands.

"Oh, Tibby," she breathed and fell senseless into her son's arms.

Behind her, a body lay sprawled on its side and stained with blood, half concealed by the two wine barrels that had fallen, crushing the head. Drew recognized the clothes immediately.

"Will."

Tal looked at Drew, his face as white as his mother's. "Drew—"

"Take her up the back way and put her to bed. I'll clear everyone out upstairs." Drew glanced at the body, another life snuffed out in an instant. "Just stay with her."

Tal nodded blankly, then realization came into his face. "You can't possibly think she—"

"I don't think anything." *What am I going to say to Carrie?* "Just take her upstairs."

Drew went up to the pantry ahead of him. Beddows the butler was peering down the stairs, the rest of the staff trying to see into the wine cellar from behind him.

"There's been an accident," Drew told him. "Clear everyone out of the kitchen, if you would, and see they stay out. And be so good as to ring up Dr. Fletcher and the police."

At the mention of the police, several of the staff stared at each other while the butler nodded.

"Very good, sir." Beddows turned to his subordinates and gave a sharp clap of his hands. "Clear the room, if you please. You all have duties to see to. You will be sent for if you are required."

Mrs. Ruggles was at the kitchen table with Beryl, sobbing against her shoulder. She looked at Drew questioningly.

"Stay there, if you will," he said to her as Beddows ushered the others out. "I need to talk to Beryl, and I'm sure she'll do a great deal better if you're here to help her along."

Beryl looked up, eyes and nose and lips red and swollen, and then she saw Tal come out of the pantry carrying his still-unconscious mother. "Oh, sir."

Tal never glanced her way, never looked at any of them. He hurried up the back stairway and out of sight.

Drew sat at the table across from the two women. "All right, Beryl, I know this is upsetting for you, but you must tell me everything you remember while it's still fresh in your mind."

"Oh, Mr. Drew, I shall never be able to forget it. And him lying there with his head bashed in."

Mrs. Ruggles made little shushing noises and pressed a dry serviette into her hands, replacing the one she had already soaked with tears.

"I'm sorry," Drew said. "We'll try to make this as brief as possible. Tell me what happened. What did you see when you went down to the wine cellar?"

Beryl sniffled and wiped her nose. "I . . . I heard that great clatter, so I went down to see what it was. And th-there he was, just like you saw him, Mr. Drew."

She began to sob again, and Drew pressed his lips together,

waiting for her to calm, knowing he had perhaps a minute or two more before the girls pushed their way in and demanded to know what the row was about. Finally, Beryl looked up at him again.

"And where was Mrs. Cummins?"

"She was up in the pantry, sir. I suppose she heard the clatter too and came down after she heard me scream."

"I see. And how do you suppose she got blood on her?"

"She was trying to help him. She . . . I didn't think to even go to him, sir, I was that upset. I don't know how she could bear it, t-touching him, but I suppose she went to see if there was something could be done."

"Did you see anything else," Drew asked. "Anything that might tell us more about what happened?"

"No, sir. I expect he was down there, and those barrels fell on him. Poor Miss Holland, she's going to be ever so cut up over it."

Drew bit his lip, not liking to think of that just yet, not liking to think of any of this. It would certainly be quite a coincidence if such an "accident" was unrelated to the murder that had already taken place at Winteroak House.

"Sir?" Mrs. Ruggles said, something in her tone telling him she had been obliged to repeat herself to get his attention. "If you've done, perhaps she ought to go lie down for a bit."

"Oh, yes. Yes, of course. I'll need a word with you when you've got her settled in."

"Right, sir. Just as you say."

The cook was just helping the maid up the back stairs when Nick stuck his head in the kitchen doorway. "There you are. What's going on? I daresay it wasn't a broken serving platter that's pulled all the color out of your face."

Drew stood and went to him, making his voice low. "It's

bad, Nick. Very bad. We have to keep Carrie and Madeline out of—"

"Keep us out of what?" Madeline said as she pushed open the kitchen door. Her expression was mild, but there was something in her eyes that would not be gainsaid.

Carrie was just behind her. "Drew, what's happened? You know Billy will have a fit if he missed out on something to do with the case. He always . . ." She faltered, looking questioningly at Drew and then at Madeline and Nick. "Tell me what's happened."

"Drew," Madeline pled, her voice barely audible.

"You'd better sit down," he said. "Both of you."

"It's Billy," Carrie cried, lunging toward the pantry. "Something's happened to Billy!"

Nick caught her before she could take more than a step. "Wait."

"What is it?" she asked, taking hold of his coat with both hands. "Nick, what is it? Where's Billy?"

"I don't know."

He looked desperately at Drew and then urged Carrie into one of the chairs at the kitchen table. Madeline sank into one across from them, and Drew sat beside her.

He took her hand and looked over at Carrie. "I'm sorry. It's . . . it's your brother."

Tears spilled down Carrie's porcelain cheeks. "Please, tell me what's happened. Has he been hurt?"

Drew shook his head. "I'm afraid he's dead."

— Eleven —

Carrie made one harsh sobbing sound and then swallowed it down. "Where is he? He's down there, isn't he?" She looked toward the pantry door. "Down in the cellar. Oh, Billy, why couldn't you just let it alone?"

"Sweetheart," Nick whispered, moving to take her into his arms.

She wrenched away from him. "I have to go to him!"

"No." Drew looked at Nick, his expression stern. "Don't let her."

Nick caught her hands. "Carrie—"

"What happened to him?" she breathed.

"Wine barrels," Drew explained. "It looks as though they fell on him."

Carrie's lip quivered, and she turned to Nick once more, clinging to him. "Why can't I see him? I need to see him."

"It's bad, isn't it?" Nick asked Drew.

Drew nodded. "I'd rather none of you went down there. There's nothing to be done for him now, and it's a sight that will stay with you. I'd rather you have better memories to keep of him."

Carrie began to weep in earnest against Nick's chest. Without a word, Madeline went over to their side of the table and put her arms around them both.

"Dr. Fletcher, sir," Beddows announced as he ushered the doctor in.

"What's happened?" the doctor asked. "All I was told is that I was wanted."

"You were quick to get here," Drew said, standing.

"I was just down the road. My office located me and sent me on here. What's happened?"

"There's been an accident." Drew led the doctor through the pantry to the top of the cellar stairs. "Down there. I don't think there's much to be done."

Dr. Fletcher pushed his glasses up on his nose. "Fatal then."

Drew nodded.

"The police have been sent for?"

Again Drew nodded.

"Very good. I'll see to things from here."

The doctor disappeared into the cellar, and Drew returned to the kitchen. Carrie and Nick were huddled together, he with his cheek pressed against her red-gold hair and she with her face buried against his neck, her slender shoulders shaking with her noiseless sobs. Madeline was rubbing her back, tears flowing down her cheeks.

Drew went to her and kissed her temple, and she slipped her arm around his waist, pulling him close. They stayed that way until the silence was broken by a decorous clearing of the throat.

"Chief Inspector Birdsong, sir."

The butler stepped aside to admit Birdsong into the

kitchen. Instead of his usual world-weary expression, there was a tautness in his mouth and something dark behind his eyes. "Where?"

Drew gave Nick a brief glance, cautioning him to keep Carrie and Madeline where they were, and then he showed the chief inspector to the wine cellar.

Dr. Fletcher looked up from where he knelt beside the body. "I haven't moved anything. I just felt for a pulse. Not any, of course. Cause of death obvious."

Brilliant. Drew bit his tongue, not wanting to voice his bitter thoughts. He supposed it was all necessary, but he wondered that they even needed to say anything more. Over and over again these two, the doctor and the policeman, dealt with death of the ugliest sort. What more was there to say?

"How long ago?" Birdsong asked in a clipped tone.

"Not long," the doctor said. "I'll know more when I've had a chance to examine the body more thoroughly."

"Right. Just let me get my photographer and fingerprint man in here, and then you can take him off." Birdsong eyed Drew. "I suppose you can give me the details."

"Not much, I'm afraid," Drew said, looking around at the rock walls and shelves of dusty bottles. "But I'll tell you all I know. That is—was—Will Holland."

"The American girl's brother."

"He was determined to help us figure out who might have killed Alice Henley."

"I see." Birdsong's mouth tightened under his heavy mustache. "And he was how old? Sixteen?"

"Seventeen, I believe. I'd have to ask Carrie to be certain."

"Seventeen," Birdsong said.

He said nothing more than that. He didn't even look at Drew, but somehow that one word ripped through Drew's heart. *Seventeen*. Just a boy. A boy who wanted nothing more than to help solve a real murder and drive a tiger-striped car. A boy who thought this was all a game. And Drew had let him.

"What was he doing in the wine cellar?" Birdsong asked.

"I'm not certain. It may have been something perfectly ordinary, but he'd been pretty keen to come have a look. The Scotland Yard chaps have searched down here a number of times and found nothing. We all figured there must be some connection to the smuggling. I suspect Will came down to have a look on his own."

"And who found the body?"

"Beryl, my wife's maid. She was asked to help serve at lunch, as the regular girl fell ill. We all heard the crash of the barrels. Beryl came down first to see what it was."

"I suppose she's the one who touched the body," Dr. Fletcher said.

There were some smears of blood on Will's left wrist and cuff, a larger stain in the center of his white shirtfront.

"That was Mrs. Cummins, I believe," Drew said. "Beryl said she was trying to see if there was anything she could do to help him."

Birdsong nodded. "I'll speak to her directly."

"I don't know if you'll be able just yet. She fainted, and her son carried her up to her room."

Birdsong's bushy eyebrows rose. "And just how was he involved?"

They were interrupted by the arrival of the photographer and two constables, who immediately began documenting the scene. Birdsong motioned for Drew to step to the back of the cellar with him where they wouldn't be in the way.

"Tell me again how your friend was involved."

"He wasn't, actually. He was with the rest of us in the dining room. We heard the maid scream, so he and I went to find out what happened. She was just running out when we stopped her. Mrs. Cummins was down in the cellar and promptly fainted."

"The maid found her standing over the body."

"No, nothing like that. She came in after Beryl. After Beryl saw the body and screamed."

"I see." The chief inspector jotted down a few notes. "I understand the house party broke up fairly quickly after the incident with the Henley girl. Besides your group, anyone else stay over?"

"Laurent, of course."

"Yes. Besides him, I mean."

"Everyone else went home. Oh, Laurent's man, Adkins, is still here, needless to say. I still don't think he's quite the article. Looks more like a street tough than a valet, if you ask me."

"Anyone been by to visit?" Birdsong asked.

Drew considered for a moment. "No one of note. Some ladies from the church came to console Mrs. Cummins and Tal. The vicar has been by a few times. I can't think of anyone else, but you might ask Beddows. I don't doubt he sees everyone who comes and goes. And anyone he doesn't see, I'm sure the cook does."

"The cook was here, was she?"

"Yes. We were just having lunch."

"I will be speaking to them both."

"Pardon me, Chief Inspector," Dr. Fletcher said, coming over to them. "Your men say they're nearly done. May I take the body now?"

"All right." Birdsong went over to the constable kneeling

beside the body. "Griffiths, I want you and Parkins to help the doctor with the deceased."

P.C. Griffiths nodded. "Right away, sir."

Birdsong turned to the doctor. "You might want to bring your car round to the back. And you, Mr. Farthering, could be a great help in seeing the ladies are in another part of the house when the boy's brought up."

"Certainly. I expect you'll want to talk to his sister."

"If she feels up to it," said the chief inspector. "If you think she does, why don't you get her and your wife settled somewhere. I'll go talk to the maid. Beryl, is it? Then I'll talk to Miss Holland."

"We'll be in the library."

"I'll drive my car round and bring in the stretcher," Dr. Fletcher said. "Then I'd best go up and see to Mrs. Cummins, poor woman."

"Perhaps I'd better lead off, Doctor," Drew suggested. "If you go back into the kitchen, I'm sure there will be questions. Let me get everyone out of the way before you come out."

"Just as you say."

Drew studied the scene one last time. The two large wine barrels lay where they had fallen, one squarely on Billy Holland's head and shoulders, the other tumbled beside it, mostly on end but leaning on the first. Over against the wall was a smaller cask Drew hadn't noticed before. There was a puddle of wine around it.

"Must have cracked when it hit the floor," Birdsong said, coming over to him.

"Could have." Drew pointed out a semicircular dent in the wood. "Could have hit one of the other barrels and bounced over here. Funny that the leak would be on the other side, if this is where it hit."

"Could have hit there, too." Birdsong turned to his photographer and the fingerprint man. "You and Parkins see to this, Tompkins, so we can move it."

"Right you are, Chief Inspector."

P.C. Parkins made quick work of the fingerprinting, and Tompkins finished up with his camera. The blue-white flash was blinding in the dimness of the cellar, and Drew spent a moment or two blinking before he could see again.

"I'd like to have a look at this leak." Drew started to turn the barrel over and then stopped himself. "All right if I move this now?"

Birdsong pursed his lips. "I'll see to it, if you please."

Careful to touch it as little as possible, he rolled the barrel toward the center of the cellar where the light was better. As Drew had suspected, there was a crack between the staves on the side opposite the dent. Birdsong had that side photographed and fingerprinted, and then Drew was allowed to touch it.

"Strange it would split that way," Drew said.

It wasn't that much of a split, only about two inches long, but it was enough to have let most of the wine drain out. Drew frowned at the puddle toward the back of the cellar where the smaller barrel had landed and glanced over to where Will Holland's body lay. Drew had seen it when he'd first come down into the cellar, a pool of blood around the mangled head and shoulders, but now he realized it was not just blood.

"Perhaps this barrel was leaking already." Drew looked at the barrels still stacked against the side wall and traced two fingers along a wet line down the front of them. "If it broke back there, there's no reason there should be wine here."

"Quite right." Birdsong stroked his mustache. "I'm

wondering if he hadn't moved that one himself, looking for something, and it was knocked out of his arms when the big ones fell on him. Could have been why the other barrels rolled off."

Drew nodded. "Might be, I suppose."

Dr. Fletcher cleared his throat. "I'd like to get the body out now, if I might, Chief Inspector."

"Yes, of course." Birdsong gestured toward the stairs. "If you don't mind, Mr. Farthering."

Drew went back into the kitchen where Madeline, Nick, and Carrie were seated at the table. The three of them looked up, a wordless plea for him to tell them something, anything, to make sense of all this.

He leaned down to kiss Madeline's hair. "Come on, all of you. We might as well move to somewhere more comfortable."

Carrie seized Drew's sleeve. "What did they say? Please, I have to know something."

"Come on."

He helped her to her feet, and Nick put his arm around her.

"Let's go to the library," Drew said. "We can talk there."

The library at Winteroak was serene and sunny and blessedly quiet. By the time Drew told the others what little he knew, Beddows was announcing Chief Inspector Birdsong.

"I'm sorry to intrude upon your grief, Miss Holland," the chief inspector said, and he seemed rather more than just professionally grave. "I will make this as brief as possible. May I sit down?"

Carrie nodded, watching him.

Birdsong took a straight-backed chair from near the hearth

and set it down in front of the sofa where she sat next to Nick. "The doctor says Mrs. Cummins is too upset to be questioned at the moment. He's given her something to make her sleep. The maid, Beryl Duncan, corroborated what you told me, Mr. Farthering, and doesn't recall seeing anyone except the cook in or near the pantry for the past hour. That was when she came to help out in the kitchen. I spoke to the cook, a Mrs.——" he paused and looked at his notes—"Mrs. Ruggles. She remembers the same."

"I . . . I wasn't in there," Carrie said. "I don't have any idea who may have seen what."

"Yes, miss, but perhaps you can give me an idea why your brother might have been down there. As far as we could see, he hadn't taken anything down there with him or touched anything in the cellar. There's no indication that anyone was down there with him before all of you heard the crash. Had he said anything to you about going into the wine cellar?"

Carrie shook her head and twisted the sodden handkerchief in her hands. "I know he wanted to find out what happened to Alice. After Mr. Cummins was arrested, he was talking to the men from Scotland Yard about the smuggling. He thought . . . he thought it was some kind of game."

She broke down again, and Nick gave Drew a brief pleading glance.

"I don't think she can tell you anything, Chief Inspector," Drew said quietly. "Perhaps, if you think it necessary, you could talk to Miss Holland another time."

Birdsong put his notebook and stub of a pencil back into his coat pocket. "I'm very sorry for your loss, miss. We will be keeping you informed of any developments in the case, and for the time being there will be a constable stationed outside the house just to see there's no other trouble." He nodded at Madeline and Nick. "Mrs. Farthering. Mr. Dennison. A word, if you would, Mr. Farthering."

Drew followed the chief inspector into the corridor and shut the door behind him.

For a moment Birdsong stood looking across into the dining room and out over the front lawn. "Following your example, eh, Detective Farthering?"

The blow more than stung. "I did my best to keep him out of it."

"I don't suppose warning you off now will do any more good than it has before."

"I promised my friend."

Drew didn't know what else to say. It seemed rather a weak motivation at the moment. At the least, some of that boy's blood was on his hands. He'd talked up his and Nick's playing detective, and this was the result. Telling Will to stay out of it had done no more good than had Birdsong's many warnings to Drew himself. If solving these sorts of crimes was truly his reason for being, it was all a cruel joke. A bit like assigning a dachshund to herd sheep.

"I saw him," Drew said. "When I came back from the grocer's, I saw him going down toward the beach."

Birdsong's heavy eyebrows went up. "Oh, yes? And what did he say?"

"Nothing, I'm afraid. Just . . ." Drew swallowed down the strangling tightness in his throat. "Just gave me a grin as though he were off on a lark and hurried on. I don't know how he got back into the wine cellar."

"And when was this?"

"About a quarter past ten, maybe closer to half past. I wish I'd asked him where he was off to."

Before either of them could say more, the bell at the front

door rang. Beddows admitted Endicott and Dane of Scotland Yard.

"We called at your office," Endicott said, "and they told us you were down here. I see the case has gotten more interesting. Care to fill us in?"

Birdsong gave him the briefest account of what had happened.

"Lovely," Endicott said, his mouth pressed into a grim line. "And your front-runner?"

"Nobody knows anything at this point," the chief inspector answered. "As usual. I'd like to know what our Frenchman has been up to this morning."

"He's been on his yacht having his lunch, a rather nice bit of roast mutton and sprouts with a cheeky little Beaujolais to set it off."

Again Birdsong's eyebrows shot up. "Oh, yes?"

"You're sure of this?" Drew asked, and he got Endicott's smug smile in return.

"We were interviewing him."

Birdsong snorted. "Charming."

"I wonder why he didn't come to lunch with everyone else," Drew said. "Seems rather a bother to have his own made separately."

"I think it was the company rather than the food," Dane put in with a smirk. He consulted his notebook. "A Mrs. Barbara Stott, twenty-eight, from Pennington."

Endicott nodded. "She left soon after we arrived. I believe we upset Monsieur Laurent's plans."

"What about his valet?" Drew asked. "Adkins."

Endicott shook his head. "No good. He was serving the mutton."

"That lets them both out," Birdsong said.

"Adkins and I had a chat last night," said Drew.

Endicott narrowed his eyes. "What exactly did he say?"

"He told me to stay out of the investigation and to keep Will out, too. He claimed he didn't like the idea of Mrs. Farthering being a widow."

"He made threats, and you didn't think that was something you ought to tell us?" Birdsong asked, his face stern.

Drew shrugged. "He didn't exactly have the most gracious way of putting it, but I got the impression he was sincere. Perhaps I was wrong."

"I'll have a word with Mr. Adkins," Birdsong said. "You can be sure of that."

Endicott shook his head. "No, I don't want you tampering with him. And he couldn't have killed the boy and been down at the yacht at the same time."

"I'll grant you that," Birdsong said, "but clearly he knows something. Or why the warning? I somehow doubt it was out of the goodness of his heart."

"That's exactly what he claimed," Drew said. "He said that, because I hadn't made things difficult for him over my wife's pearls, he wanted to do me a favor in return. Now I wish I had listened to him."

"I'm not concerned about those pearls," Endicott said. "I just want to know how Cummins was getting his cargo up to London on a routine basis. We think Adkins is our best bet for finding that out, but he's not likely to lead us anywhere if you lot keep hauling him down to the station."

"This isn't about the pearls," the chief inspector said, and his face was hard. "This is murder. If Adkins—"

"I don't care about your murder." Endicott glared at Birdsong. "Murders happen all the time. Seeing to them is your job. Mine is stopping the importation of illegal substances into my jurisdiction. If nabbing your Hampshire murderer catches me my London smuggler, I'm all for it. Otherwise, you're on your own."

"Decent of you," Birdsong said coolly. "I don't suppose your little chat with Laurent brought anything of note to light?"

"Believe you me, if I had found even a hair out of place, I'd have invited him to London for a little tête-à-tête." Endicott's heavy jaw tightened. "But no, he merely smiles and invites us to make ourselves at home on his yacht and look wherever we please."

"Did you happen to notice some little marks in the aft deck while you were there?" Drew asked. "Whitish, curved marks."

Endicott shook his head. "No. What's that from?"

"I don't know. May be nothing."

"Marks or no, if Laurent's not in this somehow, I'm a Dutchman, I swear."

Birdsong looked unimpressed. "You lot have been on this case for months already and haven't found how they're getting the drugs into the country, much less up to London."

"At least we haven't had any murders on our watch," Endicott shot back. "But you lads here in Hampshire obviously have that well in hand."

Birdsong glowered at him. "It's being seen to."

"True. True. You've said all along your murderer's Cummins, right? He's locked up tight. But perhaps you let him go out for a newspaper and a pint of milk an hour or two ago. I mean, so long as he promised to come right back, eh?"

"Perhaps if you both cooperated rather than squabbling," Drew said, "we'd be further along than we are."

"And perhaps, Mr. Farthering," Endicott said, "we'd be

further along if you and your toffy friends kept out of the way. Just for your own safety."

Drew gave him a hard look. "But we're none of us safe, are we? Not until we find whoever's done this. If Will was down in the wine cellar, it had to have been because he thought there was something there that would help crack this case."

Endicott huffed. "We've been down there. The Hampshire lads have been down there. There's nothing to see. Maybe the boy did go to see what he could find, but there's just nothing there."

"Someone thought it was important enough to kill him over it," Drew said.

"You're wrong there," Birdsong said. "If it actually was murder—"

Drew opened his mouth to protest, and the chief inspector held up one finger.

"*If* it was murder, that means only that someone wanted him dead. He might have seen something in the cellar, or in the woods, or at the pub for all we know. The wine cellar just might have been the killer's best opportunity."

No one said anything else for a moment, and then Birdsong cleared his throat. "If there's nothing else, I'll be getting back to my job." He gave them a nod and strode back toward the kitchen.

"We'll be off, too," said Endicott, replacing the hat he had removed when he entered the house. "And do leave the police work to the professionals, if you please, sir. We don't want to have to clear up another corpse by the end of the week."

Sergeant Dane chuckled and followed his superior out the front door.

Drew stood for a while, staring at nothing. These professionals had taken a rather cavalier attitude toward the death of a young boy. Amateur or not, Drew wasn't about to leave this investigation totally in their hands. Not quite yet. No matter the muddle he'd made of it all so far.

He found the cook at the sink, scrubbing clean a variety of kitchen implements. She snatched up a handful of cutlery and slammed it down into the water and then started when she realized she was not alone.

"I beg your pardon, sir. I didn't see you there." She wiped her hands on her apron and blotted her red face with it. "Is there something you were wanting?"

"I wanted to ask you about this morning, if I might. I realize it's a terribly difficult time for everyone."

"True enough." She blotted her face again. "I wish I could be some help to you, sir, as I know that's what you've come for, but I'm afraid I haven't got much I can tell. Except for going to the butcher's, I hadn't left the kitchen all morning. How that boy got in without me seeing, I'll never understand. I told the police as much."

Once again, Drew saw the grin on Will's face as he bragged about getting into the pantry without being seen. Perhaps the cook hadn't seen him, but someone else had. Drew should have sent him to Farthering Place, Will and his sister and Madeline, too.

"Quite," Drew said, forcing his thoughts back to the task at hand. "Who did you see?"

She shifted on her feet, and he pulled out a chair for her.

"Do sit down, Mrs. Ruggles."

"If you're sure you don't mind, sir." She sank into the chair with a little sigh of relief. "As I said, I didn't see anyone. When I came back from the butcher's, I started making lunch. Mrs. Cummins asked about having Mr. Tal's cake, and I told her it wouldn't be any trouble at all. Then Mrs. Farthering came in and got that dratted cat out of my pantry. I didn't see anyone else until the vicar came in to take away some of the things for his charity."

Drew took a seat across the table from her. "So he and Mrs. Cummins went into the pantry."

"Madam had already gone to lie down. Mr. Broadhurst didn't like to trouble her, with everything as has happened, you know, so he came and saw to things himself. Wasn't there but a few minutes and was gone again."

"And you're sure the boy couldn't have slipped in when you weren't looking?"

She put her fists on her broad hips. "There's my stove. And there's the back door. I think I have eyes, begging your pardon."

"Of course," he soothed. "I didn't mean otherwise. But it's a thorny problem, how he got down there, wouldn't you say?"

"It is that." She frowned contemplatively. "Him and that cat, both where they don't belong and warned off more than once, I daresay. And poor Mrs. Cummins having another shock she never deserved."

None of them deserved any of this, but he had tried to keep Will out of danger. Tried and failed. Tried and failed. What good was he doing asking questions now that it was already too late?

"You've been here some time, haven't you?" he asked. "At Winteroak House."

"Oh, yes, sir. Since Mr. Tal was a little fellow. He'd been rather sickly, you know, but he was just coming out of it and just as lively a baby as I've ever seen. The poor dear, losing Miss Alice and all, and the master being taken away. I could hardly believe it of him. He's always been such a fine man and the best of masters. And there's poor Mrs. Cummins. She shouldn't have this to bear. She just shouldn't.'"

"I take it you're rather fond of them all."

"Not everyone in service lands in so good a place. No matter what he's done, Mr. Cummins has always been good to me, and I hope no one can ever call Myrtle Ruggles ungrateful. I'm not likely to abandon Mrs. Cummins or the young master at this late date. Those gentlemen from Scotland Yard, if you can properly call them gentlemen, have no business stirring things up here. If Mr. Cummins has done wrong, well then I suppose he's got to answer for it, but they've no right upsetting Madam or Mr. Tal. And don't think I haven't told them right out."

"They have their jobs to do, I suppose. But we'll try to figure out this little puzzle and send them on their way, eh?" He glanced toward the pantry door. "It would be very helpful if I could take another look round down there."

"Go on down, sir. I've got supper to get to now."

Drew thanked her and made his way back into the wine cellar. He began looking around again, starting with the three barrels of wine that had fallen onto the stone floor.

— Twelve —

Drew switched on a reading lamp in the library, and Madeline blinked at him.

"I hadn't realized how dark it had gotten."

"Neither had I," he said. He switched on a lamp at the end of the sofa, where Nick and Carrie were sitting. Carrie looked more delicate than usual as she sat curled up next to him. Her shoes were on the floor, her legs tucked up under her. They had evidently been sitting that way for a long time, still and silent.

"Do you want me to send a telegram to your father?" Drew asked her.

Carrie shook her head. "I'll do it. I can't have it coming from anyone else."

She took the pencil and stationery he offered her and began writing. She had only partially written her father's name when the pencil lead snapped. Nick scrounged in the drawer in the end table where they kept the cards and found another one. Carrie broke it a moment later.

"Let me," he said gently, taking the paper from her and

finding a third pencil farther back in the drawer. "You tell me what you want to say, and I'll write it down for you."

She nodded, looking pitifully grateful to him. "Just tell him to please come, Billy was . . . was . . . Oh, I don't know what to tell him. How can I tell him Billy's dead? That he was most likely murdered?"

Tears pooled in her eyes, spilling over when she blinked them away.

"Perhaps we should just say it was an accident," Madeline suggested. "We don't know anything more at this point. Not really."

Drew looked up at her, feeling that knife twist of guilt again in his gut. It was true—they didn't know for certain. Not yet. But it seemed rather unlikely Billy's death and Alice's were unrelated. Still, he held his tongue. Perhaps it was for the best.

"It might be easier, sweetheart," Nick said. "By the time he gets here, we'll be much more certain about everything. The important part is just getting him to come."

She nodded. "All right. Write what you think is best."

"Give it to me," Madeline said, holding out her hand.

Nick passed her the pencil and paper, and she wrote a short message: *Please come. Billy in fatal accident. Need you. Wire sailing information.*

Drew read it over her shoulder. Short and to the point, a dagger to the heart of a loving father. It would be four or five days at the earliest before Mr. Holland knew more than that his only son was dead. *"Following your example, eh, Detective Farthering?"* Drew pushed the thought away.

"I think that's best for now, darling. What do you think, Carrie? Shall I have it sent?"

"I don't know what else to do." She looked up at Nick.

"Are you still going to find out what's going on here? It's not just Alice anymore."

"I was thinking you and Madeline ought to go back to Farthering Place until your father arrives."

Carrie's red-rimmed eyes narrowed. "While you and Drew stay here?"

Nick glanced at Drew. "Not all the time, I'm sure. What do you think, Drew?"

"I told Tal I'd do what I can to help. I may be rather useless on that front, but I have to try. But I won't keep you, old man. I know you want to be with Carrie just now."

Nick smiled faintly. "I do." He leaned over and kissed her temple. "Of course I do. But if we can help Tal while he's in this mess, I hate to turn tail now."

"If you're staying," Madeline told Drew, "I'm staying."

"Darling—"

"I mean it. I'm not going home. Not after what's happened to Billy. Nick can drive Carrie back to Farthering Place. Mrs. Devon will look after her until her father comes. Nick can go back and forth between here and there as needed. Then she won't—"

"I'm staying too."

"Carrie," Madeline breathed.

"I'm staying." Carrie's voice quavered just the slightest bit, but then she frowned and lifted her chin. "I don't know how long it will take Daddy to arrange passage. It could be a week or more. Either way, I'm not sitting over at Farthering Place by myself."

Madeline came over and sat beside her, taking her hand. "You don't have to do that. I know you're scared."

"Of course I'm scared!" In her agitation, Carrie's South Carolina accent was more pronounced than ever. "But there has to be something I can do besides leave you all to look for clues while I wait for my father to come take me home."

Nick put his arm around her, pulling her closer to his side. "I don't know if that's a good idea. I shouldn't like anything to happen to you."

"I want to stay. I want to help find whoever did this."

"Carrie—"

"Please." She turned sorrowful blue eyes up to Drew. "Don't send me back now. I can't bear sitting back there at your house, wondering what's happening, just thinking about Billy. I can't bear being alone."

Madeline gave her hand a comforting squeeze. "Please, Drew. Can't she stay? I mean, if it's all right with Tal and Mrs. Cummins."

Nick frowned. "No."

"Might not be such a bad idea," said Drew. "At least here we can both keep an eye on her. Besides that, it seems rather unlikely that the killer is going to pop by every day."

Nick studied Carrie's pensive face and then gave a reluctant nod. "All right. But only until your father gets here. And promise me you won't go off by yourself. Ever."

She nodded, her expression solemn.

Drew glanced at Madeline, and she gave him a nod. He put his hand over Carrie's. "Have you thought about what you want to do? About your brother, I mean."

"I don't know. I guess something has to be decided."

"Whether he's buried here once your father arrives or taken back to the States, the coroner will have to prepare the body. I assume that can't wait very much longer."

"Oh, no. No, no, no." Carrie shook her head, dabbing her eyes with her handkerchief. "I don't want all that. I don't want him sewed up like Frankenstein's monster and filled with horrible chemicals. Daddy will want to take him home, but I just don't want Billy having all that done to him first. And Daddy'll want to see him, and I don't want him to, especially by the time he gets here. Who knows how long that will be or what Billy would . . . would be like by then." She pressed a hand over her mouth. "It would stay with him the rest of his life, seeing Billy like that. But I don't know what else to do. I don't know what your laws say about that kind of thing. I don't know where—"

"We have a small family plot at Farthering Place," Drew said. "It's just a little clearing surrounded by a grove of oaks, but it's a quiet, peaceful place. If we can have the service soon, there would be no need for any preservation."

"Uncle Mason is buried there," Madeline said softly.

Carrie's eyes filled with tears. "You wouldn't mind? With Billy not being family?"

"Of course not." Drew squeezed her hand and then released it. "What do you think?"

She nodded rapidly. "That would be very kind of you. Do you think we could see to it before Daddy gets here? He's not going to be happy that I didn't ask him about it first, but I just can't stand him seeing Billy as he is."

"We'll see to it," Drew assured her. "Don't you worry."

She began crying in earnest then. Nick took her into his arms, gently pushing her head down to his shoulder, stroking her hair as her tears soaked into his dark jacket.

Drew stood, took Madeline's hand, and escorted her out of the room, shutting the library door behind them.

After lunch the next day, Drew walked over to the vicar's house to speak to him about arranging the service for Will

Holland. Mrs. Broadhurst came to the door and told him her son was out visiting his parishioners, but she said Drew was welcome to stop in and have a cup of tea with her. Drew declined the invitation with thanks. He wasn't in the mood for tea and cakes and inconsequential chat. He needed a stretch of quiet so he could mull over what he'd seen down in the wine cellar. There was something about those barrels that nagged at him. Clearly, Will's death hadn't been an accident, yet no one who might be considered a suspect had been unaccounted for at the time.

He turned from the lane where the Broadhursts lived and walked down along the shore for a while and then up along the Lymington River until he reached the bridge that crossed over into Lymington itself, two miles or so from Winteroak House. It wasn't far into the center of town, the church and the post office, and several respectable little shops. Mrs. Ruggles had told Madeline this would be a good place to find a collar for Eddie. Now was as good a time as any to get one.

He found exactly what he wanted in a shop down from the newsagent's, a black velvet collar with a little bell. From now on, when Eddie got into mischief, someone would know about it.

Once he'd made his purchase, he realized it was teatime. It wouldn't take long to walk back over to Winteroak, but by then it seemed fairly likely that everyone there would have already had their tea. He didn't want much more than just tea, so he went back to the newsagent's. Earlier, the girl there had directed him to the shop where he had bought the collar, and now she was kind enough to point out a tea room across the way.

O'Gorman's was small but evidently quite popular, crowded and noisy with the chatter of ladies, most of them middle-aged. Drew made up precisely one-sixth of the shop's male patrons. The place was cheery that summer afternoon and smelled absolutely divine. He was waiting for the hostess to seat him when he spotted Philip Broadhurst sitting at a table in the corner, his back to the wall. If the brooding darkness in his expression was any indicator, whatever he was thinking had put him out of his usual good humor. Even so, Drew decided it was as good a time as any to ask him about Will's burial service.

"Good afternoon."

The vicar started at the greeting and stood up. "Drew. How are you?"

The two men shook hands.

"What brings you here?"

"I came to get a collar for a cat." Drew patted his pocket, making it jingle, and then he shrugged. "Actually I had wandered over to your house to see you, but your mother said you were paying calls on your parishioners. I didn't expect to run into you here in Lymington."

"I, uh, didn't expect to see you, either." Broadhurst glanced briefly toward the door. "Always a pleasure, of course. Will you sit down?"

The table was already laid for two, so Drew waved him off. "You're expecting someone. I'll just get my own place. I would like to have a word with you when you've got a moment. About Will Holland."

"No, no. Sit. Please. I just stopped in for tea myself. So long as we're both here, we may as well talk. How are you? How are things at Winteroak today? How is Miss Holland? Please, sit down."

Drew did as he was bidden. "It's not easy for her, as you might expect. There's still the shock of the accident and dealing with the police and having to wire her father back in the States. In short, everything's rather the same as when you were by yesterday. Mrs. Cummins has done all she's able to, but there's really not much any of us can do."

"No," Broadhurst said. "The whole business is tragic. And I had spoken to the boy just that morning."

"I was wondering about that. Did he happen to say where he was going or what he was about?"

The vicar shook his head. "I regret to say he didn't. I wish now I had gotten him to come back to the house with me, but he wouldn't hear of it. Said he had business to see to. Such a tragedy."

They both fell silent as the girl brought them tea.

"Generally we'd have our own vicar, Mr. Bartlett, see to this sort of thing," Drew said when she'd gone, "but Miss Holland has specifically asked if you would handle the service. Since she knows you and since you knew her brother."

Broadhurst fidgeted in his chair. "I'm honored that she should ask for me in particular, but at someone else's church, I—"

"No, this wouldn't be at our church. Just at my estate. We have a few family graves on the property, and we all thought that would be a proper place for Will to be buried."

"I see," the vicar said, glancing again toward the door and not sounding as if the conversation was holding his full attention. He gave an almost imperceptible shake of his head. "That being the case, certainly. If it would be a comfort to Miss Holland, I would be happy to oblige. When did you think of having it?"

"Tomorrow morning, if you're not already engaged," Drew said, taking a subtle glance of his own into the large mirror that hung above the table. "Her father is due in at

Southampton on Sunday, and she wants it seen to before then. The condition of the body . . ."

"Perfectly understandable. But I'm afraid tomorrow morning is out of the question. I have, uh, other obligations then. Would the afternoon do? Say one o'clock?"

"That ought to be fine. I'll check with Miss Holland, but I don't think that will be a problem." Drew stood and shook the vicar's hand again. "Thank you. This means a great deal to her, and we don't have much to offer by way of comfort at the moment, besides the hope of eternity."

Broadhurst also stood. "It's the only true comfort we have."

"Oh." Drew fished a few coins out of his pocket, enough to cover the bill and a generous amount left over for the girl. "Thanks for letting me interrupt your tea."

"No, please," the vicar protested. "I asked you."

"Only after I imposed on your time and your table. Please, it's the least I can do. I'd be happy to walk back to the village with you if you'd like the company."

"No, I, uh . . ." Again Broadhurst's eyes flicked toward the door. "I'll just finish my tea. Sometimes it's rather nice to be where one isn't so well known."

Drew nodded in understanding. "And even here you still have people making demands upon your time. But not to worry. Next time we happen to meet, you'll have to open the conversation. Otherwise, I'll just assume you'd rather be let alone."

Broadhurst chuckled and sat down once again. "No need for that. I'm always happy to chat, and having demands upon my time is a well-known part of my job."

"Yes, I suppose it is. So tomorrow at one?"

"One o'clock. And please tell Miss Holland if there's

anything at all I can do to be of service to her before then, just let me know." There was gentle sincerity in the vicar's dark eyes. "Tell her too that I will keep her and her father in my prayers."

Drew briefly bowed his head. "I'll do just that. Good afternoon."

He left the tea room and crossed the street back to the newsagent's where he could see the door to the tea room but not be seen from inside. He bought the latest edition of the *Times* and concealed himself behind it as he waited. A few minutes later, the vicar left the shop and walked the other way down the street and crossed the bridge, ostensibly back to Armitage Landing. Once he was well out of sight, Drew folded his newspaper, tucked it under his arm, and made his way back to Winteroak House.

Drew returned in time to dress for dinner, a subdued affair where everyone struggled to converse about anything but what was on everyone's mind. Drew wanted to report on his conversation with the Reverend Mr. Broadhurst, but with Laurent being ever so polite and solicitous to the ladies, Drew decided the tale would keep until later.

"I don't know what it is," Mrs. Cummins said when they retired to the library after the meal, "but I've felt so cold lately. Nerves, I suppose."

"Are you all right, Mother?" Tal asked. "May I get a shawl or something for you?"

"If you don't mind, dear. Thank you." She gave the others an apologetic smile. "I've had the fire going in my bedroom all day, but I know the rest of you are probably too warm for that down here."

198

Laurent's eyes lit. "Nonsense. A fire would be just the thing. Come, you must have one if you are suffering the cold."

He rang for a footman, and soon there was a small but cheery fire in the grate. Mrs. Cummins sat huddled by it for a while, listening to the others' quiet conversation, but soon she was nodding off and finally retired for the night. Laurent paced about the room after that, clearly bored.

"It seems a good night for each of us to retire early," he said, looking at everyone pointedly, and then when no one seemed inclined to agree, he made a slight bow. "I will take my own advice, at any rate. Good evening, ladies and gentlemen."

Tal glared after him once he was gone. "The slimy toad, fawning over my mother that way. It makes me ill."

"At least we can talk now," Drew said, and he told them about his visit to Lymington. "I'm certain Broadhurst had been waiting for someone, but nobody went into the tea room after I left, and he came out just a few minutes later."

"'It will, I believe, be everywhere found,'" Nick quoted, "'that as the clergy are, or are not what they ought to be, so are the rest of the nation.'"

"And I wager that what our Miss Austen meant by that," Drew said, "was that they're no better or worse than anyone else, though they tend to lead their flocks into being like them. For good or ill."

"You don't suppose whoever it was the vicar was waiting for was already in the shop, do you?" Madeline asked.

"I don't think so, darling. He kept looking over my shoulder, and I could almost swear he warned someone off. It was fairly subtle, but I don't think I'm mistaken about that."

"I know the padre." Tal leaned against the mantel, staring

into the still-crackling flames. "If he was waiting for some-one, it was perfectly innocent. Probably some middle-aged lady who thinks her husband doesn't love her anymore or some such rot. Parsons have to deal with that sort of thing all the time, don't they? I mean, if it was a woman like that, she couldn't talk to him at the church or even at his home without someone noticing and mentioning it to someone else, and before long there would be all sorts of wild speculation about why she could possibly need to speak to the vicar in private. You know how small villages are."

Nick nodded. "And heaven help her if one of her neighbors was to ask her what she and the vicar talked about and she refused to say."

"Nasty gossips," Tal muttered. "We've already had half a dozen old crows come by just to poke their noses in to see what they can find out at the murder house."

Carrie looked down at her hands lying folded in her lap, and Nick, sitting close to her on the floral sofa, glanced at Drew, clearly wanting him to steer them away from the subject of murder.

"I'm sure it was nothing," Drew said. "Maybe I just imag-ined something that wasn't really there."

Carrie looked up at him again, blue eyes anxious. "But he did say he would do Billy's service. He doesn't mind?"

"Not in the least," said Drew. "He said he'd be honored. He's got an engagement in the morning, but he said if one o'clock would be all right, he will do it then."

"That would be fine. If Daddy is going to be here on Sun-day, tomorrow should be just right." She gave him a pitifully thin smile. "Thank you for taking care of the arrangements for me, Drew."

"I'm glad I could help. I wish there was more I could do."

He felt a needle prick of guilt in the pit of his stomach. *I wish there was more I hadn't done.*

"I think Tal would do much better if he didn't have Laurent about all the time," Drew said when he and Madeline had gone up to their room, "but he's a wily fellow, our Frenchman, and knows when to play up to his hostess. I can't imagine he doesn't know she is the only reason he's still here."

"Poor Tal." Madeline kicked off her shoes and stretched out on the bed. "This must be awful for him."

"There's no love lost between them," Drew said. He shed his dinner jacket and tie, not caring that Eddie immediately pounced on the tie and carried it under the bed. "I can't say I blame Tal in the least for suspecting him. I feel the same way."

"But Laurent was on his yacht, being questioned by Scotland Yard, when Billy was killed," Madeline said. "I don't know of a better alibi than that."

"Very convenient, if you ask me."

"Well, it's not as though he set up the interview. He couldn't have known Inspector Endicott would have come just then to give him an alibi."

"Ah, but you forget, he wasn't alone." Drew sat on the bed and removed his shoes. "There was that woman, Mrs. Something-or-other, on the yacht with him. He had his alibi all along."

Madeline propped herself up on one elbow, frowning. "But we all heard those barrels fall. How could he have pushed them over and still been on his yacht?"

"I don't suppose he could have." He hesitated for a moment. "I've been wondering too about this bout of food poisoning the maid has."

"Josephine?"

"Mrs. Ruggles absolutely will not allow for the possibility. Not in her kitchen."

"But what else could it be? Dr. Fletcher examined her."

"True," Drew said, "but if the food was spoilt, then why was she the only one to become ill? And if the doctor was expecting food poisoning, then naturally that's what he would see. A small portion of arsenic would produce the same effect."

Madeline's eyes widened. "You don't think someone was trying to kill her, too?"

"Not kill, but perhaps put her out of the way for a day or so."

"But why?"

"I don't know," he said, shoulders slumping. "Only it seems rather a coincidence that it should happen just now. Perhaps I'm just making something of a perfectly ordinary occurrence."

She took hold of his sleeve. "I don't like being here, Drew. We ought to get Carrie and Nick and go back home now. Billy thought this was all fun and games and now he's dead. I don't want—" She stopped, forcing a smile. "No, never mind. We're going to figure this out. And no, Carrie and I aren't going home without you and Nick, so don't even say it."

"I'd feel better if you did," he admitted, "but if you're going to stay, you stay with me from now on, eh?"

She put her arms around him and pulled him close. "I wouldn't want to be anywhere else."

— Thirteen —

Will Holland's funeral took place the next day. It was a small gathering in the circle of trees in the meadow out beyond Farthering Place—Tal and his mother, Drew and Madeline, and Carrie on Nick's arm, pale but clear-eyed. As he had at Alice's funeral, the vicar spoke gravely and yet not without hope. For those who put their trust in Christ, death was not the end but the beginning of the adventure.

Drew felt his throat tighten at those words, remembering how Will had been eager for an adventure of his own. The mystery of the pearls had been fun enough, but having a real murder case to solve was much more interesting. And now . . .

They should have all gone home, Carrie and Nick and Madeline, too. Will should have gone with them. He should have gone and stayed there until the case was solved. And then he should have gone back to America and gone to university and played American football and gotten himself a sweetheart and a little tiger-striped convertible and then lived to see a son of his own do the same.

"It's not right," Drew said.

Tal had been silent before the service, and now, as the

others were moving away from the graveside, leaving behind the mound of newly turned earth, he came up to Drew, his voice low, torment in his eyes. "It's not right," he said, echoing Drew's words.

Drew patted Madeline's hand that rested on his arm. "Excuse us a moment, will you, darling? We'll be along shortly."

She nodded, gave Tal a sympathetic glance, then hurried to catch up to Nick and Carrie and Mrs. Cummins.

"Where does it end?" Tal said once she had gone, his mouth taut and his body coiled, ready to snap. "It doesn't make sense. The police say he was killed because he saw something he shouldn't have. But my father's in jail. It's not as if whoever was in this with him can continue on with the smuggling and everything else."

"No doubt they shut down everything once your father was arrested," Drew said, "but that doesn't mean there isn't a trail to follow back to his accomplices, whoever they are."

Tal raked a hand through his hair. "I can't take this much longer. Mother's trying her best, but I can tell it's tearing her apart. Why do the police have to be so deuced slow?"

"I'm sure they're doing everything they can. We just have to—"

"Just have to be patient?" Tal snapped. "Just have to let them do their jobs? Just have to what?"

"Look here, old man, I know what you mean. It seems like they're doing nothing and all the while people are dying. It just takes time."

"They ought to make an arrest," Tal said as he stalked through the grass. "My father wasn't in this alone. And he's not the one killing people now. The police ought to make another arrest before we're all murdered in our beds."

"And whom do you suggest they arrest?"

"That rotten Frenchman, for one," Tal said, his eyes flashing fire. "A baby could see he's up to no good, him and that Adkins brute he keeps with him."

"I don't know why you don't send him off, to tell the truth," Drew said, glad the unctuous cur hadn't insisted on accompanying Mrs. Cummins to Farthering Place. "I don't like his being in the house. Clearly you don't, either."

Tal's mouth turned down in distaste. "Mother doesn't think it would be 'kind' to send him away when the police haven't found anything against him, and my father hasn't said he's involved in anything underhanded. The oily devil plays up to her monstrously, and she can't even see it."

"He *has* been a friend of your father's and hers for some years now. It would be rather a scandal if he were sent packing at this point."

Tal gave him a grudging nod. "And that's the only reason I don't send him off myself. Will's murdered and then we ask Laurent to leave? It would be seen as proof of his guilt, no matter what the police do, and likely would damage his wine business. If by some chance he's not involved in all this, it wouldn't be very fair to him, eh? No matter how great a swine he is."

"I suppose you're right. Innocent until proved guilty, eh?"

"True enough. But if your chief inspector were to put him and his man both in chokey, I'd sleep sounder, I can tell you for certain."

"He'd like nothing better, I'm sure," Drew said. "But either Laurent is as innocent as he claims or he's been extremely clever about keeping his hands clean on this side of the Channel."

"The police are too soft on him, if you ask me. Hold his feet to the fire, and he'll squawk quick enough."

"They can't very well do that, you know. Not without evidence."

"Right," Tal said, a sneer marring his face. "Two murders aren't quite enough."

"It's a bit hard for them to arrest a man they were interviewing at the time the last murder was carried out, don't you think?"

"Maybe he didn't do it," Tal considered, "but he could have had it done. Come on, Drew, you know that sort of thing happens all the time. If the police won't do anything about it, why don't you?"

Drew blinked, startled into a low laugh. "Me? Come on, old man, you know I haven't any authority here. I don't like Laurent any better than you do, but I don't have anything but my own personal distaste to hold against him."

"And Adkins?"

Drew frowned. "I'm not quite sure what to think of him. Clearly Scotland Yard think he'll lead them to something important if they're patient enough."

"And who else will be dead by then?" Tal rubbed his eyes with both hands. "Oh, never mind. Never mind any of it. Maybe it would be best if you all went home now."

Drew stopped where he was. "What?"

"You heard me. I don't want anything to happen to anyone else. You'd all be safer here at Farthering Place."

"You're most likely right. We just didn't want to leave you and your mother on your own at Winteroak. Plus I'm more likely to turn up something there rather than here."

Tal shook his head. "No. I appreciate your trying to help out, but I should never have asked you in the first place. It's not your responsibility."

"I'd like to help out all the same."

Tal looked at him for a long moment, a sudden coldness in his eyes. "Truth is, Drew, you're worse than useless."

He stalked off toward the house, and Drew could do nothing but watch him go. *Worse than useless.* It was true, wasn't it? He'd accomplished nothing at Winteroak House but let Will Holland get killed. If the case was too much for Birdsong's people and Scotland Yard to boot, who was Drew Farthering to presume he knew more than they did?

He swallowed down the tightness in his throat. Instead of heading back to the house, he turned the other way and looked out over the familiar meadow, down to the village below. He could see Holy Trinity among the other buildings and remembered the centuries-old engraving in the pulpit: *"Woe unto me if I preach not the gospel."*

Woe unto me, he thought, *if I abandon my own calling.* It was the same, wasn't it? Turning his back on the task he'd been given, whether or not it was appreciated, whether or not he saw the use in it, was not his way. He couldn't stand one day before God and say not that he had tried and failed but that he hadn't tried at all. If only just one thing in this entire muddle made any sense.

"Drew?"

He started at the voice, a voice he hadn't expected to hear again, at least not here and not now. Then he turned. "Tal. I thought . . ." He frowned, studying his friend's face. "I thought you'd gone."

"I had no place saying what I did, Drew. This whole business has me reeling, and I guess it's easiest to strike out at whoever's closest, eh?"

"I know you've had a rough go of it."

Tal exhaled heavily, the pain in his eyes nearly unbearable. "I just . . . I need to know what's going on, what happened to Will and Alice. I don't know where to start or where to turn."

Drew hesitated a moment, but there was only one place he knew to go in time of trouble. Only one.

"I don't know what I'd do if I didn't believe God was with me." He smiled just the slightest bit. "I've found He doesn't mind if we come to Him after we've made a complete shambles of things. He just wants us to come."

"And you think He cares about the nasty little messes we make?" Tal asked. "The ones we barrel straight into without a thought of Him and then come sniveling to Him to make better?"

There was no bitterness in Tal's tone, only an honest questioning and perhaps a hope that it might be true.

"I do," Drew told him. "For reasons I can't even begin to understand, He loves us and wants to walk beside us, even when we walk through places so dark we can't see Him."

Tal said nothing for a long moment, and then he looked away. "I wish I were as sure as you. I wish I could make sense of even one thing that's happened this past week." He took a quivering breath. "I suppose there's a lot I ought to think about. Please, Drew, come back to Winteroak. Help me figure this out. I didn't mean what I said. Forgive me, will you?"

"Nothing to forgive. You're absolutely right."

"Really, I am sorry. I didn't—"

"No, it's true what you said. I've been useless." Drew shook his head. "But maybe I'm just stubborn enough to keep trying anyway."

"Good," Tal said. "Very good. I want whoever's behind this to pay for what he's done. I want to know what sort of wretched creature could have killed Will and Alice just because they happened to be inconvenient. I want to look into his eyes and tell him exactly what his greed and selfishness have done." He clenched his hands into fists. "I want to help you however I can."

"The best help you can be, Tal, is by trying to think of anything, no matter how small, that might be a clue. Anything unusual. Anything that doesn't fit into the regular routine. Anyone around the house who isn't acting quite as he or she normally does."

Tal huffed. "Don't you think I've tried? The police have asked again and again what I knew and what I noticed and why I didn't realize what was happening. There wasn't anything to notice in particular. Except poor Alice . . ." His voice quivered, but he steadied himself and went on, "After she went, there were police everywhere, with Will nosing around after them. There wasn't much I noticed at all by then. I couldn't think of anything more than Alice was dead and my father was a dope smuggler."

"I know. But maybe you could think again. Anything's worth checking into at this point. It's usually the small things that end up being the best clues." Drew tapped his waistcoat pocket. "Like that scrap of label I found a while back. I still don't know where it goes or if it has anything to do with anything, but I'm keeping my eyes open."

Tal nodded, a burning eagerness in his eyes. "Right. I'll see what comes to mind."

"But not just this minute." Drew turned him back toward the house. "Come on, old man. I'm sure our housekeeper Mrs. Devon has some good strong tea waiting for us. That's enough to worry about for today."

"You'll come back to Winteroak? You won't abandon the case?"

"No." Drew clasped his shoulder. "I'm not much of an abandoner, I'm afraid. Never have been. Now come along."

There were few things more comforting than Mrs. Devon's tea and sandwiches and the "nice bit of cake" she always seemed to have ready on difficult occasions. Afterward they went back to the Cummins house.

It was rather an awkward gathering at dinner. Drew and Madeline did their best to keep the conversation going while Tal hardly spoke or ate. Carrie didn't make an appearance at all, and Nick was too distracted with worry for her to say much, either. Mrs. Cummins seemed overwhelmed by the task of playing hostess, though she seemed determined to carry it off nonetheless. Laurent was remarkably tactful in his dealings with her, helping her over the uncomfortable pauses and, for once, refraining from making sly insinuations.

"I wish the police would either arrest him or allow him to leave altogether," Drew muttered as he escorted Madeline away from the dining room. "If he gives me that 'see how innocent I am' smile one more time, I'm quite likely to beat him over the head with the copy of *Les Misérables* I found in our room. It's in French."

She squeezed his hand, not quite smiling. "Think how Inspector Endicott must feel after months of watching him and finding nothing."

"And poor old Birdsong. Truly, a policeman's lot is not a happy one."

"I beg your pardon, sir," Beddows said, coming up to them, his grave face even graver than usual. "Chief Inspector Birdsong is here to see you again. I've put him in the library."

Nick came up to them once the butler was gone. "It's a bit late for business, isn't it?"

"He must have some news," Drew said. "We'd better not keep him waiting."

"You don't suppose he's come to take Monsieur Laurent off our hands, do you?" Nick suggested, and there wasn't a trace of humor in his expression.

Drew shook his head. "I doubt we're so lucky, old man. Otherwise our chief inspector would have called for him and not me."

"I'd like to hear, too."

Drew was surprised to see Tal had joined them, but he only nodded. "Of course."

"I thought you'd like to know what Dr. Fletcher's autopsy found," Birdsong said once they were all seated in the library. "Would Miss Holland wish to hear, as well?"

Drew looked at Madeline. "Do you think she's feeling up to it?"

"I know she'll be pretty mad if we don't tell her there's news."

Nick hesitated and then he exhaled heavily. "I'll go see if she wants to come down."

He was back a moment later. At his side, Carrie was pale but determined. "Please," she said when the gentlemen rose. "Sit down."

She sat on the sofa, watching Birdsong with wary eyes, saying nothing. Nick sat next to her, Tal returned to his chair by the window, and Drew took his seat again beside Madeline.

After a moment, the chief inspector sat too, pulling his chair up closer to them. "I spoke to Dr. Fletcher this afternoon, Miss Holland. He gave me the results of the autopsy on your brother's body."

She drew a shuddering breath. "What did he say?"

"Those wine barrels didn't kill him. He was dead before that. Maybe an hour before. Maybe two."

Carrie squeezed her eyes shut and twisted her fingers together in a little knot. Madeline went to stand behind her, comforting hands on her slender shoulders. Carrie reached back to take her hand.

"What else did he find?" Drew asked, forcing the sickening image of the wine cellar back into his mind, trying to see anything in the picture that didn't fit. Anything that was wrong. That barrel with the leak . . .

"The boy was hit on the right side of the head with something heavy, something with a flat circular end. Dr. Fletcher thinks some kind of mallet most likely."

Tal caught a hard breath but said nothing.

"Death was instantaneous," Birdsong continued. "Afterwards the barrels were pushed onto him. The way he was lying—" the chief inspector paused and glanced at Carrie— "the way the neck and shoulders were damaged, the doctor says it is quite clear that he was already on the floor when the barrels hit him."

"Then there's no question about it being murder," Tal said.

"Not in the least," Birdsong told him.

"Did your people find anything in the house that could have been used?"

"There were two mallets in the garden shed, but they had clearly not been moved for some time. There were the croquet mallets as well, only they're not quite the right size. There was a mallet in the kitchen, the kind used for pounding meat, but it had been scrubbed clean." Birdsong looked only mildly annoyed. "The cook seemed rather put out that we would expect anything less in her kitchen."

Tal's lips trembled. "Does my father know about this?"

"I questioned him about it this afternoon, Mr. Cummins. He says he doesn't know who would have wanted to kill the boy or why. Obviously he couldn't have done it."

"But one of his cronies could have." Tal's voice shook, and he took three deep breaths to steady himself. "I'm . . . I'm not feeling very well, Chief Inspector. Unless you have any further questions for me, I'd like to be excused."

"No more questions, not at the moment. Do stay nearby, eh?"

Tal looked white to the gills now, and he managed only a nod before disappearing down the corridor.

"Maybe I'd better look after him," Drew said after an awkward silence. "Excuse me a moment."

He hurried out of the room, just in time to see Tal reach the top of the stairway.

"Tal. Hold on a minute, old man."

Tal stopped and turned and then started walking again. Drew picked up his pace, taking the steps almost at a run and then making his strides long and swift until he was nearly at Tal's side.

Tal came to an abrupt stop but didn't turn around. "What is it?"

His breath was coming in little gasps, and Drew gripped his shoulder, trying to steady him. "Are you all right? If there's anything I can—"

Tal's body lurched, and he quick put a hand over his mouth. "Sorry, Drew, but I'd rather not embarrass myself just now. There are better places than the upstairs hallway to be sick. Excuse me."

Not waiting for a reply, Tal sprinted down the corridor. Drew heard his door open and then shut with a faint thud. For a moment, Drew stood there at the top of the stairs, praying Tal would somehow find his way through all this, and then he turned to find Laurent walking down the corridor toward him.

"Monsieur Tal, he is unwell?"

Drew fought down the urge to strike the man's smug face. "It's very kind of you to be concerned, but it really isn't anything to do with you."

Laurent looked mildly taken aback. "You do me wrong, Monsieur Farthering, indeed you do. How can I be a friend to the father and to the poor maman so many years now and yet have no worry for the son?"

"Perhaps, Monsieur Laurent, you ought to be worried for yourself. After all, you are in a house where two murders have taken place."

"I, monsieur? What do I have to worry myself? Since I have stepped off my *Onde Blanc*, I have the innocence of the new lamb. Who could be safer?"

"Someone bashed in Will Holland's head with a mallet. I don't see how anyone could feel safe." Drew studied him for a moment. "Unless you were the one with the mallet."

Under his thin mustache, Laurent curled his lip. "A mallet? Such implements are the province of hirelings." He spread the long white fingers of one hand over his immaculate shirtfront. "What should one such as I know of them?"

There was a twinkle in Laurent's eye. He was mocking Drew just as he had mocked the police all this while. Until there was evidence . . .

Laurent made a bow. "But just as you say, Monsieur Farthering, I will withdraw myself for now. I trust you will let me know if there is any way I might be of service."

Drew gave a cold nod in return and watched him wander back down the corridor to his room. He turned his thoughts back to Tal. Clearly something about Birdsong's information

214

had upset him. Something about the mallet. It was a common enough thing to have in a kitchen, wasn't it?

Perhaps Tal was calmer now and could answer a few questions. Drew went down the hallway to his room and tapped on the door. No answer.

"Tal? I say, Tal, it's Drew. I just wanted to make sure you're all right. Anything I can do? Tal?"

For a moment there was perfect silence. Then the latch clicked, and the door opened. If possible, Tal looked worse than when he left the library. His hair was slicked back, wet. He'd removed his coat and tie and opened his shirt at the neck. His cuffs and collar were damp. There was no doubt he'd been sick just as he'd feared. The smell of it hung in the too-warm room. Tal stared at Drew, tiny beads of sweat standing cold on his upper lip, his eyes red-rimmed and empty.

"May I come in?"

Still silent, Tal took a step back to admit him.

Once inside, Drew nudged the door shut. "They'll sort it all out. The police will. These things just take time."

"And who else dies in the meantime?"

"Tal—"

"Who else dies because of my father?"

Drew took hold of his arm and made him sit down in the overstuffed chair by the window. He then pulled back the curtains and threw open the sash.

Tal covered his eyes with his hand. "Don't."

"It's stuffy in here." Drew pushed the matching armchair over to the window and sat down.

"Look here, Drew," Tal said, blotting his face with his damp sleeve, "I know you mean well. I know I asked you to help, but it's just no good. Can't you see that? My father's locked up, maybe for good, and still people die."

"I don't think he killed Alice. He certainly didn't kill Will."

"No. He couldn't have killed Will. And he loved Alice. I'm sure he did. He said she was the daughter he never had. She loved him, too. Oh, Drew." Tal dropped his head into his hands. "I just don't know. I don't know anything anymore. He couldn't have, right? He couldn't have killed Alice. He knew. He *knew*."

"Knew what?" Drew jostled his shoulder when he didn't respond. "What did he know?"

"He knew how much I loved her. How much I needed her." Tal finally looked at him. "And there's . . .." He stared at Drew for a minute and then just shook his head.

"What?"

"I don't know. She wanted to tell me something before she died, and I never gave her a chance. Maybe if I had stopped trying to be the life of the party and just taken the time to listen to her, maybe she wouldn't have died. Maybe . . ." He choked off a sob, fists and jaw clenched in determination. "Maybe nobody else would have died, either."

"What do you think she was trying to tell you?"

Tal inhaled painfully and then exhaled, forcing his hands to relax. "It had to be about Dad, don't you think? About this nasty business he was in. But why didn't she just tell me? Why couldn't she come right out and tell me instead of looking at me as if I should be able to read her mind?"

"Maybe she was afraid," Drew suggested. "She told Madeline she didn't want to hurt you. If it was about your father, someone you loved and trusted, she knew it was going to hurt you. Maybe she thought you wouldn't believe her. I wouldn't have believed it myself then."

"But what could I have done? How was I supposed to know?"

Drew considered that. "What did she say?"

"She said she wanted to talk to me, but when we had a moment alone, she didn't say much of any consequence. Said she didn't like Laurent being around, and I daresay you know why that is by now, and she wished Dad wouldn't do business with him. And I don't know what else. She was telling me something about helping to get ready for the party a few days before everyone came, and then those silly girls Violet and Georgie came to get her to look at their headdresses for the ball that night." Tal drew a couple of shuddering breaths, and once more his eyes pooled with tears. "And that was the last time Alice and I had a word alone."

It was deuced little to go on. Had she been trying to get him to go down into the wine cellar? Evidence he would have to see to believe? And had that evidence been what had also gotten Will Holland killed?

"The police have had their eye on Laurent for some time now," Drew offered. "Do you think she wanted you to know something about him?"

"I don't know anything," Tal said. "If I did, this would have been stopped years ago. Why didn't I see it? Why didn't I know about all of this? My own dad."

"He deceived everyone, not just you. Even your mother didn't know."

"Poor Mum. He was everything to her, and now he's done this? It's a rotten way to treat any wife, much less one as devoted as she is. Even now, I expect she'll stand by him to the last."

Drew managed a smile. "Wouldn't surprise me. 'Love is not love that alters when it alteration finds,' eh?"

"Alice was the same way. I never met another girl like her in that, one I could depend on. One who was meant for me."

Tal shook his head and wrapped his arms around himself. "How am I meant to do without her now, Drew? How can I ever have any peace not knowing who wanted her dead and why?"

Drew hesitated. Tal was already raw and bleeding inside, clinging with battered hands to the shreds of what he had believed all his life. Still, it had to be asked.

"Tal, are you sure? Given what you know about your father now, are you absolutely sure he couldn't have given Alice that cocaine? Perhaps because she saw something she shouldn't have?"

"No." Tal lowered his head into his hands once more, the word scarcely more than a low moan. "No, no, no. He couldn't have. I couldn't bear it. I couldn't bear knowing my own father had . . . Oh, God help me, I couldn't."

Drew gave his shoulder a comforting squeeze, not saying anything, and finally Tal exhaled and lifted his head.

"I'm all right now, Drew. Really. I just need to think things out a bit."

"Tal—"

"Really. I'm all right." He picked up the damp towel he'd flung onto the bed and wiped his face. "You'd better go back and finish up with the chief inspector."

Drew rose and went to the door.

"And Drew?"

Drew turned again.

"If I don't get a chance to tell you again, thank you."

"Tal, I haven't—"

"No, that's all. Just thank you."

Then Tal shut the door.

— Fourteen —

By the time Drew returned to the library, Birdsong had already left and Nick had escorted Carrie back to her room. Madeline was still there waiting.

"Is he all right?" she asked.

"No. He's not all right. He's not all right at all. This is tearing him up. I've got to figure this out and quickly." Drew began pacing the room. "Did Birdsong have anything more to say?"

"Not really. He said he'd be back later to ask more questions. I don't know what else anyone has to say. What else are we supposed to do?"

"Think," he told her, then sat down next to her. "We've got to think. If Billy was already dead when those barrels fell, then someone or something had to push them over."

"But Mrs. Ruggles was in the kitchen cooking, and Beryl was helping her. Even if they didn't see Billy go into the pantry, they would have seen someone coming out."

Drew nodded, again picturing the wine cellar and how everything in it had been situated. "I've been wondering about that smaller barrel for some while now. I couldn't figure out how it could have spilled out where Will was and at the back of the cellar too, not if it sprung a leak when the barrels fell."

She shrugged. "I don't know."

"And I've been thinking about how that barrel split. There's a little place between two staves where it popped open, just a couple of inches long. The rest of it is sound as a bell. How does that happen from a blow? Unless it wasn't the impact of the wine cellar floor that opened it."

"Then what was it?"

"Consider this," he said, leaning closer to her and lowering his voice. "Suppose you wanted to kill someone and not have anyone know he was dead for another hour or so."

"That wouldn't be very kind of me, but all right. Then what?"

"Perhaps you mean it to look like an accident, too. So you bash the fellow on the head and cover it up by dropping something heavy on him. Wine barrels are the perfect choice, but they're deuced loud, aren't they? You can't be anywhere near when they fall or you'll be found out right away, so you take this little cask of wine from one of the shelves and use it to prop up the larger barrels. Once you've done your dirty work, you take something—a thin blade of some kind, I'd guess—and pry open the staves of the smaller barrel, but just a bit mind you, just enough so the wine begins to leak out. And then—"

"The wine leaks out until the little barrel is too light to hold up the bigger barrels anymore, so they fall down onto the body and make a huge clatter when I'm somewhere else entirely." She caught her breath. "Oh, it makes perfect sense."

"Exactly, which is why some of the wine was puddled near

the body and some was under the barrel where it landed at the back of the cellar."

Madeline wrinkled her brow. "Then anybody could have done it."

"Anybody who was around the house."

"He'd have to get past Mrs. Ruggles, wouldn't he? She doesn't much like people in her pantry."

"I suppose that's true," Drew admitted, "but it couldn't be that hard. Will said he'd done it more than once."

"And look where it got him."

"True. And she was out at the butcher's that morning, which would give someone plenty of time to set up the barrels and then get Will to go down into the wine cellar. Now instead of there being nobody who could have done it, we're pretty much back to anyone being able. Anyone in the house or out of it, including Laurent and Adkins, their time on the *Onde Blanc* notwithstanding. I'll have to ring up the chief inspector."

Madeline nestled against him. "Can't you phone him tomorrow? I don't want you to have to worry about this tonight."

"Certainly, darling." He kissed the top of her head. "The chief inspector can wait until morning."

But sleep was elusive that night. Drew turned over again, trying not to disturb Madeline, wondering how he hadn't wakened her already with his restlessness. Even placid Eddie had gone to sleep on the window seat.

From where he lay, Drew looked out the window into the star-filled night. He couldn't help thinking about Tal. He'd lost so much: the girl he was mad about, the father he'd admired, his whole notion about life and whom he could trust, the future and what it held for him now. No doubt he'd lost even the feeling that he was safe in his own home. Everything had changed, and there was no going back to the way things were before.

At least Tal still had his mother, though all this had been as devastating for her as for him. Yet she was a typical English woman—chin up, head held high, and carrying on regardless. Tal had that to cling to. If Drew could help them both find some peace by figuring out who had killed Alice and Will and why, then he would do it. God helping him, he would.

He had to.

He let the breath seep out of his lungs, and a wave of sleepiness overtook him. He didn't have to figure it all out just now. Tomorrow he would start over again. He'd tell Birdsong his theory about the wine barrels, and then he and the chaps from Scotland Yard would take it from there. They'd figure this out, and at least then Tal would have a little peace. At least then—

There was an urgent tapping on the door.

Madeline woke beside him, blinking and bewildered as if trying to remember where they were and why they weren't in their own bed at Farthering Place.

The tapping grew more insistent.

He sat up, pulling the coverlet up to her chin. "Stay here, darling. I'll go." He switched on the lamp on the bedside table, threw on his dressing gown that was draped over a chair, and hurried to the door. "Who is it?"

"Drew, please . . ."

He recognized the voice and immediately opened the door. "Mrs. Cummins. What's the matter?"

"Oh, Drew." Her voice was hardly understandable, choked as it was with tears. "Please come. Please."

Madeline grabbed her own wrap and came to his side. "What is it?"

"Oh, my dear." The older woman caught a sobbing breath and lowered her head. "He's dead. I thought he was only sleeping, but he's dead."

Madeline took her arm, drawing her into the room so Drew could shut the door.

"Who's dead?" Drew said, trying to keep his voice low and not too harsh.

"It's Tibby!" Mrs. Cummins sank down onto the divan at the foot of the bed, drawing Madeline down with her. "Tibby . . ."

She thrust a wadded sheet of notepaper into Drew's hand. He spread it out on the bedside table under the glow of the lamp, squinting to make out the blotchy scrawl.

> *If weakness is sin, then God forgive me. I am weak. I could bear some of this perhaps, but not all of it. Not all of it at once. Not when I know it's all been a lie. All of it. All my life.*
>
> *You took her from me. You may as well have killed me yourself. I'll save you the trouble.*
>
> *God forgive me.*
>
> *Talbot Brennan Cummins*

Drew looked at the two women clinging to each other there in the half-light and wanted to be sick. *Tal. No, no, no.*

"Is he in his room?"

"Yes."

The word came out as a hardly audible sigh, and Drew peered into Mrs. Cummins's slack face. "May we go in?"

Still clinging to Madeline's arm, she led them down the corridor to her son's room. The bedroom itself was lit only by the moonlight pouring through the tall windows, spilling over the rumpled bed and the eveningwear strewn on the floor. A long, narrow rectangle of cold white light fell from the bathroom door, illuminating the body that lay in its confines.

Tal lay on his side, clad only in the bottom half of his navy-striped pajamas. His knees were drawn up slightly, one arm crumpled under him and the other more out to the side. There was a partly unfolded towel under him, and his hair and face were wet. Mercifully, his eyes were closed.

Careful to smudge the handle as little as possible, Drew shut off the still-running tap at the sink. "How did you know something was wrong?"

Tal's mother stood staring at nothing and did not answer. "Mrs. Cummins?"

She dabbed her handkerchief to her eyes. "I, uh, I heard a crash. It must have been when he fell."

The towel rack had skittered up under the sink. Four ragged holes in the wall opposite marked where it had been.

Drew knelt at his friend's side and pressed two fingers against Tal's neck. "He's still warm."

Mrs. Cummins caught her breath as Drew silently pled with heaven to let him find even the slightest sign of life. There was nothing.

He shook his head. "I'm sorry."

"Oh, Tibby. Tibby."

Mrs. Cummins reached for her son, but Drew got to his feet and held her back. "Better not touch anything until the police arrive."

"But what happened?" Mrs. Cummins asked. "How did he . . . how did he do it?"

"The coroner will have to tell us for certain. He must have taken something. Then I suppose he went to splash his face in the sink and stumbled when he reached for the towel. It looks as if he fell to his knees. He must have tried to stand again after that and couldn't make it."

Drew looked again at the towel rack and then at the sink. Frowning, he picked up two little metal rings lying by the soap. They were grimed with what looked like ash. He started to ask Mrs. Cummins if she knew what they were, but instead slipped them into the pocket of his dressing gown. This sort of trifle could wait until later.

"May I see the note again?" he asked.

Mrs. Cummins looked confused. Madeline nodded toward Drew's pocket. "You still have it."

"Oh, right." Drew pulled out the note and looked it over again, trying to find something besides disillusion and despair behind the words, behind every cutting slash of the pen. *A lie. All my life. You took her from me.* What would his father think now of his harmless little business venture?

"Are you certain this is his handwriting?" To his surprise, Drew's voice came out steady, if a little hard. "We can't afford to assume anything."

Mrs. Cummins nodded jerkily, not lifting her head from Madeline's shoulder. "It was on h-his bed."

She started to sob audibly, and Madeline tried in vain to soothe her. The older woman fumbled in the pocket of her flannel robe, and Drew thought she wanted a fresh handkerchief. He gave her his own.

"No, no," she said. "He had this, too." She pressed an envelope into his hand. It was an old one, addressed to Tal from a Bond Street tailor, but that made no difference. The envelope was empty except for minute traces of white powder.

Drew held back the oath that leapt to his tongue.

Cocaine.

"He wants to see you." Tal had told Drew this more than once, but Drew hadn't seen Mr. Cummins since that day Scotland Yard had taken him from Winteroak House. But now Drew had no choice. He had to talk to the man. There had to be more Cummins could tell him.

He stopped first to see Chief Inspector Birdsong, who seemed grudgingly impressed with his theory about the wine barrels.

"You may well be right, Mr. Farthering," Birdsong said, "but that makes our job just that much harder, don't you think?"

"Yes, it does. Sorry. But maybe this will make it up to you." Drew fished out the two metal rings he had in his pocket and handed them to the chief inspector. "These were by Tal's sink the night he died. I forgot I had them until just a bit ago."

Birdsong studied them, eyes narrowed. "What are they?"

"I hoped you could tell me that. They look as though they've been in a fire, don't you think?"

The chief inspector rubbed one of the rings between his thumb and forefinger and studied the blackened mark it left behind. "I'd say so. Hmmm. Any theories?"

"Not a one," Drew admitted, "but I'll continue to think on it."

"Fair enough. We'll be keeping these, thank you." Birdsong took a small envelope from his desk drawer, wrote Tal's name on it, and deposited the rings inside. "I suppose you'd better be getting along now. He's waiting for you."

Steeling himself, Drew nodded. "Right."

Cummins sat at a heavy-looking table, his face as gray as his prison uniform, a stark contrast to his red-rimmed eyes. With a glance at the officer at the door, Drew sat down across from him.

"Good of you to come, Drew. I know I'm the last person you want to see just now."

Drew tried to make his expression less severe, but knew he was only marginally successful. "I see they've told you about Tal. I'm sorry."

"It was never what I meant to have happen, Drew. You have to believe me."

Cummins reached one hand across the table and then pulled it back again. Drew hadn't meant to draw away from him, but it was difficult not to.

"That doesn't much matter at this point. It isn't easy when someone you've looked up to turns out to be—" Drew stopped, knowing there was no way he could finish the sentence without adding to the pain the man already carried. "Judging by the note Tal left, it was all more than he could bear. Especially knowing Alice died because of . . . because of the cocaine."

"Because of me, you mean."

Drew made no reply to that.

Cummins sighed. "What exactly did the note say?"

Drew reached into his pocket and then stopped when the guard took a warning step forward. "Just a piece of paper, Officer. You may read it if you like." He took out his copy of the suicide note and offered it to the guard, who waved him away and leaned against the wall once more. Drew then handed the note to Cummins, watching his face as he read.

"No." Cummins shook his head, his face contorted with grief. "He couldn't have believed that. I told him! He said he understood! He swore he understood!"

"Understood what?"

"About Alice." Cummins twisted his trembling fingers together. "I tell you I didn't kill her. She was a dear girl, and I was happy she made Tal so happy. I didn't give her the cocaine. I never had the stuff in the house. Never. I never wanted anyone in my family around it. I warned Tal about it more times than I can remember. Even you a time or two."

He gave Drew a pitiful, pleading smile, and Drew had to press his lips tightly together to keep from cursing the man. Cummins knew what poison he had been dealing all these years, knew the relentless hold it had on those who fell victim to it, and yet he had sold it, had grown fat on it, without a pang of conscience. So long as no one he held dear was affected, he had been content to go on. Even now . . .

Cummins winced, obviously reading Drew's feelings if not his thoughts. "Don't hate me, Drew. I know I disgust you. I disgust myself. But I know how much Tal loved Alice. I would rather have died myself than have him lose her. Whatever else I've done, I didn't kill her. I told him I didn't, and he believed me." He caught hold of Drew's sleeve and wouldn't let him pull away. "He believed me! He wouldn't have killed himself. Not like that. Not because of me."

"But the note says—"

"Listen to me, Drew. He wouldn't have! I tell you he knew I never gave her cocaine. I told him so, and he promised me he believed me."

"Then he must have found out something later. Something that changed his mind. Something that convinced him you were lying." *As you've lied about everything else all his life.*

"He couldn't have, because I didn't do it. I would never have hurt him that way. He meant more to me . . ." He looked up into the bare bulb burning over his head, and his eyes filled with tears. "All of this was for him."

Drew knew he should have forgiveness, kindness, pity for the broken man before him, knowing he himself had been given mercy rather than justice, knowing they were equally sinful before a holy God. At the very least, he ought to have sympathy for a parent grieving the loss of a child. But then again, there were other parents, hundreds, perhaps thousands over the past twenty years and more who had grieved for their own children, children whose lives had been sold for one miserable man's gain. Pity? Sympathy? Somehow, just now, Drew couldn't manage it.

"For him?" he said coldly, pulling free of Cummins's grasp. "You think this is what he would have wanted?"

"No." Cummins sniffed, blinked hard, and then sat himself a bit straighter in his chair. "Tal was a good boy. A good man. I don't think you'd disagree with me on that, no matter what I drove him to."

"No," Drew said, his own grief softening his tone. "I wouldn't disagree."

"You don't know what it's like to love a child of your own, to pin every hope and every dream on him, to know there's nothing you wouldn't give or do to keep him happy and well."

Drew folded his hands on the table in front of him, listening. Cummins, too, was silent. Then one corner of his mouth turned up.

"You wouldn't think it now, but Tal was a tiny thing when

he was born. Early too. Much too early. We thought we'd lose him those first few days. He and Margaret both had a number of medical issues, operations, multiple specialists, constant nursing. I'd had a bad time of it in my investments the year before, everything was mortgaged, I'd borrowed more than I had any right to already, and then this. What would you have done?"

Still Drew said nothing.

"I suppose better men would have let their wives and children die before soiling their precious honor. I wasn't that strong. When I found I could be paid handsomely just for turning a blind eye to what was stored in my warehouse, it seemed like a blessing from heaven. An answer to my hopeless prayers. Later, when Margaret and Tal were both well and strong, I found it wasn't so hard to expand the operation. The profits paid off my debts and made Winteroak a showplace. They sent my son to school and then to university and to study on the Continent, as well. And I didn't spend it just on my own family, Drew. You know very well how many people my charities have helped."

"And you think that makes up for everything else?"

Cummins looked away. "It was all I knew to do at the time."

"You could have left it." Drew clenched one hand into a fist. "Once Tal was well, you could have stopped."

"Come now, Drew, you're not as naïve as all that. These people aren't overly dainty when it comes to keeping their business going smoothly. Do you really think I could just turn in my notice and there be no consequences? It's a bit like climbing on a wild stallion. Once you're on, there's nothing you can do but hold on as best you're able. Even now, with Tal . . ." Cummins caught a shuddering breath and then shrugged. "I'm not going to let them hurt Margaret, and they will if I say anything. I'm going to pay for what I've done, I'm well aware of that, but I won't have my wife pay, too. I've hurt her enough as it is."

Drew nodded. "I'll do what I can to see she's looked after. This has all been rather rotten for her."

"Thank you, Drew. She deserves better than this, I know. Maybe I should have confided in her, way back when Tal was just a baby. Perhaps I would have if she hadn't been so ill and so worried about our newborn. Together, maybe she and I could have come up with a better scheme for getting out of the mess we were in. She's never failed me in a pinch, and now I've done this to her. God help me, I never meant it to come to this."

Before Drew could come up with a response, the guard cleared his throat. "Time, sir."

Drew's chair legs made a harsh scraping sound on the cement floor as he pushed it back from the table.

Once more, Cummins caught his arm. "For her sake, Drew. For Margaret's and for . . . for Tal's. Find out who killed Alice. And the boy."

Drew picked up his hat, pulling his arm free as he did. He believed the man was innocent, at least of murder. At least of *these* murders. But then he'd been certain of him before. Like Tal, all his life.

He stood there a moment more, Cummins making no more pleas except with his anguished eyes.

"Sir?" the officer prompted.

Drew put on his hat and walked through the door.

"I couldn't bear it any longer," Drew said, sitting on the bed as he fumbled with the buttons on his blue-striped pajamas. "I wasn't very kind, I'm afraid, but I just didn't feel very gracious and comforting."

Madeline came out of the bathroom with her face freshly scrubbed and her hair a little damp at the temples. "You should have let me go with you."

"No."

She looked only mildly surprised when he said nothing more. "So what are we going to do now?"

He watched her in the mirror for a moment and then blew all the breath from his lungs. "I think it's time we all went home."

Madeline turned to face him, eyes wide. "We haven't found out who killed Alice or Billy yet."

"That's a job for the police, isn't it?"

He realized one of the pajama buttons was in the wrong hole, so he yanked the fabric on either side of it until it flew off and went skittering under the bed. Eddie leapt off the dresser and dove after it. With a huff, Drew snatched off the shirt itself, wadded it into a ball, and threw it onto the window seat.

Madeline sat down at his side and slipped her arm through his. "This isn't much like you, you know."

"Maybe I've finally realized I've got no business poking my nose in this sort of thing."

She pressed a comforting kiss to his bare shoulder. "You did tell Tal you'd find out what happened to Alice."

"Fat lot I've done about that."

"It's not your fault you haven't found out anything yet. Neither have the police. That doesn't mean we should just pack up and go home."

He nodded rapidly, his smile brittle. "Oh, right. Very good. I'll just carry on being useless then, shall I?"

"Drew." She wrapped him in her arms, pulling his head

232

down to her shoulder, holding him there until he gave in and relaxed against her. "Don't say that, darling. Don't even think it. You're not useless."

"Of course I am!" He shrugged away from her. "I haven't found out who killed Alice. I've gotten Carrie's brother killed. I left Tal so hopeless he killed himself."

"None of that is your fault. And it certainly doesn't mean you're useless."

"What have I done with my life? I've never even had a proper job."

"What about all the good you've done?" she asked. "You've helped a lot of people. People who lost a loved one and needed to know why. People who seemed guilty but weren't. People who might have been killed if you hadn't exposed a murderer."

"Will Holland would be alive right now if I hadn't told him about some of our cases and let him nose around at Winteroak. If I am supposed to be a sleuth, I'm a pretty rotten one."

She gave him that pert little grin of hers, though there was a great deal of love and patience in those perceptive eyes. "You think God didn't know what He was doing when He called you to be a sleuth?"

He huffed. "But that's the whole point. *Did* He call me, or did I, in my usual insufferably self-assured way, just assume He did? I have no training for this. I'm just as likely to be killed as find a killer. I *was* nearly killed last summer, if you remember." Drew's throat tightened, and tears stung his eyes. "Tal begged me to find out who killed Alice, and I've failed him."

"You've only failed him if you quit before you do what you told him you would."

He pulled away from her again, closing his eyes. "I'm just no good at it. I've fancied myself a good judge of people, but I've blundered over and over again. Cummins was a friend of ours for years, and all that while he was a criminal. I never saw it. Never."

Once more she slipped her arm through his, not letting him escape her tender touch. "Mr. Cummins fooled a lot of people, people with much more experience and training than you. Why should you feel any more taken than them?"

"Because people *die* when I make mistakes. What if someone else dies because of me?"

She took his face in her hands, forcing him to look at her, forcing him to hear. "Alice didn't die because of you. She was murdered. Billy was murdered. Tal took his own life. None of that is your fault. It's awful, it's tragic, but it's not your fault."

"But if I could have prevented—"

"But you didn't. You couldn't. That doesn't mean you should stop trying. Who knows if you might stop this murderer from killing again?"

"And if I don't? If I can't? What if it's Mrs. Cummins the next time? Or Carrie? Or Nick?" In spite of himself, his voice shook. "What if it's . . . you?"

"Drew." She kissed the corner of his mouth, his cheek, his closed eyes, and then she held him close again. "Our times are in God's hands, and if it's my time or yours or anyone else's, there's nothing you can do to change that. All you can do is keep on doing whatever it is He's given you to do for the time you're given to do it."

"I couldn't," he whispered against the soft warmth of her throat. "If anything ever happened to you, I could never go on."

"I don't want you to worry about that. Not tonight." She tugged him down to the pillows and curled up in his arms. "I'm not going anywhere but right here."

He pressed his lips to her fragrant hair and closed his eyes. For tonight at least, that was enough.

— Fifteen —

Saturday morning was perfectly miserable. The weather was drizzly but hot, the air heavy and sticky. The church was sweltering, as were the mourners inside it, packed into the pews like tinned fish. Tal had been well liked, Drew had no doubt of that, but he wondered, with three deaths in less than a week, how many of those present merely wanted to partake of the spectacle. Drew didn't know how, under the circumstances, Tal was to be given burial in consecrated ground. But whether it was through mercy, influence, or a certain amount of money, he was glad. For Tal's sake and also his poor mother's, he was glad.

Drew walked Mrs. Cummins into the church with Laurent simpering at her other side. Nick followed them, escorting Carrie and Madeline. A murmur of sympathy and curiosity followed them up the aisle and then hushed as they came to a stop in front of the casket. In front of Tal laid out in his best suit.

Drew stared down at his friend as he lay in the narrow confines of the box and searched for something he knew was no longer there. Everything that had made Tal Cummins himself was gone. What was left was a mockery, a reminder of Drew's own failure.

He could still see Tal's face as he'd stood on the beach throwing stones into the sea. *"I have to know who killed Alice."* Drew still hadn't a clue.

"Sorry," he whispered.

Sorry he hadn't found Alice's killer as he'd promised. Sorry he hadn't kept another murder from happening at Winteroak House. Sorry he hadn't been able to give Tal even a hope of finding out something. Sorry that Tal had found it all too unbearable. Sorry that he had gotten hold of more of that miserable cocaine. Sorry, sorry, sorry . . .

An intake of breath, something between a sob and a moan, came from somewhere beside him. He didn't have to look to know whose it was.

"I'm sorry," he murmured into the soft marcelled waves of Mrs. Cummins's hair.

She leaned into him, somehow smaller and frailer than he'd ever seen her, but she made no answer. She clung to him for only a brief moment and then turned toward the front pew. He sat down with Madeline on one side of him and Mrs. Cummins on the other. If nothing else, he felt better for being there to give Tal's mother what comfort he could. On the other side of her sat Laurent. The rest of the front pew was conspicuously empty.

Nick and the other pallbearers, all of them school friends of Tal's, sat in the pew behind them. Carrie was next to Nick, looking as if she had stopped crying only moments before. Drew didn't blame her. She'd had a miserable week and probably wanted nothing more than to go home and never again hear even the mention of Hampshire. Her father would be here tomorrow to take her home, and afterward Nick would have an even worse time of it.

The sotto voce murmurs of those in attendance fell to dead silence as the last arrivals came down the aisle. Chief Inspector Birdsong in politely somber dress escorted Tal's father toward the casket. Cummins was wearing one of his own suits now, black and obviously expensive, though he seemed to have shriveled inside it. It was something of a mercy that his coat sleeves hung down a bit too long and for the most part concealed the handcuffs on his wrists.

The chief inspector escorted him to the casket, then stepped back to give him a moment with his son. Cummins stood there motionless for a long moment. Then with a wrenching sob he leaned down and kissed Tal's forehead. Drew could make nothing of the words he said afterward, but there was no denying the raw agony behind them.

After a respectful amount of time had passed, Birdsong took his prisoner's arm and steered him to the front pew. Mrs. Cummins gave Laurent a pleading look, and he was kind enough to move to the other side of the chief inspector so she could sit next to her husband. But the couple didn't look at or cling to each other as Drew expected they might. They only watched in silent resignation while the vicar came to stand behind the pulpit, nothing in his expression but sadness and pity for the bereft parents.

He spoke well, just as he had at Will Holland's funeral. He spoke of God's eternal love, mercy, and forgiveness. He spoke of His infinite patience and understanding of human frailty. And, as if he had been listening to Madeline last night, he reminded the congregation that every person's life rested in His hands, and that true peace was found only in trusting Him with it. He spoke kindly to the grieving parents and led a prayer for their peace and comfort. The casket was then closed, and their son went forever from their sight.

Seeing the vicar's nod, Drew and Nick and four other pallbearers stepped forward and lifted the casket. In slow procession they followed the vicar down the aisle. With a sympathetic word to the mother, the two constables stood. Mrs. Cummins went next, with Mr. Cummins and his guard coming after. Madeline and Carrie were next, followed by the rest of those in attendance. In what seemed to be only a few moments more, the casket was lowered into the ground in the churchyard. Soon after that, Birdsong afforded Mr. and Mrs. Cummins a private word of farewell. He had a quiet word with Laurent while the couple spoke. And then he took Mr. Cummins away.

"It seems I am to be freed at last."

Laurent came down the front stairs of Winteroak House, having shed his mourning attire in exchange for something more befitting the captain of a luxury yacht. Adkins skulked behind him carrying two large suitcases and with a portmanteau tucked under his stocky arm.

"Are you?" Drew asked, glancing at Nick.

They had just come down after changing their own clothes and were waiting for Madeline and Carrie to join them.

"Does Mrs. Cummins know?"

The Frenchman looked smug. "I left a note at her door. I am certain she will understand. I have been detained here far too long. My business will wait no longer."

"And I suppose he will agree with you?" Drew looked over at the police constable standing watch outside the front door, and Laurent's expression grew insufferably more smug.

"But of course. The chief inspector, he told me this morning I was allowed to go."

Nick scowled at the valet. "Him too?"

Adkins gave him the most disdainful of looks.

"Yes," Laurent assured Nick. "The Hampshire police as well as Scotland Yard have questioned us both several times since the unfortunate death of young Will, and of course following our most recent tragedy. But there are laws, it seems, even here, and an innocent man cannot be detained forever. So if you gentlemen would excuse me, I will take my leave. My only regret is that the charming ladies are not here to see me off."

He set his captain's hat on his head and sauntered out the front door, his valet in his wake.

Nick glared after him. "What a perfect swine. And now there's no touching him."

"Don't be so sure," Drew said. "I've been thinking about him and his *Onde Blanc*. Remember that whitish residue I told you about when we were picnicking near Claridge Rindle? I'm wondering now if that isn't caused by the same stuff I saw on the deck of his yacht, those little semicircular marks aft."

Nick frowned. "Do you think so? I don't see how."

"Neither do I. But they're too similar not to wonder about them. I tell you what, you stay here and look after the girls, and I'll take a stroll down the beach and see what I can see. Where the Rindle comes out and all."

"Oh, no, you don't." Madeline's face was stern as she and Carrie came down the stairs. "Not by yourself you're not."

"Now, look here, darling—"

"You needn't worry," Nick said. "I'm going along to see he stays out of trouble."

"Out of the question," Drew protested. "Someone has to stay here and make sure we don't have any more incidents."

"We can go with you," Madeline said.

Carrie's eyes grew rounder, though she made no objection.

"Certainly not," Drew said. "And leave Mrs. Cummins alone? I'm perfectly able to—"

"If you go by yourself, we'll just come after you."

Madeline had that determined set to her mouth he knew all too well.

"There *is* a constable on duty," Nick reminded him. "If anyone comes to menace the ladies, I'm sure he will see to them."

Drew weighed the idea of leaving Madeline and the others here with police protection versus having them with him when he was out poking his nose where it without doubt did not belong.

"If I take Nick with me, will you both promise not to leave the house?"

Carrie looked at Nick. "Are you sure either of you should go?"

"It'll be our last chance to have a look at things before Laurent sails back to France," Drew said. He took Madeline's hand. "Will you promise? It's the only way I'll feel right about taking Nick along."

Madeline pursed her lips. "All right. If that's how it has to be. If you don't go out alone, we won't leave the house. And we'll look after Mrs. Cummins too, since the servants have their half day off on Saturdays. I really don't like to leave her alone right now." She touched a kiss to his lips. "Don't be long."

Carrie took shy hold of Nick's arm. "You'll both be careful, won't you?"

"Of course we will." He squeezed her hand and then released it and turned to Drew. "Shall we?"

They collected their hats and, with a cheery word to the constable leaning against one of the front pillars, walked down the drive and around the side of the house to the path that led down to the beach.

Madeline sighed as Drew and Nick went out of sight. "I suppose we ought to go see if there's anything we can do for Mrs. Cummins. We can at least try to cheer her up."

They walked back upstairs, where Madeline tapped on their hostess's door, not wanting to wake her if she was able to sleep. But a moment later Mrs. Cummins invited them to come in, and Madeline opened the door.

Mrs. Cummins was sitting near the fire in a wing chair with brocade stripes of cream and green and soft-colored flowers, a perfect complement to the feminine room. The day was warm, the fireplace unlit, but she sat huddled next to it all the same, knitting away. Something for the charity bundle, no doubt. Madeline supposed there was something comforting about a familiar routine, about doing something for others rather than thinking solely of oneself. Dressed in black, her face pale and her eyes red-rimmed, still she held her head up and managed a weak smile.

"I thought I heard you all go out," Mrs. Cummins said.

"Just Nick and Drew," Madeline replied. "May we come in?"

"Oh, certainly, my dears. I've been lost in thought, sitting here alone." She looked around the room, listening for what was not there. "The house is quieter than ever now."

Madeline would have liked to put her arms around the

poor woman and tell her to cry for as long as she liked, but perhaps that was not what Mrs. Cummins needed just now.

"It is quiet," Madeline agreed. "That's why we thought you might like some company. Or maybe there's something we could help you with." She thought for a moment. "We could pack up the things for the charity boxes if you feel up to it."

"When is the vicar supposed to come for them?" Carrie asked. "I would like to thank him again for . . . well, for seeing to everything for Billy." Her voice caught. But she quickly composed herself and added, "He seems like such a nice man."

"A lovely man," Mrs. Cummins said. "Always willing to help. So many men would think our little charity drives were beneath them, but he's pitched in and organized the whole parish." She gathered her knitting into one hand, brow furrowed. "But, yes, perhaps that would be best. We'll sort the things that have come in over the past few days. I haven't had much chance to see to it all, and I'm certain it's in a terrible muddle. No use sitting about in a mope when there's work to do, I always say." She put her knitting aside and got to her feet. "Come along with me, then."

She linked arms with both girls, giving Carrie a pat as she did.

"We mustn't give way, my dear, no matter what we face. We can only hold our heads high and press on."

"Yes, ma'am." Carrie looked a little less strained. "Thank you, ma'am."

They went downstairs and into the pantry where Mrs. Cummins showed them a section filled with various items of food and clothing. There seemed to be no rhyme or reason to how they were shelved.

Mrs. Cummins shook her head. "Oh, dear. I have neglected it these past few days, and Josephine never puts things in decent order. But the poor girl's just getting over being ill. Still, I had no idea so much had come in." She ran her fingers over a bundle of knitted items, sweaters and socks and such, and smiled faintly. "I see our ladies at St. James's haven't been idle during our difficulties."

"I think it will all be very welcome when the weather turns in the autumn," Madeline said, her thoughts more on the door that led to the wine cellar than the jumble of food and clothing in this part of the pantry. "What should we do with it all?"

"First off, we must sort it out. Clothing in one pile, food in the other. Sometimes there are small household items, cooking utensils or cutlery perhaps, and those would go in a separate pile. We'll see to that first and then go on to the next bit."

They worked for some time, commenting now and again on various items, a shawl or a pair of gloves or a particularly well-made blanket. Mrs. Cummins, clearly making an effort to stay cheerful, told them about the ladies in her parish church who made items to donate.

"Of course," she said, "it does give us all the odd afternoon to sit in someone's kitchen or parlor and natter away. All for a good cause, mind you."

"My mother's friends were the same," Carrie said as she got up to take more items off the shelves. "The things Billy and I heard while they were quilting." There was a sudden silence, and then she forced a smile. "Does this go, too?" She held up a pasteboard package of tea, and Mrs. Cummins frowned.

"Now where'd that come from?"

"It was on the shelf, but not with the other things. Does it go with the rest?"

The older woman's mouth tightened. "The constables have been through everything in the house. They might at the least put things back where they belong." She sighed, her expression softening. "I thought that all went out in the last group. Do forgive me, my dear, yes, put it with the rest. I suppose it's as well to send it now as not at all."

Carrie balanced the box on top of the other things she'd collected and carried it all over to the table they were using for sorting.

Madeline pulled out some clothing from the stack she was going through. "Oh, aren't these sweet?" She laid out a little girl's dress and bonnet, smoothing the lace that trimmed them. "Did one of your ladies make these?"

Mrs. Cummins nodded, looking up from the pile in front of her. "Mrs. Camden. Doesn't she do a lovely job? Look at that smocking. I'll never have her way with it."

"It's precious. Did the same lady make this?" Madeline held up a jacket meant for a boy of perhaps three or four.

Mrs. Cummins reached out to touch it, her lower lip trembling. "Oh . . ." She drew back her hand and pressed it over her mouth. "Oh, Tibby." Sudden tears streamed down her cheeks, and she fumbled blindly for her pocket handkerchief.

Madeline immediately went to her. "I'm so sorry. What is it?"

"Oh, nothing." Mrs. Cummins blotted her face, struggling unsuccessfully to compose herself. "It's just . . . Tibby had one just like that. We had a photograph made of him in it. I still have it on my dresser."

She made a pitiful attempt at a smile, and Madeline put an arm around her shoulders. "I'm sure he was darling in it."

"Oh, he was," the older woman sobbed into her hand-kerchief. "He was."

Carrie sniffled, her eyes filling with tears. "Daddy has one of me and Billy when I was seven and he was two. He has on a little jacket and a tiny bow tie, and I'm holding him in my lap on our porch swing."

Mrs. Cummins nodded. "Tibby is in a swing, too. Let me go get it."

She hurried away, still dabbing at her eyes, and Madeline sat down next to Carrie.

"I'm so sorry. I didn't mean to upset either of you."

Taking out her own handkerchief, Carrie blew her nose. "No, it's good. We need to remember the good things, too." Her mouth turned up at one side. "Billy always hated that picture. You wouldn't have thought it of him now, but he had the chubbiest baby legs ever."

Madeline squeezed her hand. "I'm sure he was a doll."

"I treated him like one until he was about three and wouldn't put up with it anymore." She laughed softly. "He was awfully cute."

"Maybe we should all relax for a little while. We've got-ten a lot of this sorted out, and I bet by now we could all do with a nice cup of tea."

Carrie nodded, brightening. "That's a grand idea. And then she can tell us about when Tal was a little boy. I wouldn't be surprised if she came down with more than just one pic-ture."

They hurried into the kitchen, determined to have the kettle on before Mrs. Cummins returned. They found cups, spoons and sugar, the teapot and the kettle itself but no tea.

Madeline frowned. "It looks as if we had the last of it at breakfast. With everything that's gone on, it's no wonder."

"Would it be all right if we borrowed some tea from the charity collection?" Carrie asked.

"I don't think it would hurt. This afternoon or tomorrow sometime, I'll go into the village and buy some more. We'll send a whole crate of tea to London. How would that be?"

"I think it would be fine." Carrie grinned and seemed for a moment like her old self. "It's for the needy, and if the three of us aren't needy right now, I don't know who is."

She grabbed the box from the pile of foodstuffs and opened it. "Tea always smells so good, but I wish it was coffee."

She picked up a spoon and dipped it down into the box, and then her forehead wrinkled.

"What is it?" Madeline asked.

"I don't know." Carrie pushed the spoon down into the tea again, and her frown deepened. "There's something in there."

Madeline took the box and spoon from her and tried it herself. "There's definitely something not right."

She fished around for a moment more, but clearly the spoon was hitting something about two-thirds of the way down to the bottom of the box. She got a bowl out of the cupboard and emptied the tea into it. A tightly wrapped paper packet fell on top. It had the same dimensions of the bottom of the tea box and was about two inches high.

The two girls looked at each other, wide-eyed.

"That's . . . that's the stuff, isn't it?" Carrie stammered. "Oh, heavens, that's—"

"Shhh." Madeline glanced toward the door that led from the kitchen to the dining room and then slipped the packet into her skirt pocket. "Quick, put the tea back into the box and put it over with the other things. I'll tidy up in here."

"But Mrs. Cummins—"

"She doesn't know." Madeline thrust the empty box into

Carrie's hands. As soon as the tea was safely back in place, she swiftly rinsed the bowl they had used. "Mr. Cummins told Drew he never wanted her or Tal to know anything about this."

"But she knows now." Carrie's voice was low and urgent. "And all this will come out in time."

"I know, but she doesn't have to hear about it right this minute." Madeline wiped the bowl and returned it to the cupboard with a thump. "She's got enough to bear as it is, don't you think? Without knowing her husband was using her to carry out his filthy business."

"But how does it get in here in the first place?"

"I don't know, but at least we've found another link in the chain. We'll have to tell the boys as soon as they get back, but until then, not a word, all right? I'm sure Drew will let the police know right away. They can see to it after that."

"But you can't just leave that in your pocket."

"I'll have to. At least for a while." Madeline heard Mrs. Cummins in the dining room and grabbed Carrie's arm. "Quick."

When the kitchen door swung open, Madeline and Carrie were sitting at the table, once more sorting through the canned goods.

"Look who's come calling." Mrs. Cummins came in with a thick photo album and three or four framed pictures and the vicar. "Do come in now and sit with us. Can I get you some tea?"

"Tea? Er, no, not just now, thank you, Mrs. Cummins. I won't stay long." Hat in hand, Mr. Broadhurst nodded to Madeline and Carrie. "I hadn't much time to speak to either of you at the service, I'm sorry to say. But I wanted to see how you're getting along. I know these are dark days, but they won't last forever."

"We were just going through the things for your little collection," Mrs. Cummins said. "That is why you've come, isn't it?"

"No, no," he said, patting her hand. "Not today. Of all days, not today. Sometime later. When you're feeling up to it. Or, if you'd like, I can just clear it all away. Some of the other ladies would be happy to help me pack it all up to be shipped."

"Oh." She blinked, and her lips trembled into a smile. "I'm sorry. I didn't mean to put everything on someone else's shoulders. It's just been, well, rather a trial lately. I don't mean to complain." Her face crumpled, and she pressed her handkerchief to her mouth, trying to cover her sobs.

"No, no, no," the vicar soothed, patting her hand again. "It's not like that in the least. No one would expect it of you. Not after what you've been through. You mustn't think that."

He looked pleadingly at Madeline, and she put her arm around Mrs. Cummins's shoulders. "Maybe this was a bad idea."

"No, it's all right." Mrs. Cummins drew a shuddering breath. "It's all right. Why don't we just get away from all this." She stood and gathered up the photographs she had brought down from her bedroom. "We'll go into the morning room, and I'll bore you with all my stories about when Tibby was a little boy." She took Carrie's arm. "You can tell us all about Will too, and neither of us will mind if we shed a few tears."

Carrie nodded, looking as if those tears might come right then, and the two of them left the pantry.

"I'm terribly sorry. It's usually my job to comfort people, not drive them to tears." The vicar gestured to the jumble of items spread out before them. "Perhaps I'd best take this all away so she needn't worry over it anymore."

"I think she'll want something to do over the next few days," Madeline said. "Don't you think so?"

"No need to worry her over it." He put on his hat and glanced at the various piles they had sorted out, and then he stacked a large box of canned goods on top of the one where she'd put the tea and lifted it into his arms. "I'll take this to start and come back later for more. Do give Mrs. Cummins my apologies. I will let myself out."

— Sixteen —

Drew shaded his eyes and looked down toward the docks at Armitage Landing. "Claridge Rindle is far too small for Laurent's yacht to have sailed up to where we had our picnic. But perhaps, whatever that white residue was, it washed downstream and out to the beach. If someone from the *Onde Blanc* stepped in it and then onto the deck, that might account for the marks left there."

"That doesn't mean someone from the yacht had anything to do with whatever left that residue in the stream," Nick pointed out.

Drew scowled at him. "Don't you think I know that? But I have to do something. I have to make sense of all this for all their sakes. For Alice and Will and Tal. Something he saw, something he found. I don't know what, but something convinced him his father killed Alice. I have to know what it is."

"Right."

They were silent for a moment, and then Drew pulled up short, catching Nick by the arm.

"Hullo."

Nick looked around. "What?"

"There seems to have been some embellishment since last we were here."

Armitage Landing boasted three well-weathered docks. One of them, however, was not so weathered looking as before.

Nick blinked. "Whitewash?"

"Whitewash," Drew repeated, dragging two fingers over one of the posts and bringing them back faintly white. "A nice chalky residue."

"But that doesn't mean—"

"I don't know what it means, but it would definitely leave that kind of residue in the stream and on the deck of Laurent's yacht. I hadn't thought of it before."

"Drew—"

"It's worth finding out about." Drew walked toward the old man leaning back in an old slat-backed chair, watching them with a wary eye, the same one he'd seen about several times in the past week. "Good afternoon."

The man took a measured puff of his pipe and then nodded. "Afternoon."

"We were just admiring your dock."

"Aye." He patted the post he was leaning against. "Had the boy paint her up nice just yesterday, fresh as when she were new."

"Very nice," Drew said.

The man nodded serenely. "Aye. French paint it were, too. Whitewash. A bit fussy for a good English dock, mind you, but I weren't never one to say no to a handsome offer."

Drew tried his best to look as if he knew what the man was talking about. "Oh, no, indeed. Who would? And was it a good deal of money?"

The man frowned and tapped his pipe against the empty paint can at his feet. "Money? What money?"

"The money you were offered?"

"No, no. Weren't no money."

"Then what was your offer?"

"Paint, ye ninny. I told ye already, it were French paint. I told the boy it were a might fine for our like, but he said we may as well have it because of old Jabez."

"And who's Jabez?" Nick asked.

"Jabez? Everyone knows old Jabez, eh? Him and me, we fished these waters near sixty year, man and boy, till he took up with that Bill Rinnie after I got me palsy. I can't say nothin' about Rinnie, good nor bad, but Jabez's boys, well they never was much, but they was good lads all the same. So if young Tom give Jem this here posh French paint to do up the dock, well, I warn't to say no to that. Nor would you."

"Wouldn't dream of it," Drew said. "Would we, Nick, old man?"

Drew bent down and picked up the can, and then he caught his breath. Nick gave him a quizzical look, but Drew had to keep his racing thoughts off his face.

"French, is it? What do you think, Nick? A baffler of a label, wouldn't you say? Ever see anything like it?"

Nick's eyes widened as he looked at it, but he kept his expression mild. "I . . . I may have. Can't quite place it at the moment."

Drew returned the can to its place at the old man's feet. "Do you know the whereabouts of Rinnie and his crew just now?"

The man chewed the stem of his pipe, his stoic expression unchanging. "Aye."

Drew and Nick both looked at him expectantly as he gnawed the pipestem and said nothing.

"Can you tell us?" Drew asked.

The man nodded. "Aye."

"Well, will you?" Nick urged.

The old man looked as if he might make them extract the information like a rotten molar, but then he chuckled to himself and nodded toward the water. "Out there. Left this mornin' early, like when old Jabez and me use ter go t'earn our bread."

"Don't they usually go out early?" Drew asked.

The old man gave a wheezy laugh. "That lot spend more time up to the pub than out doing a proper. Especially the last few month. They might put out of a mornin', late mind you, seven or eight o'clock, and come back afore ten. Other times, they mightn't go out till noon or after."

Drew nodded. "And they make a good catch, do they?"

The man blew out his breath, making his rubbery lips flap. "Paltry, were you ter ask a true fisherman. Not like they use ter when they had Jabez's tub and they all three worked the day long."

"We heard Rinnie came into some inheritance money," Nick said, "and that's how he managed the boat."

"Might well be, but Irene Gallagher never had a shillin' I ever heard of."

Drew again considered Claridge Rindle and those little curved marks on the decking of Laurent's yacht.

"This French whitewash, do you know where it came from?"

The old man shrugged. "France, I expect."

"I mean, what did Tom have it for?"

"Dunno. My boy, Jem, said Tom were for dumpin' it like he allus did."

Nick glanced at Drew. "Dumping it?"

The man puffed thoughtfully and then tapped his pipe

against the battered can once more. "I allus thought they was empties he was carrying, but when Jem told me he seen Tom and Bert dumpin' out proper good paint, I said we'd have a better use of it and told him to bring it on home did he see 'em again."

"Tom had a lot of these paint cans, did he?" Drew asked, forcing a touch of nonchalance into his voice.

"Now and again."

"What did he do with them out in the boat?"

The old man shook his head. "No, not out in the boat. What sort of ninny would carry paint out in a boat? On up the shore. But I never saw him paint nothin'. Maybe a buoy oncet. Still, seems a shame to let good paint go a-wastin' out to the sea."

Drew thought once again of those faint marks on Laurent's deck and the traces of white along the waterline of the Rindle. Whitewash or *blanc de chaux* in French. White of lime.

Drew gave the old man a commiserating nod. "Might I have a word with your Jem? I won't take up a moment of his time."

"Aye, he'll tell ye t'same as me when he gets back."

Nick huffed impatiently. "Gets back? He's not here?"

"Gone up to Manchester to see the football, young sir. I wouldn't have no truck with such things, but he and his mates have gone and no stoppin' 'em. Back termorrer night."

"That's all right," Drew said. "You've been more than helpful, sir."

He pressed some coins into the old man's hand, but the fellow pushed them back again.

"Here now! What d'ye take me for? Beggin' ain't me way. Ain't never been. No, sir."

"Certainly not," Drew assured him, "and no offense meant.

I just thought you might want some fresh tobacco to fill your pipe. Just between gentlemen."

Drew offered the coins again.

"Well, put that way." The old man tucked the money into his waistcoat pocket and tugged the brim of his flat cap. "Thankee kindly, and I'll smoke it to your good health, sir, and to ye both."

Drew tipped his own hat, nudged Nick into doing the same, and then hurried him away.

"What perfect imbeciles we've all been." Drew pulled out his pocket watch and thrust the scrap of label under Nick's nose. "It's not a *D* at all. It's the top half of a *B*. Blanc de chaux. White of lime. French for whitewash. It all fits."

Nick glanced back at the freshly painted dock. "Just because it's French, that doesn't mean Laurent—"

"Then what made those marks on the deck on his yacht? Crevices still with some traces of whitewash in them. Like the traces of it along the waterline up near the house. Someone must have spilled a bit on his aft deck."

"But why haul the stuff all the way over from the Continent only to dump it? Unless . . ." Nick grinned abruptly. "Unless you're bringing in something else."

"Got it in one. They've been getting the stuff in via the paint cans. And Tom Kimlin no doubt thought it better just to give Jem the whitewash than make him wonder why he'd rather dump it."

Nick shook his head. "But Laurent doesn't bring in anything. The police have checked a hundred times. We've checked, too."

"Precisely. He drops it off before he comes into port, and Rinnie and his boys pick it up out of the Solent, sealed up in cans of blanc de chaux, neat as you please and no fuss."

"So that's why that scrap is so waterlogged."

"That's why." Drew stopped in front of the phone box next to the pub. "I think old Birdsong ought to be in on this, don't you?"

Nick nodded. "I daresay he'd like to be standing on the dock, waiting for Rinnie and his lot with open arms."

"Be a good lad and ring him up. Tell him what we've come up with, and tell him he ought to get down here before the guests arrive. I think he's likely to be in a sociable mood and want to come down directly."

"Right. And you?"

"I'm going down to see if the *Onde Blanc* is still this side of the Channel."

"Ah." Nick grinned. "The bean-and-a-half, I'll wager."

"Right. And I want to see if there's any sign of Rinnie and his mates yet. Back in a jiff. You might tell Birdsong to send someone over to pick up Laurent if he's still there when they arrive."

"I'll tell him."

Drew hurried back down the path, taking the turn away from the newly whitewashed dock and up toward the bluff overlooking the Solent and much of Armitage Landing. Just as he was about to go back down to the village, he saw *The Gull* chugging toward the dock. He hurried down to the phone box.

"Birdsong's on his way," Nick said. "He also said that if this turns out to be another fool's errand, it'll be the last he does on your account."

Drew sniffed. "He can come or not come, be it on his own head, I say. But I'm going down to have a chat with Master Rinnie and the charming brothers Kimlin."

Nick's eyes lit. "You saw them. They're coming in?"

"Right now. If we can hold them at the dock, then Birdsong

259

won't have that tiresome manhunt to see to. Maybe then he won't look down on our humble efforts."

Drew and Nick were waiting when *The Gull* pulled up to one of the unpainted docks.

"Heading out again?" Drew asked pleasantly as Tom Kimlin tied up the boat. "Rather late in the day, isn't it?"

Rinnie returned a faint sneer. "Might be. Might not. What business is it of yours?"

"We're just concerned citizens, aren't we, Nick?"

Nick gave the man a sunny smile. "Good neighbors. Here for you chaps' benefit."

"What's that mean?" Rinnie asked, scowling behind his ginger beard.

Drew held out the little scrap of label he had found, displaying it for Rinnie's benefit.

"They know," Tom whimpered. "They know everything."

With an oath, Rinnie shoved Drew away from the boat. "Gun it, Bert! Get us out of here." The little engine sputtered, and the boat began backing away from the dock.

Drew shook his head in mild reproof. "The police will be here any minute now."

"We'll be halfway to France before they get here!" Rennie shouted.

He stood, arms crossed and sneering, as the boat began chugging along the shoreline.

"Not at that speed!" Drew called back, and he gave them a cheery wave.

"He's right," Nick muttered. "Dash it all. They need only nip across the Channel."

Drew scoffed. "They'd be hours in that tub."

"It's ten to one they disappear into France never to be seen again. At least not under those names."

Drew stared after them, eyes narrowed. He couldn't lose them now, not when he had finally made the connection between them and Laurent. Not when there was so much more he wanted to know. Not if—

"Not if we can stop them. Come on."

Drew sprinted up the dock and back along the path that led along the bluff to the Cummins house. He could still see the fishing boat moving along the shoreline and hear its engine running at full laborious speed.

"You don't think we can outrun them, do you, old man?" Nick huffed behind him.

"Spit spot now, Nick. It's not so long since we ran cross-country at school, eh?" Drew lengthened his stride. "We don't have to beat them to France, just to the dock at Winteroak House." There was a little skiff pulled up on the beach, and Drew angled toward it. "Quick now. Before they're out of reach."

"Oughtn't we wait for the police?" Nick asked as they clambered down the bluff and then along the beach. "This isn't strictly our boat, you know."

Drew didn't spare a glance back. "Tal would have said to take her, I've no doubt of it."

They leapt aboard, and a moment later, engine racing, they were headed along the coastline.

"There they are!" Nick said, pointing not far ahead of them. "Good thing that tub of theirs doesn't have much of a motor."

Drew grinned. "Good thing this one does."

They were quickly making up the distance between them and Rinnie's boat. Bert Kimlin was at the wheel, brow furrowed as he hunched forward, urging the little fishing boat to give him all the speed she had. His brother hung on to the rail, leaning out to better see their pursuers. Rinnie himself stood in the stern, fists on hips, fixing Drew and Nick with a killing glare.

Drew gave him another wave. "It's a fine effort, Rinnie, I'm sure," he called, "but I'm afraid you're outclassed. Make it easier on yourself and head back to the dock."

Rinnie spat a curse at him.

"Temper, temper," Drew shouted, "but I really must insist. It's either that or we run you aground here, and then what happens to your nice new boat?"

"You're not the police!" Rinnie shouted back. "You got no right to interfere with us going about our business! Let us alone or wish you had!"

"They'll be here soon enough. May as well make it easier on everyone. I understand they go easier on those who are cooperative."

Rinnie set his bearded jaw and did not reply.

"May as well head into shore," Drew said. "The game's up already, and the police are on their way."

"Full throttle, Bert," Rinnie snapped.

Bert glanced back toward their pursuers. "I've already got it wide open."

"Give her more!"

"She won't take it! She's burning up as it is!"

"Get out of my way!"

Rinnie shoved Bert aside and took over at the helm, and *The Gull* lurched forward, forcing Tom to clutch the railing or be thrown overboard. Bert staggered back to the stern.

"They're gaining on us, Bill! We've got to heave to!"

The engine purred as Drew angled the skiff closer to the other boat. "You ought to listen to him, Rinnie. You'll save yourself a lot of grief in the end."

"Not so much as I'll give you if you don't leave us be!" Rinnie barked.

"Bill," Tom whined, "do something!"

"You shut your miserable gob, Tom Kimlin! If you're staying aboard, shut up."

He jammed the throttle forward, and the engine gave a terrific roar. Then a coil of black, foul-smelling smoke curled out of the engine compartment, and with a bang and a sputter it fell silent.

— Seventeen —

Tom Kimlin looked at Bill, mouth hanging open, and Bert stormed toward the wheel. "What did I tell you? Now you've gone and fixed us sure!"

With a whimper, Tom heaved himself over the side of the boat into the Solent, thrashing through the shallow water and onto a narrow strip of beach, making for the dense trees beyond.

"Tom!" his brother called, and then with a desperate look at Bill, he vaulted over the rail. "Wait up, Tom!"

"Come back, you yellow dogs!" Bill howled.

"You may as well do as he says," Drew said, slowing the skiff next to the fishing boat. "You can't get far."

He nodded toward the road, and the three fugitives looked in that direction. Two police cars, bells jingling, screeched to a halt, and a number of sturdy-looking constables piled out with Chief Inspector Birdsong right after them. Tom and Bert trudged to a stop and stood, slump-shouldered, awaiting their fate. On the deck of *The Gull*, Bill Rinnie kicked the still-smoking engine compartment and then grimaced and swore as he leaned down to rub his foot.

"All right, Rinnie," Birdsong called. "Make it easy on all of us." He motioned toward one of his men. "Go on and get him, Parkins."

"Never mind," Rinnie groused. "I'm coming." He climbed over the side and dropped into the water where he stood for a moment, glaring at the boat. "Stupid tub. Drift out to sea and sink for all I care."

"Oh, no," the chief inspector said, looking rather pleased with himself. "That's evidence, that is. We'll see she's well taken care of."

Police Constable Parkins took hold of Rinnie's arm once he was on the beach and fastened handcuffs around his wrists. Two other officers were doing the same for the Kimlins.

"What's this about?" Rinnie demanded. "Can't a man go about his own business anymore?"

"Seems your business has become our business," Birdsong said. "Mr. Dennison here tells me you and your two mates have been conducting yourselves in a manner that lies contrary to established law."

"Him and his nibs there, eh?" Rinnie sneered at Drew and Nick. "What's a load of toffee-nosed prigs got to do with it?"

Nick climbed off the skiff and waded ashore, catching the line Drew tossed to him and securing it to a heavy bit of driftwood. Drew followed him onto the beach.

"You might ask them about this, Chief Inspector." He gave Birdsong the scrap from the whitewash label. "Laurent too."

"Ah, yes." Birdsong took it from him. "Actually, the monsoor should be with us any minute now. I've sent two of my men to invite him to meet up here so that we can all go up to Winchester for a soirée."

266

"What do you want with that paper?" Rinnie demanded. "That don't mean nothing."

"Have a look at the deck of the *Onde Blanc*," Drew told Birdsong as if Rinnie hadn't spoken. "I'd wondered what made those marks on the deck and why there was a residue left at the waterline at the lower end of Claridge Rindle. That's the connection right there."

Birdsong's forehead wrinkled. "And just what is it?"

"Blanc de chaux. You ask Monsieur Laurent if he doesn't recognize it."

The chief inspector tucked the scrap into his coat pocket. "I'll do that. But first we'll see what these fine fellows have to tell us about how they've been bringing their goods up into Winteroak House and what they have to do with the murders up there."

Tom Kimlin made a little squawk and looked pleadingly at his brother, but Bert was only staring at Birdsong, open-mouthed.

"Here now! We none of us had anything to do with those killings, and you can't say as we did. Tell 'em, Bill. We couldn't'a done. We weren't never close to the place."

Birdsong looked unimpressed. "That's more than I know. But I do know anyone who was to tell us how you lot got the goods from the Solent into the warehouse in London might find the judge a bit more lenient than usual."

Drew nodded. "A bit less likely to need his black cap, eh?"

Tom Kimlin's eyes went wide. "You can't hang us! Not for smuggling! Not for just bringing the stuff in! It's the Frenchman gets the money off it. We got hardly anything."

"Shut up, Tom," Rinnie growled. "You say another word and I'll kick your teeth in, I swear."

"What'll it hurt now?" Drew asked. "You may as well tell

us everything. It's not as if you'll be able to keep at your little trade after today."

Rinnie grinned humorlessly. "It's more than our lives are worth, mate. You find what you find. Heaven help you, but we won't." He glared at his two confederates. "None of us."

Birdsong shook his head. "We've been over this whole place, Mr. Farthering, caves and all, and more than once. Not a thing. But at least these three won't be bringing anything in that way or any other way. Not for a very long time." He looked back toward the road, seeing another police car had pulled up. "That'll be Laurent. I'll send these three along to Winchester, but we'll have a chat with our Frenchman before he goes. Take them up to the station, Parkins. I'll see to our foreign guest." He waved to the constable driving the recently arrived car. "Down here, Maxwell."

Maxwell escorted his prisoner down to where Birdsong, Drew, and Nick awaited him. Laurent looked only mildly curious as he passed the three fishermen. Rinnie walked by him, head held high, jaw defiantly set, making no acknowledgment whatsoever. Bert turned his face away, careful not to make eye contact. Tom, looking as if he might burst into tears, fixed pleading eyes upon him, but Laurent looked down his nose at the pitiful sight and then turned a bland smile on the chief inspector.

"I did not expect we would meet again, sir. I was told I was free to go, yet I am once again treated like the basest of miscreants?"

"Where's his man, Adkins?" Birdsong asked.

Constable Maxwell shook his head. "He wasn't there, sir. The prisoner said he'd gone to see to some things before they returned to France."

"Where?" Birdsong demanded.

Laurent huffed. "He went to purchase the white tea I prefer. The foolish man had allowed our store on board to run out."

"Where?" Birdsong repeated.

"Southampton. The shop is in the High Street. Bayard's. What is it now that you want?"

Birdsong nodded toward the car Rinnie and the Kimlins were getting into. "I thought you might want to hear what those three had to say about certain . . . activities here in the area."

Laurent shrugged. "What would I know of such men? They could not begin to appreciate my wares, much less pay for them."

"And what, monsoor, would you know of this?" He took the waterlogged scrap out of his pocket and showed it to Laurent.

Laurent frowned contemplatively. "And this is what?"

"Blank de show," Birdsong told him. "Right, Farthering?"

"More or less," Drew said. "Blanc de chaux, Monsieur Laurent. Nice and tidy little cans of whitewash dropped off into the Solent for our local fishermen to pick up. They dump the paint into Claridge Rindle and remove the contraband from the bottom of the can, and then you come into port with nothing but your fine wares, all duty paid of course, and nothing to touch you."

Laurent gave a guileless smile. "But the police have nothing to tie me to such a practice. And what good would it do me to give these men this contraband, whatever it may be? The cocaine, yes?"

Birdsong narrowed his eyes. "And how would you know that if you weren't involved?"

Laurent put up both hands and shrugged. "The girl, I am told it is what killed her. And the police in their very annoying way asked me about it at the time. It is a natural conclusion."

"What good it would do you," the chief inspector said, "is once the locals have collected the contraband, they bring it up to the house, and from there it goes up to London to be sold. And you are paid handsomely for your part in it."

"That seems very unlikely, does it not, monsieur? The fellow from Scotland Yard, Endicott, he says he has people watching Winteroak House for some months now. When the lovely Mademoiselle Henley, she dies, they searched the whole house, attic to cellar, and again found nothing. How then does this supposed contraband come in and come out?"

Drew glanced at Nick, then looked back at Laurent. "Why don't you tell us?"

Laurent laughed. "Monsieur Farthering, you are a most amusing fellow. It may be that these fishing men have done just as you say and by some miracle brought their goods to Monsieur Cummins to sell in London. But again you have nothing to show I have been involved in the matter."

"Nothing but Bill Rinnie and Bert and Tom Kimlin," Birdsong said. "And you can be sure one of them will talk before long."

"But evidence," Laurent said. "I am given to understand even in so barbaric a place, there must be evidence for an arrest to be made. What do you have against me? A scrap of a label which could have come from anywhere, and the testimony of three ne'er-do-wells? It is less than nothing. You cannot possibly hold me with nothing more."

"We can question you," Birdsong said stubbornly, and then he fixed Drew and Nick with a sour eye. "Was there anything more you had to tell me on this?"

"The cans," Nick said, but Drew stopped him.

"Perhaps you ought to send Monsieur Laurent back to the car, Chief Inspector. No need tipping our hands quite yet, eh?"

Birdsong nodded at Maxwell. "See he has a nice comfortable seat. I'll be there straightaway."

"Right you are, sir." Maxwell took Laurent's arm. "All right, Frenchie, come along with me."

Laurent sighed. "As you say, Officer, but you will find your time is wasted, and mine as well."

He followed Maxwell placidly enough, and Birdsong said nothing until he had been put back into the car that had brought him.

"All right then, Detective Farthering, I want to know what other evidence you have that links Laurent to the smuggling operation."

"The cans," Nick said. "We were aboard his yacht last week. Drew saw some marks on the aft deck, just little curves, and we couldn't figure out what made them. A bit of white in the crevices. Well, whitish stuff, I suppose. It was rather faint. But then we found out about the cans of French whitewash, and the rest seems fairly obvious. Isn't it, Drew?"

Drew smiled. It did seem a rather frail chain of events put that way. "You can see a white mark all along the waterline in Claridge Rindle, farther up, out behind Winteroak House. Rinnie and his lot had to have been pouring out the whitewash there. Tom Kimlin was seen dumping some. Put that with the marks on the deck of Laurent's yacht and the waterlogged labels on the cans, and it all makes sense."

Birdsong looked at him, eyebrows arched. "That's it?"

"But it's the connection between them. It has to be. Tom Kimlin practically blurted it all out not five minutes ago."

"The Frenchman's protected himself fairly well on this. If

they don't talk—and at this point I can't tell if Tom Kimlin is too scared to say anything or too scared not to—we won't likely be able to hold Laurent. He's a cool one, isn't he?"

"You will see to Adkins while you're at it, won't you?" Drew asked. "He bears watching if anyone does. I don't much care for him running loose at this point."

Birdsong huffed. "I expect Scotland Yard know more about that one than they let on. But we'll see to him, no fear. I have to wonder, though, why he and that whole lot didn't clear off the minute they were allowed to. Laurent's been nattering about leaving for a whole miserable week."

"And now I've tossed a spanner into the works."

Birdsong managed to look only mildly annoyed. "No, the bit about the whitewash is interesting. A sound theory as far as it goes, but then there's the matter of getting the stuff up to the house or at least up to London. Until we find how that's done, the rest of it isn't likely to matter. They'll just figure another way to bring it over from the Continent."

"True," Drew muttered.

"Besides," Nick put in, "it does seem unlikely that any of our fishermen had anything to do with the murders. No opportunity."

"Yes, dash it all." Drew lifted his eyes to the roofline of Winteroak House, just visible above the bluff. "But they're all tied to this smuggling ring, there's no doubt of that."

"I'll agree with you there," Birdsong said. "Get that all sorted, and we'll have a good idea who our murderer is."

"It has to be going through from here somehow." He looked around the narrow beach and then peered into the trees. "What do you say, Nick? Shall we have a look round?"

"I'm game," Nick said.

"We've had men all over this area," Birdsong said, "and

never found a thing. But if it makes you two happy, by all means. If you find anything of interest, just ring me up at my office. I'll be trying to get whatever information I can out of Rinnie and his mates. If nothing else, with them in custody and all, you two ought to be able to stay out of mischief out here." He gave them both a stern glance. "Try at least, eh?"

"Will do, Chief Inspector." Drew nodded toward *The Gull*. "You might want to have someone come take that away. I don't expect she'll move just now, at least not under her own power."

"Right. We'll see to it." Birdsong studied the beach and the trees above it, shook his head in disgust, and then made his way back up to the road. He got into the car he'd come in, and after a moment it pulled away, leaving only Drew and Nick standing on the narrow beach.

"So where do we start?" Nick asked, breaking the silence.

He looked up at the house, and Drew followed his gaze. There was little more of it visible than the roof and the chimneys and a curl of smoke from the kitchen fire that quickly dissipated in the cloudless sky.

"It's got to be somewhere down here," Drew said. "However they've concealed it, it's got to be here. Why else would those men have been involved? I've watched them. They go down to the Channel and then up as far as here, where Claridge Rindle comes out. No farther. What good would they do Laurent if they weren't a link in his chain?"

"Decoys?" Nick thought for a moment. "Suppose Laurent is bringing it in himself somehow, and these fellows are there only to draw attention away from him."

"No, if that were the case, they were doing it very badly. The police have been watching him since long before they picked up on Cummins." Drew looked up and down the beach. "I think we've got everything but that last elusive half bean that makes it all add up to five."

"It's only a couple of miles over to Lymington. If we get there and haven't found anything, I say we'd best go back up to the house, collect the girls, and head home to Farthering Place. Leave the rest to the proper authorities."

"Fair enough." Drew exhaled heavily. "You know, these caves ought to be perfect for smuggling, in a protected little cove like this and all, but the police have searched them a hundred times already. I just don't know what good we'll do looking into them again."

Nick grinned. "But we'll do it anyhow, eh? Now that we know about the whitewash, maybe we'll see another sign of it somewhere that will tip us off." He jogged over to the skiff they had borrowed from Winteroak House and grabbed the torch stored there. "Might need this in the dark there."

Drew clapped him on the back. "Good old Nick. Never say die. Well, come on then."

— Eighteen —

By the time Madeline reached the morning room, Carrie and Mrs. Cummins were laughing and crying over an album of Tal's school photos. At the back was one of him and Alice together, taken, she said, just three months earlier.

"Oh, the poor dears, and both of them gone now. Truly, it's too cruel. Too hard for anyone to bear."

"Shall I make us all some coffee?" Madeline asked, careful not to make eye contact with Carrie. "Or maybe get us some of the shortbread Mrs. Ruggles left for us?"

Mrs. Cummins blotted her eyes and nose. "No, dear, it's sweet of you, of all of you, but I think I'd do better just to lie down a while. Just till I can get my feet under me, you understand."

"Of course," Madeline said. "I'll help you upstairs."

"No, no. You girls make yourselves comfortable in here. There's the wireless, if you care to listen, or one of the books might interest you. You know where the playing cards are. I'll . . . I'll be all right. Just give me an hour or two to collect myself. I suppose the boys will be back before long to keep you company."

"I'm sure they will." Madeline gave her a comforting hug. "You have a good rest. We'll be just fine right here."

She watched as Mrs. Cummins made her way down the corridor, heard her ascend the stairs, then the sound of her bedroom door opening and closing.

Madeline shut the morning room door and plunged ahead. "He took it. The vicar. He took the box with the tea in it."

"No," Carrie breathed. "Do you think it was a coincidence? Or do you think he knew what was in there?"

"I don't know." Madeline patted her skirt pocket, making certain the packet was still there. "Oh, Carrie, surely not. He couldn't be in on this. He and Mr. Cummins both? It would be just too awful."

"We've got to tell the boys."

"As soon as they get back," Madeline said. "But for now I think we should have another look in the pantry."

Carrie's eyes widened. "What good will that do? The police have looked at everything in there. There's nothing else to see."

"Maybe not. But maybe there is. They didn't find the bad box of tea. Who knows what else might be in there. Mr. Cummins swears that Tal believed him when he said he didn't kill Alice, but the note Tal left behind makes it sound as if he found out something that changed his mind. Something that implicated his father, and maybe something that could tell us who killed Billy."

"But you don't know that he saw something in the pantry. It could have been anything anywhere in the whole house or even somewhere else."

"That's where we found the tea. What would it hurt to

have another look around, this time without anyone looking over our shoulders?"

Carrie glanced toward the door and then nodded. "If we're going to do it, we'd better do it quickly."

They scurried through the kitchen and into the pantry. It didn't look much different from when they were there before. Madeline and Carrie searched bags, boxes and bins, cupboards and drawers, even the larder, but with no result.

Madeline huffed, blowing a strand of hair out of her face. "There has to be something. What could he have seen? More important, where did he get the cocaine he took?" She scanned the pantry once again, then looked at the door that led to the wine cellar. It was a possibility that whatever Tal had discovered was on the other side of it. "I'm going down there."

Carrie's already pale face turned even paler.

"You stay up here. There's no need for you to go, too. I'm just going to have a look around, in case there's something down there everyone's missed."

"We promised we'd stay out of trouble," Carrie protested.

"We promised we wouldn't go out," Madeline said, "and I don't plan to. I won't have a better opportunity. We're practically alone in the house. Notice I said *in the house*. I won't step a foot outside."

"And what if someone sees you?"

"Like who?"

"I don't know. Anybody. Mrs. Cummins could wake up. Mrs. Ruggles could come back."

"And she'd never let us in here again."

"Oh, I just thought . . ." Carrie glanced around as if she feared she would be overheard. "What if she's part of it, as well? She's never wanted anyone around the kitchen or the pantry. What if—"

Madeline tightened her jaw. "She won't be back for hours. If she's part of it, she'll never know we even suspect."

"And you're determined to do this?"

Madeline nodded.

"Then I'm going with you."

Madeline blinked. "Do you think that's a good idea? I don't know if there's, well, if they've completely cleaned up down there. There will probably still be traces. Of the place where Billy was, I mean."

Carrie lifted her chin. "I know. Nick's been herding me away from there ever since it happened. I want to see it for myself."

"Carrie, are you sure—?"

"I want to go. I know the police have looked at everything down there, but I can't help thinking they must have missed something. Billy wouldn't—" her lips trembled, but she refused to cry—"he wasn't down there for no reason."

"I know. If we're going to have a look, I guess it's now or never. We probably won't have the house to ourselves like this ever again."

Carrie managed a half smile. "And we sure won't have another chance without the boys looking over our shoulders."

"Okay then."

Madeline peered down to where the stone steps vanished into darkness and wished she had that little Webley revolver Drew kept locked in the desk in the study at home. He'd made sure she knew how to handle it safely and that she could fire it with reasonable accuracy and confidence, but she never liked the thought of it. She was always afraid she would freeze if the time came to actually use it, and then what if her opponent turned the weapon on her? Still, it would be good to feel its comforting weight in her hand right now. It would be better to have Drew himself beside her. Well, she wasn't going to be a big chicken about it now. "Stay together, all right?"

Carrie drew herself up to her full not-quite five feet. "Right."

Madeline reached the bottom of the steps, but then scurried back to the pantry.

"Hey!" Carrie protested.

"Just hold on a minute." Madeline snatched up the flashlight sitting with some other sundries on a pantry shelf and hurried back down to where Carrie stood. "We don't want to get stuck where a light bulb is burned out or something. Ready?"

"Ready." Carrie drew a deep breath and took Madeline's arm. "Stay together, right?"

"Right."

Madeline turned on the switch at the bottom of the steps, and the wine cellar was bathed in a yellowish light. Until yesterday, the police hadn't allowed anyone down here, but the cellar looked just as it had before the incident, except there were some empty racks now and barrels missing. There were also a few spots on the stone floor that had been scrubbed more vigorously than others.

Her face grim, Carrie seemed determined not to look at the floor at all. "What could Billy have been looking for?" she asked for the hundredth time.

"What could he have found?" Madeline said, shining the flashlight into a dark corner. "Someone killed him over it, so it must have been pretty important. If he—" She drew a quick breath and then laughed. "What are you doing here?"

The light had caught a greenish sparkle on one of the upper shelves, and both girls went over to it.

"What's she doing down here?" Carrie asked, one hand

over her heart. "You little rascal, Eddie. You scared the life half out of me."

The cat blinked, stretched, and then scratched herself on the side of the neck. The airy jingle of her collar seemed oddly out of place in the hush of the wine cellar.

"You stay out of trouble, miss," Madeline warned her, turning the flashlight once again on the bottles and barrels and casks stacked around them. "This doesn't look right."

She pointed the light into the corner just left of the entrance where there was a stack of crates bearing a French wine maker's trademark.

"What's wrong with it?" Carrie asked. "They're just empty crates. I'm sure the police would have already checked them."

"Well, it wouldn't hurt to see for ourselves, now, would it? Help me."

Madeline and Carrie dragged the crates toward the center of the room, but no matter what they tapped or pressed or banged, there was nothing behind them but solid stone floor and solid stone wall.

Madeline sighed. "Okay, I'm sure you're right and the police already did that. Let's check the rest of the cellar."

Hearing a little *prrt* and another jingle of bells, Madeline turned to see the shelf where Eddie had been was now empty.

"She shouldn't be down here. The little pest will fall asleep and get locked in or something. Come on, Eddie."

She and Carrie went around one of the floor-to-ceiling wine racks, but there was no black-and-white cat on the other side.

"Now where is she?" Carrie listened for a moment and then made a clicking noise with her tongue. "Eddie? Eddie. I know she was over here."

Madeline heard the faintest jingle of a bell. "This way, I think."

They went farther back into the cellar, Madeline shining the flashlight into every nook and hiding place. No sign of Eddie.

"I know I heard her." Carrie stopped and listened again. "Back here."

They squeezed between a couple of very large casks and found themselves face-to-face with another stone wall. Unlike the other three walls, this wall was rough, carved from the natural rock surrounding the cellar.

"Well, she didn't go this way," Carrie said.

"Yes, she did," Madeline insisted. "Listen."

The jingling was fainter than ever, but Madeline could still hear it. She pointed the flashlight toward the sound and drew a startled breath. "Look."

At their feet, shadowed by one of the casks, was an opening in the rock, roughly square and just large enough to accommodate the cat. Madeline sank down in the tight space between the cask and the wall, yet she couldn't get low enough to see inside the opening. Slowly she stuck her hand inside, hoping if the cat did go through here, there wasn't anything nasty waiting to latch on to her fingers.

Her eyes widened. "Oh!"

"What is it?" Carrie asked.

Bracing herself, Madeline pressed the switch she'd found inside the opening. With no more than a slight vibration, a two-foot-wide section of the lower half of the wall swung back and up, revealing a dimly lit passageway.

"Amazing," Madeline said. "The seam is perfectly hidden in the way these false stones are laid out." She shone the light on it more closely, revealing the join to be covered by a subtle trompe l'oeil paint treatment that even the wariest eye was unlikely to detect, especially in the shadow of the casks in the wine cellar's low light. "The police have searched in here many times. How could they have missed this hole where the switch is?"

"We'd better go back now," Carrie whispered. "You don't know what's in there."

"We know Eddie's in there, and we can't just leave her. Not if someone else is in there, too." She took a deep breath, calming herself. "I'm going after her. Are you coming?"

"Madeline—"

"Just to get Eddie. I don't hear the bells anymore. Either she's stopped somewhere or something's happened to her."

Carrie's face was white in the dimness, her blue eyes enormous as she looked up at Madeline. She nodded. "All right, let's go. But we have to stay together."

"Stay together," Madeline repeated.

They ducked into the passageway and found it was actually a tunnel, wide and tall enough for them to walk through single file. It was lit by a string of small low-wattage bulbs strung from a wire, primitive but efficient.

"It's got to lead down to the shore," Madeline said just loud enough for Carrie to hear. "They had to have been bringing the cocaine up to the house from Monsieur Laurent's boat through here. We need to find Eddie and get out."

Carrie nodded and then held up one finger. Ahead of them was the sound of little bells, and a cold shiver ran down Madeline's spine. What if there was someone down here?

Please stay still, Eddie, Madeline pled silently. *Just stay where you are for another minute. Oh, God, please make her stay still.*

"She's just up ahead," Carrie said. "Hurry."

Madeline nodded, trying hard to keep her breathing even and silent, knowing she was failing miserably. *Oh, dear Jesus, be with us. We shouldn't be here. We shouldn't be here. We shouldn't be here.*

She quickened her pace around a bend in the tunnel and then choked back a shriek. Someone was huddled there against the rock wall. She clutched her flashlight, ready to use it as a weapon, but there was no need. The man was dead.

Carrie put a hand over her mouth, looking as if she wanted to scream, too. "Who is it?"

Madeline knelt at the man's head, turning his face to the light. She looked at Carrie. They both recognized him.

Laurent's valet, Adkins. He had been stabbed in the back.

"We have to leave," Madeline whispered. "Now."

Again came the sound of bells, moving toward them now. Madeline scrambled to her feet. Thank God, Eddie was coming back. Madeline would grab her, and she and Carrie would run as fast as they could back up the tunnel, out of the cellar and out to the constable posted in front of the house.

The jingling sounded closer still, coming from around a bend in the tunnel.

Madeline froze. It was the collar, but no cat.

"Mrs. Cummins?"

Margaret Cummins stood in the passageway with Eddie's belled collar dangling from one finger, a pistol in her other hand. "I really wish you had listened to me, my dear. I did try my best to keep you both out of it."

Carrie clutched Madeline's sleeve, "You wouldn't—"

"What have you done?" Madeline asked, trying her best to appear unruffled while her blood raced and leapt in her veins. "What did you do to Mr. Adkins?"

"Adkins? He wasn't Adkins, not at all. He's been spying on us all along. Valet? No. Detective Inspector Asher of Scotland Yard. Well, he'll tell no tales now, will he? It's a pity really. I didn't like to do it, you know, but he did follow me down here and, well, there it is. Poor man. He could as well have let us all alone. I mean, Sterling was already caught. I couldn't possibly run things up in London. It would have all ended. But he *would* keep poking his nose in. Your brother too, Miss Holland. Oh, and he was such a nice boy, but he wouldn't listen to me either, and it just couldn't be helped."

"You were in it with your husband from the start," Madeline said, scrambling to think of some way out of the jam she and Carrie were in. "The two of you killed Alice and Billy. Did you kill Tal, too? Your own son?"

Mrs. Cummins's chin quivered, but her expression didn't change. "Alice was a foolish girl. She got into the charity things and found the packets my husband was putting into them. I knew she didn't want to hurt Tibby. Perhaps she was afraid he wouldn't believe her. That's why she didn't tell him directly. She wanted him to see for himself. Well, I couldn't have that, could I?"

"You gave her the cocaine?" Carrie asked in a quavering voice.

"In her drink, if you must know."

"But Dr. Fletcher said it loses its effect if ingested," Madeline said. "It has to be sniffed or injected."

"Oh, he's right. He's quite right," said Mrs. Cummins. "It takes a much larger amount of the drug to do any good if it's taken by mouth. But I also know that something like lime helps."

Madeline glanced at Carrie. "That's why you made limeade."

Mrs. Cummins nodded. "I couldn't have her spoiling things, could I? It seems she did anyway, didn't she, my dear? I hated to have to break poor Tibby's heart, though."

The hand holding the pistol shook, and Madeline took a quick step forward. Just as quickly she stepped back. Mrs. Cummins, smiling sweetly, had the pistol pointed at her heart. Then she straightened her shoulders, remembering Elizabeth Bennet saying she was too stubborn to be frightened or intimidated by anyone, remembering her every breath was in the hand of God, and she felt her own courage rise.

"It's not too late," she said, holding tightly to the hand Carrie had slipped into hers. "Tal is gone, but I don't think he would have wanted you to hurt us. I don't think even Mr. Cummins would want that, no matter what you've both done."

Mrs. Cummins chuckled softly. "No, my dear, he wouldn't want that. He couldn't stomach violence. He really was never cut out for this business. He doesn't know I've known about it all along. Almost from the very beginning. He would have been found out fairly quickly too, if I hadn't been there to clean up his little messes now and again. But isn't that a wife's place? Quietly seeing to things for her husband and letting him think he did it all himself? You girls . . . well, it doesn't matter now. You won't need to worry about it." She jingled the collar again.

Madeline forced her voice into steadiness. "What are you going to do?"

— Nineteen —

Drew shone the torch against the back wall of the cave, hunching over to avoid hitting his head on the downward sloping ceiling. "Another dead end."

"Are you certain?" Nick came up to him, squinting into the darkness. "We're not that far from Claridge Rindle. If that's where they were dumping the whitewash, they must have brought in the cocaine somewhere round here."

"You'd think so." Drew carried the torch around the sides of the cave and then faced the opening again, considering. "Why dump it in the Rindle, anyway? Why not dump it in the Solent? Or down their own kitchen drains?"

"They dump it in the Rindle," Nick said, "because it's not far from where they keep the stuff."

"Exactly. They dump the paint and bring the cocaine into the house through some sort of tunnel."

Drew took a step backward and then jumped when he heard a squawk of feline protest.

"Eddie!" He picked up the cat, and she looked at him

with her usual equanimity. "How did you get down here? And what did you do with your collar?"

Nick scanned the rocks once more. "Pity she can't tell us. The way in has to be here somewhere, don't you think?"

Drew looked into the cat's docile green eyes, and one side of his mouth turned up. "Perhaps she can tell us. Stand there by the opening so she doesn't get out."

"What are you going to do?"

"Just don't let her out that way."

When Nick was set, Drew put the cat on her feet in the middle of the cave. Then he clapped his hands and ran toward her. She appeared puzzled and didn't budge.

Nick laughed. "What was that meant to be?"

"A normal cat would have turned and ran. She should have dived back into the hole she came out of." He picked her up again. "Why can't you be just an average cat for once?"

Eddie blinked at him.

Scowling, Nick came over to them. "Great lot of help you are. Now we'll have to—"

"Wait!" Drew said, tugging Nick's arm. "Did you hear that?"

They both stood stock-still. There it was again—the faint jingling of a bell. It was Eddie's bell, Drew recognized it, but Eddie wasn't jingling it.

Drew crept toward the sound, waiting for it to come again, and then he looked at Nick, brow wrinkled. "Behind there." Shading the torch with one hand, he moved behind a large rock at the back of the cave and found a gaping opening in the seemingly solid stone wall, an opening that led to a tunnel.

Nick's mouth dropped open. "How could they have missed—?"

Drew shook his head in warning. Even Nick's low whisper

might be heard. Surely whoever had left this open was still in there. It would have been closed otherwise. Closed and invisible. Again he and Nick were still. Listening. Waiting . . .

They heard the bell again, not far up the tunnel, from somewhere beyond where it curved. Then someone spoke.

"What are you going to do?"

Drew's heart began pounding against his breastbone. That was Madeline's voice, and he could hear the fear in it. Laurent and his local toughs had been taken away, though Adkins, his valet, was still unaccounted for. Then a second voice drifted back to them.

"I'm going to have to see you don't cause me any further trouble, my dear. I hope you can understand my position. There's really nothing else I can do."

That was Mrs. Cummins's voice, sweet and serene as always.

All the pieces then dropped into place.

"I suppose you'll have to join poor Mr. Asher," she said. "Can't have you telling tales."

Who was this Asher she was talking about? Whoever he was, Drew was sure he must be dead. Just the tone of Mrs. Cummins's voice was enough to tell him that. He'd have to get Madeline out of there somehow.

"We won't be needing the tunnel anymore as it is," Mrs. Cummins continued. "May as well get some final use of it, don't you think? Now, both of you, turn and face the wall."

Both? Drew glanced at Nick, realization striking them both in the same instant. Who would be with Madeline but Carrie? Nick lunged forward, but Drew stopped him, warning him to caution with an upraised hand.

Together they moved slowly forward, Mrs. Cummins's voice growing louder and more distinct.

"It's a pity all of you didn't go after Alice died. It would have saved so much trouble."

Nick took another step, jostling a large suitcase sitting unexpectedly in the dim light. He and Drew both froze as the sound echoed down the tunnel.

"Who's there, please?" Mrs. Cummins called. "I must ask you to come over to where I can see you. I should hate to have to do anything untoward to the young ladies."

Drew stayed still for another moment. He closed his eyes and pressed his lips against the back of Eddie's head, lifting a fervent silent prayer. Then he set her on her feet and gave her a push.

For a moment, she just stood there looking bored, but then she stretched herself and sauntered around the bend and out of sight.

"Who's there?" Mrs. Cummins repeated, not taking her eyes off Madeline and Carrie. "I do have a gun, and I am quite capable of using it."

There was another almost imperceptible sound down the tunnel, and she glanced back toward it. Madeline steeled herself to try to take the gun from her. But the older woman turned back, lips pursed as if she were about to scold a naughty child.

"No, no, now. That would hardly be wise." She raised her voice once more and said, "I will give you to the count of three to show yourself." She paused, listening. "One. Two."

With a little gasp, she started, almost dropping the gun, and then made a wry face and picked up Eddie. "Little devil. I nearly trod on you again. I have a feeling you're the cause of all this mess." The collar jingled as she shifted the cat more securely against her. "Can't have that happen again, can we?"

"What are you going to do?" Madeline asked again, not liking the stiff determination in the older woman's eyes. "She's no threat to you."

"We can't have her leading others down here. Especially not if there are certain unpleasant . . . remains to be found. Best to just be certain, I always say." She thrust the cat into Madeline's arms. "You'd better hold her. It will be easier that way."

"Madeline," Carrie whispered, shrinking closer to her. "Oh, God help us."

"Sit down. It will be easier than having to fall all the way to the ground." Mrs. Cummins gestured with the pistol. "Go ahead. I'll wait."

"I don't think so, ma'am."

By the time she realized he was behind her, Drew already had a firm grip on the hand that held the pistol and on her other arm, twisting her around, pointing the gun toward the ceiling of the tunnel and away from Madeline and Carrie.

"Get it away from her, Nick," Drew said.

Nick wrenched the pistol out of Mrs. Cummins's hand and pointed it at her. "All right, Drew."

Drew released her, and she pulled back from him, holding up her hand in a delicate gesture of defense. "You needn't be rough. I'm not violent, you know."

Nick pulled Carrie to his side and wrapped his arm around her, still keeping the older woman covered. "Oh no. Not at all."

He glanced down at the body huddled against the tunnel wall, and Carrie turned her face against his shoulder.

Mrs. Cummins lifted her chin. "Well, he would nose about everywhere. I had the other end of the tunnel open and he found it, the nasty little weasel. After all this time, the police walking right past it, he found it. But it's not as though I came after him with a butcher knife. Same with these two." She nodded toward Madeline and Carrie. "They could have stayed quietly in the morning room until I had a chance to leave. Instead they had to nose about, and what else could I do?"

What else, indeed?

She glared at Eddie nestled in Madeline's arms. "I should have drowned that rat weeks ago. I've always hated the sly little beasts, but Tibby adored them. How could I say no?"

Drew remembered his friend lying cold on his bathroom floor. "He found out about you, didn't he? He was going to tell the police that you were involved as well as Mr. Cummins."

"No." Mrs. Cummins shook her head. "He wouldn't have. He couldn't have. We did it all for him, Sterling and I, but he couldn't see that. He didn't understand. He saw me burning that mallet. The one from the wine cellar. I don't think he noticed what it was at first. Then when that horrid policeman told you all what had been used to kill the boy, he went through the ashes in my fireplace. The mallet itself was all burnt up, but he found those rings, those foolish little bands around the handle. They were all that was left, but they were enough. It all came out then. He knew I was the one who'd given Alice the cocaine. He said such dreadful things to me. To me! After all I'd done for him. He'd forgiven his father, but he wouldn't forgive me. He said he'd rather die. Poor Tibby."

"And that," Drew said, "is how many beans make five."

The words from Tal's note made perfect sense now. He'd lost the girl he loved and the father he'd trusted. But to find his own mother was a cool-headed killer . . . *"I could bear some of this perhaps, but not all of it. Not all of it at once. Not when I know it's all been a lie. All of it. All my life."* Not his father, but his mother. *"You took her from me. You may as well have killed me yourself. I'll save you the trouble."*

Mrs. Cummins stood there staring into nothingness.

Drew took her arm. "Better come along now. It's all over."

Her rounded shoulders began to shake, then tears traced down her cheeks. "I . . . I know it was wrong. It was just so easy at first. So easy to grow dependent on the money." She trudged toward the light in the wine cellar, her steps shuffling and unsteady. "It seemed such a little thing to do, simply passing the packets along. And then . . . then we couldn't get out of it. Now Sterling's in that horrible prison and Tibby's dead, my poor Tibby. My poor . . . poor . . ."

Her eyes fluttered closed, and she started to sag. Drew moved to catch her before she fell, but she lunged toward Nick instead. In an instant she had the gun in both hands, the muzzle pointed squarely at Carrie's head.

"Back away," she said, jaw clenched. "Just back right away."

"Nick," Carrie breathed, still clutching his hand. "Nick."

"Don't," Drew said. "Hasn't there been enough death already?"

"More than enough," Mrs. Cummins said, her eyes shrewd and narrow.

"This isn't what Tal would have wanted."

She nodded, her expression hard as ever. "He would have wanted to go on with his life. With a father he respected and a mother he trusted. With the girl he loved beside him. It oughtn't to be too much to ask. But sometimes things don't end quite as we plan, do they?" She motioned at them with the gun. "I was going to leave. Actually, Monsieur Laurent was going to take me over to the Continent on his yacht, and I was going to disappear. But it's all a bust, as you young people say, and I'm rather tired of the whole thing now."

"Mrs. Cummins . . ." Drew began.

She gestured toward the tunnel wall. "All of you. Face that way."

They did as she said. Carrie started to cry, but Nick wisely did not take her into his arms. Drew caught his glance, and Nick returned the subtlest of nods. They were agreed then. They would not stand quietly and be murdered. Surely between the two of them they could overpower one little middle-aged woman. Then again she did have a fairly powerful equalizer in her hands. He prayed she wouldn't have time to shoot more than one of them.

He turned to look at Madeline. She still had Eddie clutched to her heart, but her eyes were fixed on him. She had seen the silent communication between him and Nick. Six months a bride and he had brought her to this? *Lord, have mercy. Christ, have mercy.*

He glanced back at Mrs. Cummins, and she cocked the pistol, her expression still cool and hard. "The wall, Drew, dear. I don't want to grieve you more than I must. Death is so ugly a thing to see."

Drew faced the wall again, bracing one hand against it where Nick could see but Mrs. Cummins could not. He put up three fingers, knowing Nick would read his meaning. A countdown. *Three.* He lowered one finger, the roar of blood in his ears almost drowning out Carrie's sobs and Nick's quick breathing. *Two.* He lowered another, darting one last glance at Madeline, who stood with her cheek against the top of Eddie's head, her eyes closed and her mouth moving almost imperceptibly, praying. Praying. *And—*

The shot roared and echoed in the tunnel, the deafening sound pierced with Carrie's scream as she dropped to the ground. With a wordless cry, Nick flung himself toward Mrs. Cummins, but Drew grabbed his arm, dragging him back.

"Wait!"

Mrs. Cummins stood with her back to the opposite wall, the gun curled in her fist, and her fist pressed to her heart. That same cool smile was on her lips, but her eyes . . . the light in them had been snuffed out. She sank with surprising grace to the ground, a dark stain slowly spreading across the front of her blouse, dyeing red the demure string of pearls.

Nick blinked. He opened his mouth, swallowed hard, and then opened it again. The air rushed from his lungs as he sank to his knees at Carrie's side. "Sweetheart! Carrie, please . . . come on now."

She came to with a little muffled sob, and then her arms were around Nick's neck. Neither of them said anything more. He lifted her up and carried her through the tunnel and into the house.

"Idiot," Madeline murmured, walking into Drew's arms. "Were you trying to get yourself killed?"

"Just trying to make sure you weren't. Oh, my ears are ringing."

He held her tightly. Then, feeling a slick wetness against his neck, he stepped back just a bit. "Darling—"

She put her hand to the three deep scratches on her throat and looked at her bloodied fingers with a shaky laugh. "I guess we've finally found something Eddie's scared of."

He gave her his handkerchief, which she crumpled in her hand as she pressed herself into his arms again. He held her until they were both steady. "Where did Eddie go?"

"Took off back toward the wine cellar. She's probably

basking in the library window by now, calm as ever." Madeline glanced at the figure huddled against the tunnel wall and then put both hands to her head. "You're right about the ringing." She tried again to smile, but instead crumpled into tears. "Oh, Drew."

— Twenty —

T he lady of the house." Inspector Endicott of Scotland Yard shook his head. "As cool a killer as ever I've seen, and done in by a cat. One for the books, eh?"

Drew stroked Eddie's sleek head as she lay in a square of sunlight on the arm of the library sofa, grooming one already immaculate white paw. "I don't know how we'd have ever found that tunnel without her." He looked at Madeline seated next to him, and then at Carrie who sat in the wing chair across from her, with Nick standing behind her. "Any of us."

Chief Inspector Birdsong of the Hampshire constabulary leaned against the marble fireplace. "Cummins said more than once that his wife always stuck by him no matter what. I guess he was more right than he knew. She wasn't going to let him fail, no matter what she had to do."

"I suppose we'll never know how many people she actually killed," Madeline said softly. "And paid for it as much as anyone. Does Mr. Cummins know? About his wife, I mean."

Endicott nodded. "Told him myself not half an hour ago. Seems he's ready to talk now."

"Now that the damage is done," Nick muttered to no one in particular.

Carrie reached up and took his hand. "I'm just glad it's over."

"And it is, miss," Birdsong assured her. "We have your statement and shouldn't need to bother you again. But you all might like to know we finally got the last piece of our puzzle. He liked his hidden doors did our Mr. Cummins."

Drew thought for a moment. "The warehouses."

"Exactly. Go into the broom closet on the ground floor of the charity side and come out through a disused boiler down in the cellar of the book side. The night watchman for Cummins's books, the one who swore blue he never saw a thing, would slip over to the other side on the right evenings and find the stuff all packed up for him to take back to Cummins's warehouse, put it in with the book shipments, and send it all over Great Britain." Birdsong glanced at his watch and nodded at Endicott. "Your lads likely have him in custody by now, but I reckon I half believe him when he says he didn't know what was in those packets."

The Scotland Yard man snorted. "I remember him. We've had our eyes on him before now, but we couldn't pin him down on anything before. Just like Laurent."

Drew glanced at Madeline. "Cummins implicated Laurent?"

"In fine fashion. Monsieur will not be returning to the Continent for the foreseeable future."

Drew nodded. The Frenchman wouldn't have so much to be smug about now.

"I expect Cummins will have a few more holes to fill for us," Endicott added, "but that's the biggest of them. Now all he has before him is a long stretch in prison with no one waiting for him on the outside."

"You can come visit him anytime," Birdsong said. "He'll be in."

Endicott got to his feet. "Come on, Dane. There's work to be done. Somebody's got to tell Asher's parents. Poor blighter didn't know how close we were till the very last. Well, good afternoon, ladies. Gentlemen."

He put on his hat and led his sergeant out into the corridor and out of the house.

"He's right," Birdsong said, rising as well. "There's work to be done. I understand Dr. Fletcher has seen to things here."

"He's taken the bodies for autopsy," Nick said. "Though there's really nothing to doubt about the causes of death."

"Well, we of the constabulary must do things decently and in order, young Dennison, never mind what you lot get up to behind our backs." He peered at Drew and Nick. "For the sake of the ladies, try and stay out of trouble at least until you get back up to Farthering St. John."

Once everything was more or less settled, everyone decided it was too late to do anything but try to get a good night's sleep. The next day, a fresh, sunny Sunday, they prepared to return to Farthering Place. Josephine brought them tea and told them their things were packed and ready to go. She also brought Carrie a telegram, which stated that her father's boat had come into port. And no more than five minutes later, she informed Carrie her father was on the telephone. By the end of the brief conversation, they had decided it would be best for him to come by taxi directly to Winteroak and take her back to Southampton with him. They had berths reserved on a passenger ship leaving at eight-thirty that evening.

Madeline went upstairs to help Carrie get ready to sail. Nick was busy packing his own things, as well as making sure Drew and Madeline's were seen to. Eddie had wandered off somewhere, most likely to the kitchen, and Drew sat alone in the library a moment more, feeling the profound emptiness of the not-yet-empty house. It was just a house now, not a home, like the oddly unfamiliar body of a loved one after the life had gone from it.

"Rather sad now, isn't it?"

Drew looked up to see Philip Broadhurst in the doorway, hat in hand.

"Vicar." Drew stood, extending his hand. "Sorry, I didn't hear you come in."

"That's quite all right. The staff are rather at sixes and sevens at the moment."

He took the seat Drew offered, and Drew returned to his own.

"I stopped by to see Mrs. Ruggles," the vicar said, "well, all the staff, to speak the truth, after I heard what happened. She said I might come on in here and speak to you. You know, I don't feel bad for the younger ones as much. They'll find other places, I expect, but Mrs. Ruggles has been at Winteroak House for years now. I don't know what she'll do. She hasn't anyplace or anyone."

"I don't suppose we ever quite realize how every choice we make, good or bad, affects someone else. I hope you'll let me know if she ends up in difficulty. I'd like to help."

"I'll do that," Broadhurst said. "The parish will do its best for her, too. And all the others. The place will be sold, I don't doubt, and it might be that the new owners will take it staff and all."

"Might be," Drew agreed.

The two of them were silent for a while, and then the vicar cleared his throat.

"I'm sorry to see you go, Drew. Even with all this mess, it's been a pleasure getting to know you and Madeline."

"And you, Vicar. Next time we have a grand bash up at Farthering Place, I'll make sure Madeline puts you on the guest list."

"I'll look forward to it."

Drew sighed, looking around the library once again, feeling as if it and the whole house had been unoccupied for a terribly long while. "I wish I could have done more to stop some of what happened here in Armitage Landing, but I suppose all that's rather out of my hands."

Broadhurst smiled. "I think we're not so far apart in our callings. And don't think I haven't often felt the very same as you, as if I'm gunning my engine and going nowhere. But we're neither of us God, nor can we see everything He's doing."

Drew winced. "Now you're sounding like my wife."

The vicar chuckled. "She's a fine woman. My mother often tells me there aren't many in the world and so I'd best hurry and lay claim to one." He looked around and then lowered his voice. "Don't tell anyone, but I may be taking her advice sooner than later."

"Really?"

"Her name's Helen Martin. She's the organist at St. John's in Turner's End near Hordle. And she's one of the ladies there who does ecclesiastical embroidery. She was good enough to repair a vestment that our vicars have worn on special days for the past one hundred and fifty years. We got talking about her needlework and her music and the church. Her father was a bishop for ages, and we found we have rather a lot in common."

Drew laughed softly. "So that's what you've been about

all this time. We were fairly sure you were involved in the smuggling and maybe even the murders."

The vicar blinked. "Me? Not really."

"It made perfect sense. You seemed to always show up when something had just happened, you have a connection to the warehouse up in London, and you were deuced elusive about what you were doing when you'd disappear for hours at a time."

"I . . ." Broadhurst shook his head. "I suppose I was. Good heavens, I never thought it would be taken like that."

"You were very nearly hauled into Chief Inspector Birdsong's office to give good account of yourself. Why all the mystery? About the girl, I mean."

"My good fellow, do you know what a commotion there would be if any of the fine ladies of my flock knew I was calling on someone? Half would be ready to plan the wedding for next week, half would be holding emergency meetings to decide how best to deliver me from the scarlet woman's clutches, and the other half would be furious for my not choosing a lady of the parish."

Drew nodded sympathetically. "That's three halves, you know."

"We wouldn't be left in peace for a single minute. There are those who would assume all manner of impropriety, and heaven help the poor girl if she and I should eventually decide we aren't meant for each other. It would be a scandal no matter how circumspectly we conducted ourselves."

"Yes, I can see that."

"Anyway, we decided we'd best be fairly sure we're serious about each other before we make it public."

"And are you?" Drew asked. "Fairly sure?"

A hint of a smile softened Broadhurst's face. "Fairly sure.

302

As in almost absolutely. Nearly positively. Unshakably lean-ing in that direction."

"And what was in that packet you dropped when we were on Laurent's yacht?"

"The packet? Ah, the packet." The vicar patted his coat pocket. "My grandmother's ring. I'd just picked it up from the jeweler's in Lymington." He turned faintly red. "Hav-ing it sized, you know. In case there should be an opportune moment. It would slip out of my pocket right there in front of my mother."

Drew chuckled. "An engagement ring. Excellent. And when Madeline sends out that invitation, you let us know if it ought to be for two. Your lady fair will be most welcome."

The vicar stood and shook Drew's hand once more. "God bless you and your good wife. Don't let anyone despise the gifts you've been given, and don't you do so, either. They may not fit anyone else's idea of a calling, but the world has all sorts of needs, and God has provided for each of them to be filled, if we all do our part. It would be a shame if your part were left undone."

"Perhaps you're right," Drew said, and the emptiness of Winteroak House didn't seem quite as overwhelming as be-fore. "I'll bear that in mind."

After the vicar had left, Drew made his way back up to the room he and Madeline had occupied for the past two weeks. He would be pleased never to see it again.

Plumfield had stacked all the luggage in the middle of the room, ready to be taken down and loaded into the Rolls. Sitting primly on top of it all with her long tail wrapped around her feet was Eddie.

Madeline sighed when she saw her. "What's going to happen to her, Drew?"

He put his arm around Madeline's waist. "I'm not entirely sure. The house is to be closed up. I suppose someone will find her a new home."

"Or just turn her out to fend for herself."

He frowned. With all the turmoil around Winteroak House, that latter seemed most likely. Drew didn't like to see it. Yes, cats were natural hunters, but those that had been raised as house pets were woefully unprepared for life on their own, especially when winter came.

He went over to scratch the cat behind her whiskers. "And just what are your plans, mademoiselle?"

Eddie gave him a look that plainly said if he didn't know the answer to that by now, it was his own fault and not hers.

"She's not ours, you know," he told Madeline. "I mean, legally we haven't the right to take her off anywhere."

She gave him that indulgent smile that had been on her face ever since they'd come into the room.

"You're no help," he muttered, and he turned back to the cat. "What do you think, Miss Eddie? Would you like to come stay at Farthering Place? I have a feeling you and old Chambers, once he decides you haven't actually ruined his life, will get along famously. Shall we just stroll off together and see how we fare?"

Purring, Eddie leaned up and rubbed her face against his chin. It seemed the bargain was made.

"I'll send a note round to Cummins's solicitor," he told Madeline. "Cummins isn't likely to want her anyway, but at least we'll have everything on the up-and-up."

Madeline wrapped her arms around his neck. "Thank you, darling."

"For what? I want her at least as much as you do."

"No, not for Eddie. Well, yes, for Eddie, but mostly for doing what you do."

He kept his eyes fixed on the cat. "Alice and Will and Tal—"

There was a decorous tap on the door.

"Pardon me, sir," Beryl said, "but the taxi's come and Miss Holland is leaving."

"All right. We're coming." Drew took Madeline's arm. "Carrie will want to say goodbye."

Madeline gave him a bittersweet smile. "I think saying goodbye is the last thing she wants to do."

Carrie and Nick were at the top of the front steps, their voices soft and urgent as they took leave. She sniffed and then turned to walk down to the car. He caught her arm.

"Couldn't I come with you?" he asked, obviously not for the first time. "Just to the ship, I mean."

Her black veil was turned back, away from her face, and it quivered just the slightest bit when she shook her head. "I wish you could. I'd feel so much better if you did. But Daddy doesn't want anyone else right now, just me."

Her father was sitting in the back of the car, staring straight ahead, stone-faced, nothing like the jovial man who'd come to Drew's wedding and given away the bride. Once more Drew had to swallow his anger at the waste and evil of it all, remembering again Cummins's words. *I'm not evil, Drew. People are going to take the stuff anyway. I'm not to blame if they're hurt because of it.*" It was a sad and broken world, God help them all, and there was little Drew could do to make it better.

Madeline squeezed his hand more tightly, and he gave her the slightest of smiles, the intimate smile he kept only for her as he read the reminder in her eyes. Maybe it wasn't much. Maybe it wasn't always perfect. But, God helping him, he would do what he could to see that more families like Carrie's, like Alice's, like Tal's weren't torn apart by greed and murder.

Broadhurst was right. He didn't have to take on the whole world. He just had to see to the tasks that were put into his hands. He had failed, it was true, painfully true, but at least here the influx of contraband had been stopped, and Mrs. Cummins would never kill again. More than all of that, Carrie was alive. Madeline was alive. In spite of his failures, he couldn't count that as nothing. He couldn't help but be thankful. And maybe someday Carrie—

As if she had somehow sensed his thoughts, Carrie came over to him and, standing on tiptoe, kissed his cheek. Then she hugged Madeline fiercely and hurried down the steps to the car. Nick was right after her.

"Carrie, can't you . . . ?" He ducked his head, his voice dropping to a ragged whisper. "Can't you stay? I know it's been awful for you here, but it won't always be this way."

"I know." Her voice was just as broken as his. "I know it won't. But I need to go home. I need to get over this. I need to help Daddy get over this. If I were to stay, he'd be all alone there. I can't do that to him. Not now." She leaned up to touch her lips to his. "I'm sorry, Nick. I'm so sorry."

For a long moment he didn't move, didn't look at her. Then suddenly he had her in his arms, his cheek and then his lips pressed to her red-gold hair. "Don't be sorry. Just come back. Please come back."

She pulled away from him, only enough to look into his pleading eyes, and then she touched her lips to his in the tenderest of kisses. She whispered something in his ear and hurried to the car. It pulled out of the drive with her looking out the back window at him as he stood on the bottom step, their eyes locked until the car turned onto the road and disappeared.

Drew watched from a distance, waiting for him to come back to the house. But Nick just stood there, his eyes on the empty drive, hands shoved in his pockets.

"Shouldn't we go talk to him?" Madeline said. "I hate to leave him just standing there."

"Let me, darling."

She gave him a kiss on the cheek. "You're a good friend, Drew."

Once she had gone into the house, Drew went down the steps. "You all right, old man?"

Nick didn't answer right away, but then after a minute he nodded and said, "Yes. All right."

Drew moved closer, sensing that Nick had more he wanted to say.

"I know now how Mr. Knightly must have felt in *Emma*. 'If I loved you less, I might be able to talk about it more.'" He looked again down the road where Carrie had gone. "I feel as though I should have . . ."

"You should have done just as you did, Nick. She's lost her only brother. Her father's lost his only son. They need to grieve. Together."

"I know." Nick drew a heavy breath. "I just wanted to be with her. To give her whatever comfort I could."

"You've done that, and no doubt she appreciates it." Drew put his arm around his friend's shoulders and turned him back toward the house. "And I'll wager that whatever she whispered to you at the last, it wasn't goodbye forever."

A grin tugged at the corners of Nick's mouth as they walked up the steps. "No, not goodbye forever. Not by a long shot."

ACKNOWLEDGMENTS

To all the wonderful people at Bethany House who keep Drew polished up and at his best.

To John Mattos and Faceout Studio for the amazing cover designs for this series. Your 2014 ECPA Award for *Murder at the Mikado* was very well deserved.

To Kimberly Rogers who understands the writing life and doesn't mind playing "what if."

And to my dad who somehow manages to put up with me even when I'm on deadline.

Thank you and thank you and thank you.

Julianna Deering, author of the acclaimed *Murder at the Mikado* and *Death by the Book* in the DREW FARTHERING MYSTERY series, is the pen name of novelist DeAnna Julie Dodson. DeAnna has always been an avid reader and a lover of storytelling, whether on the page, the screen, or the stage. This, together with her keen interest in history and her Christian faith, shows in her tales of love, forgiveness, and triumph over adversity. A fifth-generation Texan, she makes her home north of Dallas, along with three spoiled cats. When not writing, DeAnna spends her free time quilting, cross-stitching, and watching NHL hockey. Learn more at JuliannaDeering.com.

More From
Julianna Deering

Visit juliannadeering.com for a full list of her books.

Drew Farthering loves a good mystery. So when a body is discovered on his country estate, he decides to do his own investigation. Trying hard to remain one step ahead of the killer, Drew must decide how far to take this dangerous game.

Rules of Murder
A Drew Farthering Mystery

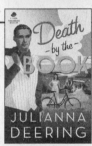

Drew finds himself caught up in another mysterious case when the family lawyer is murdered and found with an unusual clue. Can he and Madeline Parker solve the case before the hatpin murderer strikes again?

Death by the Book
A Drew Farthering Mystery

Answering a plea for help from an old flame, Drew and his fiancée, Madeline, discover murder and more behind the scenes of a theater production of *The Mikado*.

Murder at the Mikado
A Drew Farthering Mystery

You May Also Enjoy . . .

Former Columbus police officer Michael Keane has no trouble relaxing into the far less stressful job of deputy sheriff in his small hometown. After all, nothing ever happens in Hidden Springs, Kentucky. Nothing, that is, until a dead body is discovered on the courthouse steps.

Murder at the Courthouse by A. H. Gabhart
The Hidden Springs Mysteries #1
annhgabhart.com

When Brook Eden's friend Justin, a future duke, discovers she may be an English heiress, she travels to meet her alleged father. Once she arrives in Yorkshire, Brook finds herself confused by her emotions and haunted by her mother's mysterious death. Will she learn the truth—before it's too late?

The Lost Heiress by Roseanna M. White
Ladies of the Manor
roseannamwhite.com

⟡BethanyHouse